ORCAS ISLAND LIBRARY DISTRICT
EASTSOUND, WA 98245
3 3628 02026 2753

O9-AIE-319

DIE BY THE GUN

DIE BY THE GUN

WILLIAM W. JOHNSTONE
with
J.A. JOHNSTONE

KENSINGTON BOOKS
http://www.kensingtonbooks.com

KENSINGTON BOOKS are published by

Kensington Publishing Corp.
119 West 40th Street
New York, NY 10018

All Kensington titles, imprints, and distributed lines are available at special quantity discounts for bulk purchases for sales promotion, premiums, fund-raising, educational, or institutional use.

Special book excerpts or customized printings can also be created to fit specific needs. For details, write or phone the office of the Kensington Special Sales Manager: Attn. Special Sales Department, Kensington Publishing Corp., 119 West 40th Street, New York, NY 10018. Phone: 1-800-221-2647.

Library of Congress Card Catalogue Number: 2018932829

ISBN-13: 978-1-4967-0822-9
ISBN-10: 1-4967-0822-9
First Kensington Hardcover Edition: June 2018

10 9 8 7 6 5 4 3 2 1

Printed in the United States of America

Chapter 1

Dewey Mackenzie spun away from the bar, the finger of whiskey in his shot glass sloshing as he avoided a body flying through the air. He winced as a gun discharged not five feet away from his head. He hastily knocked back what remained of his drink, tossed the glass over his shoulder to land with a clatter on the bar, and reached for the Smith & Wesson Model 3 he carried thrust into his belt.

A heavy hand gripped his shoulder with painful intensity. The bartender rasped, "Don't go pullin' that smoke wagon, boy. You do and things will get rough."

Mac tried to shrug off the apron's grip and couldn't. Powerful fingers crushed into his shoulder so hard that his right arm began to go numb. He looked across the barroom and wondered why the hell he had ever come to Fort Worth, much less venturing into Hell's Half Acre, where anything, no matter how immoral or unhealthy, could be bought for two bits or a lying promise.

Two different fights were going on in this saloon, and they threatened to involve more than just the drunken cowboys swapping wild blows. The man with the six-gun in his hand continued to ventilate the ceiling with one bullet after another.

Blood spattered Mac's boots as one of the fistfights came tumbling in his direction. He lifted his left foot to keep it from getting stomped on by the brawlers. A steer had already done that a month earlier when he had been chuckwagon cook on a cattle drive from Waco up to Abilene.

He had taken his revenge on the annoying mountain of meat, singling it out for a week of meals for the Rolling J crew. Not only had the steer been clumsy where it stepped, it had been tough, and more than one cowboy had complained. Try as he might to tenderize the steaks, by beating, by marinating, by cursing, Mac had failed.

That hadn't been the only steer he had come to curse. The entire drive had been fraught with danger, and more than one of the crew had died.

"That's why," he said out loud.

"What's that?" The barkeep eased his grip and let Mac turn from the fight.

"After the drive, after the cattle got sold off and sent on their way to Chicago from the Abilene railroad yards, I decided to come back to Texas to pay tribute to a friend who died."

The bartender's expression said it all. He was in no mood to hear maudlin stories any more than he was to break up the fights or prevent a disgruntled cowboy from plugging a gambler he thought was cheating him at stud poker.

"Then you need another drink, in his memory." When Mac didn't argue the point, the barkeep poured an inch of rye in a new glass and made the two-bit coin Mac put down vanish. A nickel in change rolled across the bar.

"This is for you, Flagg. I just hope it's not too hot wherever you are." Mac lifted the glass and looked past it to the dirty mirror behind the bar. A medium-sized hombre with longish dark hair and a deeply tanned face gazed back at him. The man he saw reflected wasn't the boy who had been hired as a cook by a crusty old trail boss. He had Patrick Flagg to thank for making him grow up.

A quick toss emptied the glass.

The fiery liquor burned a path to his belly and kindled a blaze there. He belched and knew he had reached his limit. Mac had no idea why he had come to this particular gin mill, other than he was footloose and drifting after being paid off for the trail drive. The money burned a hole in his pocket, but Dewey Mackenzie had never been much of a spendthrift. Growing up on a farm in Missouri hadn't given him the chance to have two nickels to rub together, much less important money to waste.

With deft instinct, he stepped to the side as two brawling men crashed into the bar beside him, lost their footing, and sprawled on the sawdust-littered floor. Mac looked down at them, then let out a growl. He reached out and grabbed the man on top by the back of his coat. A hard heave lifted the fighter into the air until the fabric began to tear. Mac swung the man around, deposited him on his feet, and looked him squarely in the eye.

"What mess have you gotten yourself into now, Rattler?"

"Hey, as I live and breathe!" the cowboy exclaimed. "Howdy, Mac. Never thought our paths would cross again after Abilene."

Rattler ducked as his opponent surged to his feet and launched a wild swing. Mac leaned to one side, the bony fist passing harmlessly past his head. He batted the arm down to the bar and pounced on it, pinning the man.

"Whatever quarrel you've got with my friend, consider it settled," Mac told the man sternly.

"Ain't got a quarrel. I got a bone to pick!" The drunk wrenched free, reared back, and lost his balance, sitting hard amid the sawdust and vomit on the barroom floor.

"Come on, Rattler. Let's find somewhere else to do some drinking." Mac grabbed the front of the wiry man's vest and pulled him along into the street.

Mayhem filled Hell's Half Acre tonight. In either direction along Calhoun Street, saloons belched customers out to continue the battles that had begun inside. Others, done with their recreation outside, crowded to get back in for more liquor.

Mac brushed dirt off his threadbare clothes. Spending some of his pay on a new coat made sense. He whipped off his black, broad-brimmed hat and smacked it a couple times against his leg. Dust clouds rose. His hair had been plastered back by sweat. The lack of any wind down the Fort Worth street kept it glued down as if he had used bear grease. He wiped tears from his cat-green eyes and knew he had to get away from the dust and filth of the city. It was dangerous on the trail, tending a herd of cattle, but it was cleaner and wide-open prairie. He might get stomped on by a steer but never had to worry about being shot in the back.

He knew better than to ask Rattler what the fight had been over. Likely, it had started for no reason other than to blow off steam.

"I thought you were going to find a gunsmith and get some work there," Mac said to his companion. "You're a better tinkerer than most of them in this town."

Mac touched the Model 3 in his belt. Rattler had worked on it from Waco to Abilene during the drive and had turned his pappy's old sidearm into a deadly weapon that shot straight and true every time the trigger was pulled. For that, Mac thanked Rattler.

For teaching him how to draw fast and aim straight, he gave another silent nod to Patrick Flagg. More than teaching him how to draw faster than just about anyone, Flagg had also taught him when not to draw at all.

Rattler said, "And I thought you was headin' back to New Orleans to woo that filly of yours. What was her name? Evie?"

"Evangeline," Mac said.

"Yeah, you went on and on, even callin' out her name in

your sleep. With enough money, you shoulda been able to win her over."

Mac knew better. He loved Evangeline Holdstock, and she had loved him until Pierre Leclerc had set his cap for her. Leclerc's plans included taking over Evie's father's bank after marrying her—probably inheriting it when he murdered Micah Holdstock.

Being framed for Micah's murder had been enough to convince Mac to leave New Orleans. Worse, the frame had also convinced Evie to have nothing to do with him other than to scratch out his eyes if he got close enough to the only woman he had ever loved.

His only hope of ever winning her back was to prove Leclerc had murdered Holdstock. Somehow, his determination to do that had faded after Leclerc had sent killers after him to Waco.

Mac smiled ruefully. If he hadn't been dodging them, he never would have signed on with the Rolling J crew and found he had a knack for cooking and cattle herding. The smile melted away when he realized Evie was lost forever to him, and returning to New Orleans meant his death, either from Leclerc's killers or at the end of a hangman's rope.

"There's other fish in the sea. Thass what they say," Rattler went on, slurring his morsel of advice. He braced himself against a hitching post to point at a three-story hotel across the street. "The House of Love, they call it. They got gals fer ever' man's taste there. Or so I been told. Less go find ourselves fillies and spend the night, Mac. We owe it to ourselves after all we been through."

"That's a mighty attractive idea, Rattler, but I want to dip my beak in some more whiskey. You can go and dip your, uh, other beak. Don't let me hold you back."

"They got plenny of ladies there. Soiled doves." Rattler laughed. "They got plenny of them to last the livelong night, but I worry this town's gonna run outta popskull."

With an expansive sweep of his arm, he indicated the dozen saloons within sight along Calhoun Street. It was past midnight and the drinking was beginning in earnest now. Every cowboy in Texas seemed to have crowded in with a powerful thirst demanding to be slaked by gallons of bad liquor and bitter beer.

"Which watering hole appeals to you, Rattler?" Mac saw each had a different attraction. Some dance halls had half-naked women willing to share a dance, rubbing up close, for a dime or until the piano player keeled over, too drunk to keep going. Others featured exotic animals or claimed imported food and booze from the four corners of the world.

Mac had become cynical enough to believe the whiskey and brandy they served came from bottles filled like all the others, from kegs and tanks brought into Hell's Half Acre just after sunrise. That's when most customers were passed out or too blind drunk to know the fancy French cognac they paid ten dollars a glass for was no different from the ten-cent tumbler filled with the same liquor at the drinking emporium next door. It was referred to as poor man's whiskey.

"Don't much matter. That one's close enough so I don't stagger too much gettin' to it." The man put his arm around Mac's shoulders for support, turned on unsteady feet, and took a step. He stopped short and looked up to a tall, dark man dressed in black. "'Scuse us, mister. We got some mighty hard drinkin' to do, and you're blockin' the way."

"Dewey Mackenzie," the man said in a hoarse whisper, almost drowned out by raucous music pouring from inside the saloon.

"Yeah, he's my friend," Rattler said, pulling away from Mac and stumbling to the side.

When he did so, he got in the way of the dark man's shot. Mac had never seen a man move faster. The Peacemaker cleared leather so swiftly the move was a blur. Fanning the hammer sent three slugs ripping out in a deadly rain that tore into Rattler's body. He threw up his arms, a look of surprise on his face as he collapsed backward into Mac's arms.

He died without saying another word.

"Damn it," the gunman growled, stepping to the side to get a better shot at Mac.

Shock disappeared as Mac realized he had to move or die. With a heave he lifted his dead friend up and tossed him into the shooter. The corpse knocked the gunman's aim off so his fourth bullet tore past Mac and sailed down Calhoun Street. Almost as an afterthought, someone farther away let out a yelp when the bullet found an unexpected target.

Mac had practiced for hours during the long cattle drive. His hand grabbed the wooden handles on the S&W. The pistol pulled free of his belt. He wasn't even aware of all he did, drawing back the hammer as he aimed, the pressure of the trigger against his finger, the recoil as the revolver barked out its single deadly reply.

The gunman caught the bullet smack in the middle of his chest. It staggered him. Propped against a hitching post, he looked down at a tiny red spot spreading on his gray-striped vest. His eyes came up and locked with Mac's.

"You shot me," he gasped. He used both hands to raise his six-gun. The barrel wobbled back and forth.

"Why'd you kill Rattler?" Mac held his gun in a curiously steady hand. The sights were lined on the gunman's heart.

He never got an answer. The man's pistol blasted another round, but this one tore into the ground between them. He let out a tiny gurgling sound and toppled straight forward, like an Army private at attention all the way down. A single twitch once he hit the ground was the only evidence of life fleeing.

"That's him!" a man shouted. "That's Mackenzie. He gunned down Jimmy!"

Another man said, "Willy's not gonna take kindly to this."

Mac looked up to see a pair of men pushing hurriedly through the saloon's batwing doors. It didn't take a genius to recognize the dead gunman's family. They might have been chiseled out of the same stone—broad shoulders, square heads, height within an inch of each other. Their coats were of the same fabric and color, and the Peacemakers slung at their hips might have been bought on the same day from the same gunsmith.

Even as they took in how the dead man had found the quarry Leclerc had put a bounty on, their hands went for their guns. Neither man was too quick on the draw, taking time to push away the long tails of their coats. This gave Mac the chance to swing his own gun around and get off a couple of shots.

Flying lead whined past both men and into the saloon they had just exited. Glass broke inside and men shouted angrily. Then all hell broke loose as the patrons became justifiably angry at being targeted. Several of them boiled out of the saloon with guns flashing and fists flying.

The two gunmen dodged Mac's slugs, but the rush of men from inside bowled them over, sending them stumbling out into the dusty street. Mac considered trying to dispatch them, then knew he had a tidal wave to hold back with only a couple of rounds.

"Sorry, Rattler," he said, taking a second to touch the brim of his hat in tribute to his trail companion. They had never been friends but had been friendly. That counted for something during a cattle drive.

He vaulted over Rattler's body, grabbed for the reins of a black stallion tethered to the side of the saloon, and jumped hard, landing in the saddle with a thud. The spirited animal tried to buck him off. Mac had learned how to handle even the proddiest cayuse in any remuda. He bent low, grabbed the horse around the neck, and hung on for dear life as the horse bolted into the street.

A new threat posed itself then—or one that had been delayed, anyway. Both of the dead gunman's partners—or brothers or whatever they were—opened fire on him. Mac stayed low, using the horse as a shield.

"Horse thief!" The strident cry came from one of the gunmen. This brought out cowboys from a half dozen more saloons. Getting beaten to a bloody pulp or even shot full of holes meant nothing to these men. But having a horse thief among them was a hanging offense.

"There he is!" Mac yelled as he sat up in the saddle and pointed down the street. "The thieving bastard just rounded the corner. After him!"

The misdirection worked long enough for him to send the mob off on a wild goose chase, but that still left two men intent on avenging their partner. Mac put his head down again, jerked the horse's reins, and let the horse gallop into a barroom, scattering the customers inside.

He looked around as he tried to control the horse in the middle of the sudden chaos he had created. Going back the way he came wouldn't be too smart. A quick glance in the mirror behind the bar showed both of the black-clad men crowding through the batwings and waving their guns around.

A savage roar caught his attention. In a corner crouched a black panther, snarling to reveal fierce fangs capable of ripping a man apart. No wonder the black stallion was going loco. He had to be able to smell the big cat.

The huge creature strained at a chain designed to hold a riverboat anchor. The clamor rose as the bartender shouted at Mac to get his horse out of the saloon. The apron-clad man reached under the bar and pulled out a sawed-off shotgun.

"Out, damn your eyes!" the bartender bellowed as he leveled the weapon.

Mac whirled around and began firing, not at the panther but at the wall holding the chain. The chain itself was too strong for a couple of bullets to break.

The wood splintered as Mac's revolver came up empty. When the panther lunged again, it pulled the chain staple free and dragged it into the room. The customer nearest the cat screeched as heavy claws raked at him.

Then the bartender fired his shotgun and Mac yelped as rock salt burned his face and arm. Worse, the rock salt spooked the horse even more than the attacking panther.

The stallion exploded like a Fourth of July rocket. Mac did all he could do to hang on as the horse leaped through a plate glass window. Glittering shards flew in all directions, but he was out of the saloon and once more in the street.

The sense of triumph faded fast when both gunmen who'd been pursuing him boiled out through the window he had just destroyed.

"That's him, Willy. Him's the one what killed Jimmy!"

Mac looked back at death stalking him. A tall, broad man with a square head and the same dark coat pushed back the tails to reveal a double-gun rig. Peacemakers holstered at either hip quickly jumped into the man's grip. Using both hands, the man started firing. And he was a damned good shot.

Chapter 2

Dewey Mackenzie jerked to the side and almost fell from the horse as a bullet tore a chunk from the brim of his hat. He glanced up and got a quick look at the moon through the hole. The bullets sailing around him motivated him to put his heels to the horse's flanks.

Again the horse bolted through the open door of a saloon. This one's crowd stared at a half-naked woman on stage gyrating to bad piano music. They were too preoccupied to be aware of the havoc being unleashed outside. Even a man riding through the back of the crowd hardly pulled their attention away from the lurid display.

Mac slid from the saddle and tugged on the reins to get the horse out of the saloon. He had to shoulder men aside, which drew a few curses and surly looks, but people tended to get out of the way of a horse.

Finally he worked his way through the press of men who smelled of sweat and lust and beer. He emerged into the alley behind the gin mill. Walking slowly, forcing himself to regain his composure, he left the Tivoli Saloon behind and went south on Throckmorton Street.

The city's layout was something of a mystery to him, but he remembered the wagon yard was between Main and Rusk, only a few streets over. He resisted the urge to mount and ride out of town. If he did that, the gang of cutthroats would be after him before dawn. His best chance of getting away was to fade into the woodwork and let the furor die down. Shooting his way out of Fort Worth was as unlikely to be successful as was galloping off.

Where would he go? He had a few dollars left in his pocket from his trail drive pay, but he knew no one, had no friends, no place to go to ground for a week or two. Mac decided being footloose was a benefit. Wherever he went would be fine, with the gunmen unable to track him because he sought friends' help. He had no friends in Fort Worth.

"Not going to get anybody else killed," he said bitterly, sorry for Rattler catching the lead intended for him.

He tugged on the stallion's reins and worked his way farther south along Rusk until he reached the wagon yard. He patted the horse's neck. It was a strong animal, one he would have loved to ride. But it was distinctive enough to draw attention he didn't need.

"Come on, partner," Mac told the stallion quietly. The horse neighed, tried to nuzzle him, and then trotted along into the wagon yard. A distant corral filled with a dozen horses began to come awake. By the time he reached the office, the hostler was pulling up his suspenders and rubbing sleep from his eyes. He was a scarecrow of a man with a bald head and prominent Adam's apple.

"You're up early, mister," the man said. "Been on the trail? Need a place to stable your horse while you're whooping it up?"

"I'm real down on my luck, sir," Mac said sincerely. "What would you give me for the horse?"

"This one?" The liveryman came over and began examining

the horse. He rested his hand on the saddle and looked hard at Mac. "The tack, too?"

"Why not? I need some money, but I also need another horse and gear. Swap this one for a less spirited horse, maybe? And a simple saddle?"

"This is mighty fine workmanship." The man ran his fingers over the curlicues cut into the saddle. "Looks to be fine Mexican leather work. That goes for top dollar in these parts."

"The horse, too. That's the best horse I ever did ride, but I got expenses. . . ." Mac let the sentence trail off. The liveryman would come to his own conclusions. Whatever they might be would throw the gunmen off Mac's trail, if they bothered to even come to the wagon yard.

He reckoned they would figure out which was his horse staked out back of the first saloon he had entered and wait for him to return for both the horse and his gear. Losing the few belongings he had rankled like a burr under his saddle, but he had tangled before with bounty hunters Pierre Leclerc had set on his trail. The man didn't hire stupid killers. Mac's best—his only—way to keep breathing was to leave Fort Worth fast and cut all ties with both people and belongings.

A deep sigh escaped his lips. Rattler was likely the only one he knew in town. That hurt, seeing the man cut down the way he had been, but somehow, leaving behind his mare, saddle, and the rest of his tack tormented him even more.

"I know a gent who'd be willing to pay top dollar for such a fine horse, but you got to sell the saddle, too. It's mighty fine. The work that went into it shows a master leather smith at his peak, yes, sir." The liveryman cocked his head to one side and studied Mac as if he were a bug crawling up the wall.

"Give me a few bucks, another horse and saddle, and I'll be on my way."

"Can't rightly do that till I see if I can sell the stallion. I'm runnin' a bit shy on cash. You wait here, let me take the horse and see if the price is right. I might get you as much as a hundred dollars."

"That much?" Mac felt his hackles rise. "That and another horse and tack?"

"Don't see horses this spirited come along too often. And that saddle?" The man shook his head. "Once in a lifetime."

"Do tell. So what's to keep you from taking the horse and riding away?"

"I own the yard. I got a reputation to uphold for honesty. Ask around. You go find yourself some breakfast. Might be, I can get you as much as a hundred-fifty dollars."

"And that's after you take your cut?"

"Right after," the man assured him.

Mac knew he lied through his teeth.

"Is there a good restaurant around here? Not that it matters since I don't have money for even a fried egg and a cup of water." He waited to see what the man offered. The response assured him he was right.

"Here, take five dollars. An advance against what I'll make selling the horse. That means I'll take it out of your share."

"Thanks," Mac said, taking the five crumpled greenbacks. He stuffed them into his vest pocket. "How long do you think you'll be?"

"Not long. Not more 'n a half hour. That'll give you plenty of time to chow down and drink a second cup of coffee. Maggie over at the Bendix House boils up a right fine cup."

"Bendix House? That's it over there? Much obliged." Mac touched the brim of his hat, making sure not to show the hole shot through and through. He let the man lead the horse away, then started for the restaurant.

Only when the liveryman was out of sight did Mac spin around and run back to the yard. A quick vault over the fence took him to the barn. Rooting around, he found a serviceable saddle, threadbare blanket, bridle, and saddlebags. He pressed his hand against them. Empty. Right now, he didn't have time to search for food or anything more to put in them. He needed a slicker and a change of clothing.

Most of all he needed to leave. Now.

Picking a decent-looking mare from the corral took only a few seconds. The one who trotted over to him was the one he stole. Less than a minute later, saddle and bridle hastily put on, he rode out.

As he came out on Rusk Street, he caught sight of a small posse galloping in his direction. He couldn't make out the riders' faces, but they all wore black coats that might as well have been a uniform. Putting his heels to his horse's flanks, he galloped away, cut behind the wagon yard's buildings, and then faced a dilemma. Going south took him past the railroad and onto the prairie.

The flat, barren prairie where he could be seen riding for miles.

Mac rode back past Houston Street and immediately dismounted, leading his horse to the side of the Comique Saloon. He had to vanish, and losing himself among the late night—or early morning now—imbibers was the best way to do it. The wagon yard owner would be hard-pressed to identify which horse was missing from a corral with a couple dozen animals in it. Mac cursed himself for not leaving the gate open so all the horses escaped.

"Confusion to my enemies," he muttered. Two quick turns of the bridle through an iron ring secured his mount. He circled the building and started to go into the saloon.

"Door's locked," came the warning from a man sitting in a chair on the far side of the door. He had his hat pulled down to shield his eyes from the rising sun and the chair tilted back on its hind legs.

"Do tell." Mac nervously looked around, expecting to see the posse on his trail closing in. He took the chair next to the man, duplicated his pose, and pulled his hat down, more to hide his face than to keep the sunlight from blinding him. "When do they open?"

"John Leer's got quite a place here. But he don't keep real hours. It's open when it's needed most. Otherwise, he closes up."

"Catches some shut-eye?"

The man laughed.

"Hardly. He's got a half dozen floozies in as many bawdy houses, or so the rumor goes. Servicing all of them takes up his spare time."

"You figuring on waiting long for him to get back?"

The man pushed his hat back and looked over at Mac. He spat on the boardwalk, repositioned himself precariously in the chair, and crossed his arms over his chest before answering.

"Depends. I'm hunting for cowboys. The boss man sends me out to recruit for a drive. I come here to find who's drunkest. They're usually the most likely to agree to the lousy wages and a trip long enough to guarantee saddle sores on your butt."

"You might come here and make such an appealing pitch, but I suspect you offer top dollar." Mac tensed when a rider galloped past. The man wore a plaid shirt and jeans. He relaxed. Not a bounty hunter.

"You're the type I'm looking for. Real smart fellow, you are. My trail boss wouldn't want a drunk working for him, and the boss man was a teetotaler. His wife's one of them temperance women. More 'n that, she's one of them suffer-ay-jets, they call 'em. Can't say I cotton much to going without a snort now and then, and giving women the vote like up in Wyoming's just wrong but—"

"But out on the trail nobody drinks. The cook keeps the whiskey, for medicinal purposes only."

"You been on a drive?"

"Along the Shawnee Trail." Mac's mind raced. Losing himself among a new crew driving cattle would solve most of his problems.

"That's not the way the Circle Arrow herd's headed. We're pushing west along the Goodnight-Loving Trail."

"Don't know it," Mac admitted.

"Don't matter. Mister Flowers has been along it enough times that he can ride it blindfolded."

"Flowers?"

"Hiram Flowers, the best damned trail boss in Texas. Or so I'm told, since I've only worked for a half dozen in my day." The man rocked forward and thrust out his hand. "My name's Cletus Grant. I do the chores Mister Flowers don't like."

"Finding trail hands is one of them?" Mac asked as he clasped the man's hand.

"He doesn't stray far from the Circle Arrow."

"What's that mean?" Mac shifted so his hand rested on his gun when another rider came down the street. He went cold inside when he remembered he hadn't reloaded. Truth to tell, all his spare ammunition was in his saddlebags, on his horse left somewhere behind another saloon in Hell's Half Acre.

When the rider rode on after seeing the Comique was shuttered, Mac tried to mask his move by shifting in the chair. He almost toppled over.

He covered by asking, "You said the Circle Arrow owner was a teetotaler. He fall off the wagon?"

"His missus wouldn't ever allow that, no, sir. He upped and died six months back, in spite of his missus telling him not to catch that fever. Old Zeke Sullivan should have listened that time. About the only time he didn't do as she told him." Cletus spat again, wiped his mouth, and asked, "You looking for a job?"

"I'm a piss poor cowboy, but there's no better chuckwagon cook in all of Texas. Or so I'm told, since I've only worked for the Rolling J in my day."

Cletus Grant's expression turned blank for a moment, then he laughed.

"You got a sharp wit about you, son. I don't know that Mister Flowers is looking for a cook, but he does need trail hands.

Why don't me and you mosey on out to the Circle Arrow and palaver a mite about the chance you'd ride with us to Santa Fe?"

"That where the herd's destined?"

"Might be all the way to Denver. It depends on what the market's like over in New Mexico Territory."

"That's fair enough. I might be willing to go all the way to Denver since I've never been there, but heard good things about the town."

Cletus spat and shook his head sadly.

"Too damn many miners there looking to get rich by pulling skull-sized gold nuggets out the hills. The real money comes in selling them picks, shovels . . . and beeves."

"Which is what the Circle Arrow intends," Mac said. "That suits me." He thrust out his hand for another shake to seal the deal, but Cletus held back this time.

"I can't hire you. Mister Flowers is the one what has to do that." The man looked up and down the street, then rocked forward so all four legs hit the boardwalk. One was an inch shy of keeping the chair level. When Cletus stood, his limp matched the uneven chair. He leaned heavily on his right leg. "Let's get on out to the ranch so's he can talk with you. I don't see much in the way of promising recruits."

Mac mounted and trotted alongside Cletus. The man's horse was a fine-looking gelding, well kept and eager to run. From the way the horse under him responded, Mac thought it would die within a mile, trying to keep pace.

"Yup," Cletus said, noticing Mac's interest. "The Circle Arrow has the best damned horses. Mister Flowers says it pays off in the long run having the best. We don't lose as many cattle—or drovers."

"That's good counsel. There're too many ways of dying on the trail without worrying about your horse dying under you." Mac thought a moment, then asked, "What's the trail like? The Goodnight-Loving?"

"The parts that don't kill you will make you wish you were dead. Drought and desert, Injuns and horse thieves, disease and despair."

"But the pay's good," Mac said, knowing the man tested him. "And if I'm cooking, the food will be even better."

"You got a wit about you, son. Let's hope it's not just half a one." Cletus picked up the gait, forcing Mac to bring his horse to a canter.

As he did so, he looked behind and saw two of the black-coated riders slowly making their way down the street. One pointed in Mac's direction but the other shook his head and sent them down a cross street. Being with Cletus Grant might just have saved him. The bounty hunters thought he was alone. That had to be the answer to them not coming to question them about one of their gang getting shot down.

The thought made Mac touch his S&W again. Empty. He kept reminding himself of that. The saddle sheath lacked a rifle, too. If they caught up and a fight ensued, and he couldn't bite them, he was out of luck.

"You got a curious grin on your face," Cletus said. "What's so funny?"

"Drought and desert, Indians and—"

"I get the drift. And I wasn't joking about them. The trail's decent enough, but the dangers are real."

"Nothing like I'm leaving behind," Mac said. That got a frown from Cletus, but he didn't press the matter. That suited Mac. He didn't want to lie to the man.

Not yet. Not unless it became necessary to escape the killers Pierre Leclerc had set on his trail.

Chapter 3

Hiram Flowers spun the tip of his knife a few more times, bored the hole in the pinewood, and finished carving himself a spinner to make a new horsehair lariat. His old lariat had worn out during the last trail drive. At the memory of that drive the prior year, he looked up and saw his boss's widow come out onto the ranch house porch and begin sweeping.

She had hired help for that. A maid. But Mercedes Sullivan preferred to keep her hand in running the house, the ranch, everything about the Circle Arrow. A tiny smile curled Flowers's chapped lips as the fiery redhead bent to flick away a bit of debris stuck between the porch boards. The sight of her made his heart race a little faster, and it wasn't just from how her perky rear end poked up into the air or the gentle sway under her blouse. He knew those emerald eyes of hers were bright and clear and hid none of her razor-sharp intelligence. She was a handsome woman, and a capable one when it came to business.

She was also his boss.

Flowers forced himself to pull his eyes away from her trim

figure and mesmerizing ways. Her husband had been his best friend, no matter that Flowers had worked for Ezekiel Sullivan for more than fifteen years. He had struck up an immediate friendship with the man because of who he was, not just because of his wife.

Zeke had been his boss then. Mercedes was his boss now that the fever had taken Zeke six months back.

He muttered that over and over. Boss, boss, boss.

"You say somethin', Mister Flowers?"

He turned to Howard "Messy" Messerschmidt, a drover hired away from an adjoining ranch. Jake Church ran that spread in a slapdash way, hardly ever turned a profit but somehow kept stumbling along, and he treated his hired hands worse than he did his steers. That made it easy to hire away the best of the drovers, men like Messerschmidt and his partner, Klaus Kleingeld, who didn't speak much English. That didn't bother Flowers overly. He had found some good men, hard workers and dedicated cowboys among the men from down in New Braunfels. He wished he could hire one of those German women as a cook. He'd never found a single one who couldn't whip up a meal fit for a king.

"I was reflecting on how lazy you and Kleingeld are. You have chores to do out in the barn."

"Every bit of the chores are done, Mister Flowers. We rode through the cows corralled on the south forty, looking for any trace of splenic fever. Not a trace, not even a tick bite on the lot, and those are the last of the herd to be examined."

"You look in on Cassidy?" Flowers saw how the cowboy's face became a poker mask. That told him more than he wanted to know.

"He's still sleeping off his bender."

Both of them looked at the clear blue Texas sky and the sun hanging high in it. They had been up by sunrise, doing all the chores necessary to keep the ranch running and to prepare for the drive. Cassidy hadn't stirred, other than to roll over in his bunk and snore even louder.

"Mister Flowers!"

He looked up at the call and saw Cletus Grant waving at him. Cletus rode toward the house with another man on horseback beside him.

"He found a sucker," Messerschmidt said. "Be happy about that. We need all the trail hands we can find after so many of them went south to work on the railroad."

"What's a cowboy know about laying iron track?" Flowers stuck his knife in the bench beside him and stood. He ignored whatever Messy said in response. The man went on and on when he should have kept his yap shut. More important was the man riding alongside Grant.

He sized him up fast. Wherever did Grant find such losers?

The two men reined in, and Grant started to make the introductions. "Mister Flowers, this here's . . ."

Grant's words trailed off. It was apparent he hadn't bothered finding out the man's name, or if he had, he'd already forgotten it. Considering his age, either was possible.

"Dewey Mackenzie," the young man said. "Cletus here says you need cowboys, but my experience is more with cooking."

"You're a trail cook?" Flowers spat. The day was turning sourer the higher the sun got in the sky. "You don't look like one."

"I worked for Sidney Jefferson of the Rolling J, down around Waco. If you want to send him a telegram, he might not answer right away. He's mighty sickly and—"

"Not wasting time or money on a telegram. You don't have the look of a man willing to sit astraddle a horse all night long."

"I've ridden night herd and don't take much to it. Like I told Cletus, my skills are elsewhere."

Flowers took in the youngster. The revolver tucked into his belt had the look of being used hard and often, but he wasn't a gunfighter. Any gunslick worth his salt wore his iron on his hip. A gambler might use a shoulder rig, but having a pistol thrust into the belt like this spelled death if the hammer or cylinder caught on a vest or waistband during a quick draw. The only man he had ever heard of who carried his six-gun in a coat pocket and used it that way was a marshal out in El Paso. And he lined the pocket with leather to keep from getting the hammer tangled in cloth.

Dewey Mackenzie was no gunman, and he wasn't a cowboy.

"Can't use you. Sorry Cletus dragged you all this way for nothing."

"I can cook. I make the best darned biscuits any cowpoke ever ate. Keep the men happy and you get twice the work from them."

"He's right about that, Mister Flowers." Cletus shifted weight off his gimp leg and looked from one man to the other and back. "I'll work an extra hour just for a decent meal. Remember the last drive when—"

"Shut up, Cletus." Flowers tried to keep his shoulders from sagging. He faced Mac and said, "We got a cook. If you can't ride night herd as a wrangler, there's no place on the Circle Arrow drive for you."

He watched a curious ripple of emotion cross the young man's face. Mac took off his hat. The hole in the brim was fresh. There wasn't any fraying yet from wind or rain. His long dark hair was plastered down from sweat, although the day wasn't that hot. Something riled him, and whatever it was wouldn't surface. He had the look of a man with harsh secrets to keep. That meant a history Flowers had no desire to learn or have catch up with either the young man or anyone else on the drive. It was hard enough getting across West Texas and up into New Mexico Territory along the Goodnight-Loving Trail without keeping a close eye on your back trail.

"I can ride herd. I'm not too good, and I'd rather go as cook. I *am* good at that."

"Sorry." Flowers glared at Cletus Grant. The man had expected a finder's fee for another rider.

"But, sir, I—" Mac's words were drowned out by three quick gunshots, followed by a loud whoop like an Indian on the warpath coming after a scalp.

Flowers saw he was wrong about the boy not being handy with his revolver. He had it out and cocked in the blink of an eye, the muzzle pointed up at the bunkhouse roof. Slower to turn, Flowers only touched the butt of his six-gun and didn't throw down when he saw Cassidy teetering on the edge of the roof, buck naked with a gun in one hand and a bottle in the other.

"I'm a ring-tailed, rootin' tootin' son of a bitch from Pecos, and I kin take any man on this godforsaken ranch." Cassidy raised his six-gun again. The motion unbalanced him and caused his feet to slip from under him. He sat hard, then slid down the shingled roof. He landed awkwardly, sprawled in the dirt, and didn't move.

He hadn't killed himself, though. His breath still wheezed and bubbled in his throat.

Cletus cringed at the inelegant sight of Cassidy's bare butt and muttered, "I ain't pulling the splinters from his cracker ass."

"Messerschmidt, get this drunken fool back into the bunkhouse and sober him up," Flowers ordered. "I don't care if you have to pour ten gallons of coffee down his throat. I want him sober before sundown."

"Can't see how that's possible, Mister Flowers. He's never sober. I declare, he's got whiskey instead of blood flowing through his veins."

Flowers glared. Messerschmidt kicked the pistol from Cassidy's unsteady hand, caught his wrist, and pulled the man to his feet. As the drunk toppled forward, he got a shoulder into Cassidy's belly and hoisted him like a sack of grain. A quick kick of his heel opened the door. He made no effort to keep from banging Cassidy's head against the frame as he carried him into the bunkhouse. In his drunken condition, the man never noticed.

"That's our cook," Cletus said. "Mister Flowers, you can't depend on Cassidy. No, wait, I'm wrong. That's exactly how you'll see him along the trail since he'll have the liquor supply under lock and key."

"Hush up. And you," Flowers said, spinning on Mac, "clear out."

He closed his eyes when a soft voice from the direction of the ranch house summoned him. Resolute, he left his problems with the men and went to see what Mercedes Sullivan had to say. Every step closer to the porch—where she stood with arms crossed over her breasts, foot tapping, and an expression just this side of a hellfire and brimstone sermon—convinced him climbing a gallows to be hanged was easier.

Disappointing Mercedes was worse for him than a noose around his neck.

"Yes, ma'am," Flowers said, stopping at the foot of the steps leading to the porch. From here he looked up at her.

"That's enough ruckus from Cassidy. He's drunk again, isn't he? I won't stand for that. No man who works for the Circle Arrow can be as soused as he is right now."

"I need him, Miz Sullivan. He's our cook."

"I heard about the trouble you had with him on the last drive. Zeke said he got into the cooking stores constantly and was seldom sober. If you hadn't stopped him, my husband would have sent Cassidy packing."

"It's not good to be on the trail and fire men, especially the cook. I can ride scout, and Messerschmidt is as good with the herd as any man I've seen."

"Yes, yes," she said impatiently. "And Cletus Grant can soothe any horse in the remuda." She relaxed a little, her arms dropping. She sat down on the top step and pointed to a spot beside her. She pointed more emphatically when he hesitated to sit beside her. Flowers sighed and lowered himself stiffly to the plank step, being careful not to sit inappropriately close to her.

"It's a long drive," he said. "If we go all the way to Denver with this herd, I'll need seasoned men, and plenty of 'em."

"Hiram, you have to fire Cassidy."

"I—"

"I know he's your nephew, and it would break your sister's heart for her youngest to get fired. Do you want me to do your job for you? I will no longer permit a man to be that drunk and remain in my employ."

Flowers began, "Your work with the temperance league is—"

"That has nothing to do with firing Cassidy. He's a poor worker, plain and simple, and I have heard the men grumbling about his cooking. Whether he does a poor job because he's drunk—or not drunk enough—doesn't matter."

"Yes, ma'am." Flowers sighed heavily again. "I'll send him back to his ma."

"Hiram, trust me. She knows what a wastrel he is. Now. When do we hit the trail?"

"I'll be ready at dawn in two days."

"Good. That'll give me time to get my gear together. Have one of the men see that Majestic is ready then."

"Majestic? But that's your horse. I don't need to take your horse. We've got fifty head for the remuda, and what'd you ride here?"

She looked at him, redheaded, beautiful, and absolutely determined as she said, "You misunderstand me, Hiram. I want my horse ready because I'm riding along with you on this drive."

Flowers opened his mouth, then snapped it shut. No words came out. He stared at her, and all he could see were the high cheekbones, fair skin, and that flowing, long red hair. She might have been an Irish elf she was so pretty.

"Zeke always went with the herd. Since he's gone, it's my duty as owner."

"You can't!" He blurted out the denial. The shock on her face that he would speak to her that way turned to stubbornness he knew couldn't be changed. She was downright mulish when she set her mind to something. "Miz Sullivan, it's dangerous on the trail. Hard going every inch of the way. It's not like running the ranch and having a nice soft bed at night."

"You think so little of me, Hiram? I'm tough enough. I need to go along to get the best deal I can. You're not much of a haggler."

"Never had to be, not with Mister Sullivan along. I swear, I never saw a man better able to squeeze an extra dime out of a cattle buyer."

He realized as soon as he said it that he had played right into her hands.

"Since you lack the experience, it will be good for you to see me use my feminine wiles to accomplish the same ends that Zeke achieved." She sounded smug, satisfied, as if she had practiced that line to recite for him. He refused to be convinced.

"Ma'am, all you have to do is bat those long eyelashes of yours and hearts melt."

"Like yours?" Her expression became unreadable. The words were light and joshing, but Flowers heard something else there he dared not believe.

"I won't be a party to you going. I'll quit. I'll take half the men with me, too."

"You'd leave me your nephew and no one else?" Anger rose now, turning her milky cheeks rosy. Her lips thinned to a line, and her green eyes flashed like warning beacons. Flowers had to tread carefully, or she might fire him and try to lead the drive by herself.

"I'll get rid of Cassidy. I promise you that. But I'll need a cook."

"And for me to stay at home, tallying accounts and minding the home fires?"

"Yes, ma'am, exactly." Flowers almost sagged in relief. He had convinced her to stay. The trail was no place for a lady like her. Then she drove another knife into his gut and twisted it around.

"I will remain behind on one condition. Desmond rides with you."

"Your son?" Flowers swallowed hard. It was almost better if he took Cassidy. He could deal with a drunk.

"His father's death hit him hard. It's time for him to snap out of the funk he's been in since the funeral and learn how to run a ranch. Watching you with the herd on the trail will stand him in good stead."

"Desmond?" The name came out in a croak. "He's not even here. He went back to town."

"I wondered where he had gotten off to. Fetch him. Get him outfitted and teach him what he needs to know. Otherwise, I must go along with you."

"I think I know where to find him," Flowers said, his voice hardening. "There's a special place in Fort Worth where he ends up after . . . after spending time there," he finished lamely. He didn't have the gumption to tell Mercedes Sullivan her son frequented whorehouses and raised such holy hell that many had banished him. Being banned from a brothel in Hell's Half Acre took a special amount of hell-raising.

"Then it's all settled. Thank you, Hiram." She bent over and lightly kissed his stubbled cheek.

"Ma'am, not where the men can see." He blushed under his weather-beaten hide.

"So I should kiss you when the men can't see?" Her joking tone had returned.

"I better go right away if I want to get back before midnight." He climbed to his feet and almost ran from the ranch house. Damn the woman! She got under his skin so quick.

He poked his head into the bunkhouse. Messerschmidt had pinned Cassidy to the floor, his knees on the drunken man's shoulders. He tried to pour a cup of coffee into the gaping mouth. Only a few drops made it in.

"Cassidy, you're fired," Flowers said. "Get your gear out of here by the time I get back from Fort Worth. Tell your ma you're a drunken, no account, lazy weasel. If you can't remember, I'll tell her myself."

Cassidy choked and sputtered on the little bit of coffee that had gone down his throat, then stared up at Flowers in drunken befuddlement and said, "But Uncle Hiram, you can't fire me. You pr-promised my ma."

"Out. Now." He motioned for Messerschmidt to get off the man. "Messy, I want you to tell your partner to get the horses ready. Dawn, day after tomorrow. We're hitting the trail."

"Yippee!" Messerschmidt took off his hat and waved it around his head. "We don't like it here on the ranch. We're cowboys meant to be on the trail."

Flowers left, grumbling. He saddled his horse and galloped after Cletus and that whippersnapper he'd found in town. When he overtook them, he drew to a halt and stared hard at Mackenzie.

"You weren't lying about being able to cook?"

"No, sir, I was not," Mackenzie said. He showed no sign of lying. He either believed his own lies or could serve as chuckwagon cook.

"You're hired, but I swear, if you poison my crew, I'll hogtie you and drag you the entire way to Santa Fe behind the ugliest, meanest longhorn in the herd."

"I won't disappoint you, Mister Flowers." Mackenzie grinned from ear to ear.

"There's one chore you got to do before getting all the grub together for the drive."

"Mister Flowers, you can't ask him to—" Cletus Grant clamped his mouth shut when he saw how resolute Flowers was.

"Both of you will fetch back Desmond."

"Who's that?" asked Mackenzie, looking from Flowers to Cletus and not getting an answer from either.

"You're coming with us, aren't you, Mister Flowers?" Cletus was all choked up. Flowers smiled wickedly.

"You two will drag him out of that whorehouse by his heels, and I will be in a saloon drinking my fill of whiskey to shore up my resolve to face him."

Hiram Flowers liked the sound of that plan, but he knew he would go with Grant and the newly hired cook. It was his job as trail boss. More than that, Mercedes had asked him to bring her wastrel son back to the ranch, and whatever she wanted, he did. Anything.

Chapter 4

Mac shifted uneasily in the saddle. The signpost he'd just ridden past said Fort Worth was only three miles away. He had hightailed it from town and thought escape from the gang of bounty hunters was possible. Tempting fate by riding back so soon gave him the fantods.

"Look here, Mister Flowers, if I'm going to be your cook, why don't I get on back to the ranch and be sure the chuckwagon is all packed up proper-like? We both know how important it is for everything to be in its right place, secured when we hit rough terrain and—"

"We're going to pry Desmond loose from whatever hellhole he's crawled into. I need help with that."

"Hellhole?" Cletus Grant snickered. "Is that what you call them purty lil' things' private parts now?"

"I can cut that flapping tongue of yours out and stuff it in your ear," Flowers said. Mac tried to find even a hint of joking in what the trail boss said. He couldn't hear it. The man was deadly serious. From the look of the thick-bladed knife sheathed at his left side, it had seen hard use. Slicing out tongues might have been the least of what that steel had seen and done.

"Didn't mean anything by it, Mister Flowers. You know me. I'm always joshing, keeping a lighter way of seeing things."

Mac and Grant exchanged glances. Cletus shrugged and looked ahead down the road.

There was plenty of daylight left and that worried Mac. The owner of the wagon yard had undoubtedly taken the black stallion with the flashy tooled saddle straight to the bounty hunters. That told the gunmen their quarry was still around town. Mac had expected that and figured to use it as a diversion. He had been clever using Cletus as a shield to get out of the city before, but coming back to Fort Worth only stirred up the pot again.

"We had to come to town tomorrow anyway. Old man Mason at the mercantile's got the rest of the supplies I ordered for the drive," Flowers said. "We can lasso Desmond and take everything back. That'll save a trip in."

"I can go check the supplies. Making sure everything's ready is my job." Mac hoped he could lose himself in the commercial section of Fort Worth, away from the saloons and brothels in Hell's Half Acre where the bounty hunters were most likely to be prowling. Then again, they might have some of their gang watching the general stores to be sure he didn't buy supplies for the trail.

His head began to hurt. Too many ideas crowded in, jumbled up, and tried to spill out in some sort of escape plan. Sticking with the Circle Arrow foreman gave him the best chance of avoiding trouble. At least he hoped so, but if necessary, he could take some of the supplies slated for the Circle Arrow trail drive and ride out of town. Stealing like that worried his conscience a mite, but getting caught by the bounty hunters and killed—or worse, taken back to New Orleans to hang for a murder Leclerc had committed—had to be a lot worse.

"Mason knows Cletus. You sign for the goods, then meet us just beyond the train station. It'll be dawn by then."

"Dawn?" Mac perked up. "You thinking it'll take us all night to find Miz Sullivan's son?"

Cletus laughed harshly, then tried to cover up with a fake cough.

By the time they crossed the railroad tracks, the sun had set and a brisk wind blew across the prairie, coming up from the south. Mac fancied he caught the salty scent of the Gulf of Mexico in the wind. If so, that meant a storm brewed somewhere out of sight. The way it rained here wiped out tracks within minutes. Travel became impossible in the driving rain, but having his trail washed away mattered more.

"Mason won't shut up shop for another half hour," Cletus said, fumbling open a pocket watch and holding it up to catch the light from a gas lamp. "I can get everything you bought and be waiting for you long before dawn."

"Git," Flowers said. Cletus wasted no time galloping away. When the man was out of earshot, Flowers spoke in a weary voice. "The last time I found Desmond he was in the Frisky Filly Sporting House. From the ruckus he put up as I dragged him out, he might have a favorite whore there."

"We can start there," Mac said. His head swiveled back and forth, jumping at every cowboy and rider dressed in a black coat. Either none was in the gang hunting him or they ignored a man with a partner. Mac doubted he had a big enough store of luck to use the same trick twice. Having Cletus riding with them would have given more, better, cover.

"You're as jumpy as a long-tailed cat on a porch full of rockin' chairs," Flowers commented. "What kind of trouble did *you* get into here in Fort Worth?"

"Some of Miz Sullivan's teetotaler ways must have rubbed off on me, maybe. All these drinking emporiums make me a tad uneasy." As they rode past every saloon, Mac glanced inside, worrying he would see the square-headed, broad-shouldered men hunting him down.

"Why do I doubt that?" Flowers asked dryly as he drew rein in front of a fancy three-story building.

Lights burned in every window on the top floor. Half-dressed women sat on a balcony circling the second story. They waved and hooted at anyone passing by. The ground floor had stained glass windows, cut crystal fixtures visible through the open front door, and a parlor that was about the ritziest thing Mac had ever seen. He wouldn't have thought this was a frontier cathouse but rather one pulled up by the roots from Storyville in New Orleans and transplanted. It seemed out of place in a rough and tumble section of town like Hell's Half Acre, but Mac knew the rich folks liked to sneak down to the "wrong" part of town and revel in the danger.

Mac touched the revolver tucked into his belt to remind himself he had six empty chambers. The sight of a huge black man in a tailored, pearl-gray, swallowtail coat standing just outside the door, acting as gatekeeper, reminded him of his lack of firepower. There wasn't any way he could take a man that size and strength in a bare knuckles fight. From the way the mountain of a man stood, he had plenty of weapons of his own tucked away in a shoulder rig, in his coat pockets, and unless Mac guessed wrong, a couple of sheathed knives hidden under the broad lapels of his fancy jacket.

"We have to get past him?" Mac asked in awe.

"You man enough to bull past him?" Flowers laughed. This was as close to humor as Mac had heard from him, and it had to come at his expense.

"A full-grown bull's not bull enough to get past him."

Flowers nodded once.

"You might be a good hire, after all. You're the first one of the men I ever brought who's shown good sense."

"How loco are your cowboys? Who'd tangle with him?" Mac stepped down to stand beside his horse. He pressed close to hide his face from riders in the street. They shouted obscenities back at the ladies of the evening on the porch just above the street. In return, the Cyprians passed judgment on their manhood and anatomical endowments.

"We full up right now," the ebony giant said, stepping up and pressing a hand the size of a dinner plate against Flowers's chest.

"You mean we don't have the money to even get into the parlor. I know that. We're here to take Mister Sullivan home. He is here, isn't he?"

"That'd be tellin'. The boss don't like that none. Our customers deserve—and get—all the privacy we can give 'em."

Flowers lifted his shoulders and dropped them as he stepped forward. Mac almost laughed when he saw the servant's expression. Flowers might be the man's name, but he wasn't in the least bit fragrant like one. If he had taken a bath in the past week, it would have been a surprise.

"That'd be Harrison Judd?" Flowers said.

The broad, flat face betrayed no emotion.

"Who's inquirin' after me, Obediah?" On the heels of the question, a dapper man twirling a cane came from inside the whorehouse. The light caught the gold knob at one end of the cane and the steel tip at the other.

Mac had seen canes like this before. A sword inside the length came out with the twist of the knob and presented a formidable weapon. He began to get antsy at so much deadliness facing him and Flowers. His empty revolver taunted him now and made him wonder if a plot in the potter's field waited for him.

"Just the gent I want to see," Flowers said. "Come on out for a minute, Mister Judd. We wouldn't want to disturb any of the paying customers." Flowers pointedly looked at the well-dressed men in plush chairs with a drink in one hand and their other arm around trim waists of pretty waiter girls.

"This is becoming tedious," Judd said. "Let the boy sow his wild oats. You got no call dragging him out by his heels just when he's beginning to enjoy himself."

"Unless I miss my guess, Desmond is so drunk there's not a whale of a lot he can enjoy right now. Has he passed out?"

"Doesn't matter one bit to me. He pays for a lady's company. That's between the two of them."

"So you aren't the pimp running this whorehouse? You don't take the money from the gals and get them hooked on laudanum?"

Mac put his hand on Flowers's arm to quiet him. The man was building up a head of steam, and the safety valve wasn't going to hold much longer. Obediah moved his hand under his coat to get nearer the revolver in his shoulder holster. If lead started flying, Flowers would be the first to drop. Mac would be a close second.

Flowers jerked away from Mac angrily. He thrust out his chin and bumped his chest against Harrison Judd. The brothel owner, though considerably smaller, stood his ground.

"Might be we can come to an arrangement," Judd suggested. "I only learned recently that Desmond's last name is Sullivan. He wouldn't be the son of Mercedes Sullivan, would he? The widow owner of the Circle Arrow? That must mean he's actually as rich as he makes out with the girls."

"He doesn't have a penny to his name," Flowers said.

"But his ma does. What's it worth to her not to have him dragged through the streets naked as a jaybird and humiliated? Or maybe the marshal comes by and arrests his ass for disturbing the peace."

"Peace? That's not what he's here for. He—"

"Arrested and his picture bannered on the front page of the *Fort Worth Daily Gazette* would cause his poor old ma considerable heartache. Why, she wouldn't be able to hold her head up if she ever came into town again. How'd such publicity help her with her temperance crusade? Makes her look like a hypocrite, doesn't it?"

"She'd disown him so it wouldn't reflect on her," Mac said. He squeezed harder on Flowers's arm to keep the man quiet. It didn't work.

"You go drag him out here this minute or we're going in and find him," Flowers declared.

"The Frisky Filly is a big place. You think you can find him before you get tossed out? Or worse?"

Hiram Flowers reared back to launch a haymaker. A dozen things flashed through Mac's head at the same instant. The black guard was pulling his revolver. Judd worked his hand over to a vest pocket where the butt of a derringer poked out. The argument had drawn the attention of the women on the balcony above them. Worse, Flowers shouting at the pimp drew a crowd of men who were flowing into town for a night's debauchery.

Mac looped his arm around the foreman's and twisted hard. This kept the punch from landing and unbalanced Flowers enough for Mac to steer him away. The foreman cursed and raged until they were across the street.

"What'd you stop me for, you young idiot? I could have taken him."

"It wouldn't have been a fair fight. Look upstairs."

Flowers sputtered and tried to deny that several of the scantily clad women had pistols of their own. Even if they aimed at Flowers and missed, hitting their pimp, the torrential downpour of lead would have been deadly.

"Get yourself killed and what good's that to Desmond?" Mac saw Obediah's attention fixed on them. He kept his hand hidden under his coat, resting on his revolver.

Then the guard had his hands full of cowboys trying to crowd into the Frisky Filly to sample the fleshy wares.

"He's in there. You heard what that snake said. He wants to blackmail Mercedes!"

"That makes it easier on us that Desmond is a man of habit." Mac studied the layout of the building. There had to be a back entrance. Judd didn't look to be the kind of man willing to pay for a guard on each door. Obediah was probably alone, his size and menacing look intended to keep out anyone who could be intimidated.

That included Mac, but he felt the pressure of time working on him. The bounty hunters wouldn't give up after he had plugged one of them. The way they had chased him through the saloons and up and down the streets the night before told him they were persistent, both from the need for revenge and the huge reward on his head. Either of those would be enough to keep them looking for him. Both insured they'd wear down the shoes on their horses chasing him to the ends of the earth.

"What's he look like? Desmond?"

"You're not going in there without me. I swear, I'll thrash him within an inch of his life for putting his poor ma in such a position. She'd die if he got his picture in the newspaper for doing half what he's likely doing in there." Flowers balled his hands into knobby fists as he ranted.

"Come around back. Let me do the talking," Mac said.

"I want that young reprobate out of there. If he doesn't ride with us on the drive, Mercedes said she'd come along."

"And you want her to stay safe and sound on the ranch," Mac said. He eyed Flowers closely, then shook his head. The grizzled old cowhand and the lovely ranch owner were as mismatched a pair as he could imagine. Still, he understood unrequited love and what it did to a man.

Evie had thrown him over for Pierre Leclerc and, so help him, Mac still loved her. Deep down, he still loved her although he knew fate had driven them apart for all time.

He didn't wait to see if Flowers was going to play along. Crossing the street, he went around the side of the building until he reached the far end of the balcony on the second floor. He waved to a young girl there.

"You can't—" Flowers started, then shut up when Mac shot him a cold look.

"Hello up there," Mac called. "You've got quite a view from that balcony."

"You want a better view? Here, mister, take a gander at this." The woman hiked her skirts and fluttered them about. She wasn't wearing anything under them.

"I'm a bit nearsighted. I'm not sure what I saw. Fact is, I do better fumbling around in the dark. My hands are a lot better at finding secret places than my eyes. Why not let me in?"

"Come on around to the front and tell Obediah it's all right."

"You didn't see the misunderstanding I had with him. He didn't think this was enough." Mac took out every bill he had left from his earnings. Folded triple and spread out in the dark, it looked like a wad of greenbacks big enough to choke a cow. "And that's just one pocket." He thrust his hand in and pulled out the same roll of bills, making it seem he was rolling in dough. "It'd all be yours 'cept he won't let me in."

"Come on, Mackenzie," Flowers said, tugging on his arm. "We can figure something else to get inside."

"My friend says there's a better house down the street. Too bad since you're real purty." Mac made no move to go after Flowers. He knew what the soiled dove's reaction would be. And he was right.

"Come on around. There's a door painted all red. I'll let you in there, but you got to give me all that money."

"Honey child, it's all yours."

Mac tried not to look too eager rounding the cathouse and standing in front of the red door the whore had mentioned. Flowers stood close.

"We rush in and—" the foreman began.

"And nothing," Mac broke in. "If she raises a ruckus, finding Desmond will be impossible." He heard someone fumbling with the doorknob. "There she is now. Keep quiet and follow me."

"You're mighty bossy for a hand I just hired this afternoon. I can fire you, you know."

"That's up to you, isn't it? I learned that a chuckwagon cook's got to take charge or he'll get walked on. Nobody walks over me."

"You got quite a mouth on you." Flowers sounded ready to fight again.

"Stop being so riled you've got to pull Desmond's chestnuts out of the fire." Mac saw the slow realization dawn on Flowers that his anger was misdirected. He relaxed a little, but his fists were still ready for a fight.

The door swung open. "You all hot and ready or you just gonna talk?" The soiled dove stood with one hand on a cocked hip and tried to look alluring "Don't matter to me, as long as I get paid."

Mac went to her and pushed the door open more so he got a good look down the hallway. They were at the rear of the building and a staircase led upward just inside the door.

"Why don't you go to your room and get ready for me?" he suggested. "I like to make a grand entrance."

"Like an actor coming on stage?"

"Exactly like that," Mac said. He held out a few of his greenbacks. She snared them and made a big point of tucking them into her bodice.

"I'll expect the rest after you make that big entrance." She walked down the hall, putting as much of a hitch in her behind as possible to entice him. She paused a moment at a door, shot him a sultry look and batted her eyelashes, then went in.

"Come on. We don't have much time to find Desmond," Mac said. He worried that Obediah might make a round through the halls to be sure everything was all right. Or Harrison Judd might check on his girls. Or any of a dozen other problems.

Flowers started up the stairs. Mac hung back and seriously considered hightailing it. He had gotten out of Fort Worth and away from the bounty hunters once. The more times he had to escape their six-guns the more likely his luck was to run out.

"Come on. I can't find the son of a bitch by myself." Flowers motioned urgently for him.

This decided Mac. He wanted the job with the Circle Arrow cattle drive, not only as a way to elude Leclerc's killers. He enjoyed being out on the trail, as dangerous as that could be.

He took the steps two at a time to reach the upper floor. Mac stared at the lavish decorations. Plaster statues of nude women lined the hallway. A soft carpet deadened the sound of Flowers's boots as he tromped along, opening each door as he went to take a quick look inside. Twice Flowers got furious cries to stop spying. At the third door he opened he simply stood and stared. Mac hurried to join him.

"That's Desmond?" Mac almost burst out laughing.

The rust-haired boy was only a year or two younger than Mac but had the look of being unfinished, soft . . . and drunker than a lord. He sprawled on his back across a big bed. His long johns had been put on backward so the drop flap was in the front and open.

"You boys want to join us? That'll be extra." A nude, blond strumpet perched on the edge of the bed, one foot up on the mattress and the other on the carpeted floor. She lounged back to expose herself.

"Come on, Desmond. Time to go." Flowers swung Mercedes Sullivan's son up and over his shoulder. He staggered a bit under the weight, then got his balance. "Get his clothes, Mackenzie."

Mac did as he was told, letting Flowers slip past into the hallway. He faced the harlot, who showed every sign of putting up a protest.

"What's he owe you?"

"A hundred dollars!"

"That's a lot of money."

With a sullen pout on her face, she said, "I'm worth it."

Mac pondered a moment, then said, "One of your friends down on the first floor's got the money."

"Angie? Bethany?"

"Yeah," Mac said, edging to the stairs. "She's the one."

Before the woman complained, he followed Flowers down the steps and out back.

"That's his horse. Bring it here," Flowers ordered Mac.

Running now, Mac grabbed the reins of the horse and tugged, getting it moving. Flowers met him halfway back to the whorehouse, heaved, and dumped Desmond belly down over the saddle.

"Let's get the blazes out of here," Flowers said. "I've had all of Fort Worth that I can stomach."

Chapter 5

Quick Willy Means sat in the corner of the dance hall, watching the ebb and flow of customers. Most came in to get drunk. Some came in to pay a dime and dance with the girl of their choice. Only a few did both.

This was one of the more expensive watering holes in Fort Worth, being right at the edge of Hell's Half Acre. It catered to a richer clientele but also saw some of the cowboys on their way to the dives and brothels south along Throckmorton Street. He liked the different types of men who came in. It gave him a chance to cover more territory in his hunt.

He slipped his revolver from his holster, snapped open the gate, and clicked the cylinder. Every chamber carried a fresh round. Another move closed the gate. He laid the pistol on the table next to the bottle of decent Kentucky whiskey.

Farther south, he couldn't get whiskey that didn't make him puke. In other parts of Fort Worth, he had to pay too much. This was just right. Plus he could reach any part of town in a flash, being centrally located. That suited him just fine after Jimmy Huffman was cut down. He had never liked Jimmy, or his brothers, but they were the best trackers he had ever hired and had no qualms about using their revolvers if the need arose.

And it did often. Means was the most efficient bounty hunter in the West. In eight years of hunting criminals, he had failed to find only two, and he thought one of them had died in a spring flood, his body washed all the way down the Mississippi to the Gulf of Mexico.

The other one he considered still to be found. Being hired by the shipping magnate in New Orleans added to the work, but the price Pierre Leclerc paid in advance made up for the detour from Kansas City and a man with a thousand-dollar reward on his head to this piss pot Texas town. Being derailed irritated him, but having Mackenzie cut down Jimmy Huffman caused a hatred to build. Quick Willy Means did not lose men working for him.

Ever.

He moved his gun a few inches on the table, poured himself another shot of the acceptable whiskey, and knocked it back before the rangy blond man crossed the dance floor to stand in front of him. Arizona Johnston might do to replace Jimmy Huffman. He had a quick hand, sharp eye, and didn't give much lip. Mostly Means appreciated that he was a thinker without being a jackass. But he really didn't know the man yet.

"I've got a line on him," Johnston said without preamble. "He and two others rode into town from the south. One went off on his own, but Mackenzie and his partner made a beeline to a whorehouse." He smiled crookedly. "A fine one by the look, too, not just a crib like most of them in that part of town."

Means used the muzzle of his revolver to push a shot glass in Johnston's direction and said, "Have a drink."

"Later, when we've corralled him."

"You won't drink with me?" Means sat a little straighter.

"I will when we catch Mackenzie and have the bounty riding

high in our pockets. Keeping my head clear now lets me enjoy a celebration later."

Means gave the gunman another once-over. The trail clothes he wore varied considerably from those worn by the Huffman brothers. Arizona Johnston wore a sand-colored duster, with canvas pants poking out from under the frayed hem. A plain brown cloth coat, paisley vest, and a boiled white shirt showed some taste, but nothing out of the ordinary. His Stetson with a snake-skin hatband was pushed back on his head.

The only thing that interested Means about the man's attire were the two revolvers. One hung low on his right hip just about the proper place for a quick draw. The other rode high in a cross-draw holster on his left side. Two guns but he wasn't rigged to fire one in each hand.

"Let's go after our fugitive from justice," Means said, pushing back from the table. He made a big show of picking up the gun with his left hand, doing a border shift to his right, spinning it around, and slipping it expertly into his right holster.

He watched for Johnston's reaction. There wasn't one. He either was unimpressed or he hid his admiration for a man so adroit with a shooting iron. Means needed to find out which it was before they hit the trail together.

As they walked out side by side, Johnston asked, "Is it true you have a pack mule so loaded down with wanted posters that it walks bowlegged?"

"I've got a couple hundred posters in a banker's folder. Any of those varmints might show up at any time, at any place. It's my duty to study them and to be sure new posters are added."

Means kept his voice level as he answered, but the flippant question peeved him. Hunting men was a business and one he took seriously. There was never room for joking.

"Where'd the Huffman boys get off to?" Johnston swung up into the saddle and waited for him to step up.

Means settled himself in the saddle, pushed back his coattails to expose the butts of both revolvers, then said, "They're mourning their brother. Lead the way. We can take Mackenzie ourselves."

"Do we split the reward with the Huffmans?"

"They're part of the crew."

"Not that good a part," Johnston said, eyes ahead as he rode. "One got himself cut down and the other two are drowning their sorrows."

"They're partners. My partners. Are you looking to take the entire reward for yourself?"

"Of course not. You've got the contact back in New Orleans. I just wanted to make sure where I stood. Equal share, right?"

"We're in this together," Means said. "You found him, so you've earned your share."

"And the Huffmans? How'd they earn theirs?"

"Being my partners," Means said, his ire rising now. "We've ridden together for quite a spell. Most bounty hunters concentrate on a lone outlaw at a time. We go after entire gangs."

"Loyal," Johnston said softly, almost to himself. "I can appreciate that."

Means tilted his head to one side when he heard the shouts ahead. A couple of shots made him reach for his left-hand gun, but he checked the move. All around him and Johnston flowed men like a bucking, churning ocean, running in the direction of the whorehouse.

"What's going on?" Means asked.

"I'll find out," Johnston said. He bent low and grabbed the collar of a man stumbling along. With an impressive show of strength he pulled the man off his feet. His boots kicked feebly in the air scant inches above the dirt. "Where are you going, partner?"

"Big fight. Riot. Men gonna get themselves kilt. I want to see."

"Where's this fight?"

"Somebody said it was at the Frisky Filly. Harry Judd's place." The man belched and turned slowly in Johnston's grip. "He don't like bein' called Harry. He's all stuck up and snotty. Harrison Judd, he says, 'cuz he runs the fanciest fancy house in the whole damn town."

Johnston dropped the man, who fell to his knees, then scrambled up and joined the flow of the crowd.

"Do you reckon it's Mackenzie causing the uproar?"

"There's one way to find out," Means said. He kept his horse walking through the crowd until the men were packed too close for any further progress.

Ahead rose the house of ill repute with a second-story balcony filled with whores all egging on the fighting down below. Means stood in his stirrups and tried to see who was responsible for the loud hoots and hollers, both from the women and from the crowd.

"See him?" Johnston asked.

Means didn't bother answering. He settled down and thought hard. Getting closer to the house wasn't possible. Hundreds of men barred his way. Worse, identifying Mackenzie in such a crowd would be like finding a particular straw stick in a haystack.

"There's nothing we can do with a crowd this big. If we tried to grab Mackenzie, the crowd would turn on us just for the hell of it."

"What are we going to do? Lose him?"

"Johnston, you haven't thought this through. He'll ride out of town. We follow. We'll grab him out on the prairie."

"What aren't you telling me?" Arizona Johnston craned his neck. "There's three men riding off. That might be them."

"I saw. One's Mackenzie, sure as rain. The old pelican riding with him is Hiram Flowers, about as tough a man as you'll ever run across."

"Does he have a reward on his head?"

Means shook his head slowly.

"Not that I ever saw, but that doesn't mean he hasn't done plenty that's against the law. With Mackenzie beside him, the two must be up to something."

With that, Means skirted the crowd and began riding slowly in the direction Mackenzie and Flowers had taken. They had come to rescue the third man. Was Flowers getting a gang together? It had been five years since he'd run afoul of the man over in Abilene. There hadn't been any hint that Flowers broke the law, but Means always wondered. Seeing him with Dewey Mackenzie firmed up his opinion. They were up to no good.

"Willy, over there. A man with two pack mules."

He started to correct Johnston and order him to call him Mister Means, then saw what the man already had. One man didn't need so much in the way of supplies. This might be the target for Mackenzie and his gang.

"Go back and get the Huffman brothers. If Mackenzie is planning a robbery, I might need a passel of guns backing me up."

"You're not going to take them on by yourself? If Mackenzie is half as dangerous as you said that Leclerc made out, you'd have your hands full. With two others backing him in a robbery, there'd be no way any one man stood a beggar's chance of capturing them."

"I don't intend to ambush them since I'd have to know where the man with the pack mules is headed. Get Charles and Frank. If they try to rob him, they'll do it around dawn. I would."

Johnston started to make another comment about such craziness, then wheeled around and trotted away, finding a side street to avoid the crowd outside the Frisky Filly. It had grown even larger.

Quick Willy Means made sure his revolvers rode easy in their holsters, then gave his horse its head to walk along parallel to the drover with the pack mules. When the man disappeared over a rise, Means cut across the terrain and found the road leading to the southwest.

He kept his distance, wondering what the drover had in his packs that Mac and Flowers might want. Men like that would steal pennies off a dead man's eyes. It took all his willpower not to ride up to the man with the mules and offer to guard his shipment, hoping Mackenzie attacked anyway. Let the murderous outlaw come to him.

But he held back. Dawn began poking into the sky by the time Johnston and the Huffman brothers joined him.

"I let the drover get a mile ahead. Even if Mackenzie robs him, we can overtake him, especially if he tries to keep what all he's stolen."

"We want him dead, boss. He killed Jimmy."

Means ignored whichever of the Huffman brothers spoke. It made no difference to him if Mackenzie was taken back alive or dead, although Leclerc had promised a bonus if he was returned to New Orleans alive to stand trial. Leclerc had an ax to grind. For Means, it was a matter of expediency. Mackenzie might surrender right away. Cowards did that. If so, he'd be obligated to take him to Leclerc for justice. More likely, especially with Hiram Flowers at his side, Mackenzie would try to shoot it out.

That never came out good for the outlaws. Means had been returning escaped prisoners and road agents for eight years. Not one had survived a shoot-out with him. From all he could tell about Mackenzie, he was just starting his criminal career. That made him a greenhorn, a greenhorn outlaw and easy prey. His instincts would be wrong, and his skill with a gun would be lacking.

Means glanced over at Arizona Johnston. Even if Mackenzie went against Johnston, he had no chance. The Huffman boys were a different matter, but it wouldn't come to that. He wouldn't let it.

They topped a low rise and had a panoramic view of the dawn-lit Texas prairie. He caught his breath.

"They're riding together, the three from Fort Worth and the

man with the supplies." Frank Huffman sounded confused. Means shared some of that puzzlement.

"It might be they're all in cahoots," he said, finally coming up with a new plan. "We won't try to grab Mackenzie now. We'll trail them for a while and see what they're up to."

"That might be dangerous, Willy," said Johnston. "With the supplies on those two mules, they can feed a small army. We could be up against a couple dozen outlaws."

Frank Huffman drew his pistol and aimed it in Mackenzie's direction. "You turning chicken, Arizona? We don't care. That son of a bitch murdered our brother. Even if he's backed up by a thousand men, we're gonna take him down."

Johnston said something under his breath about being stupid. But Means knew Frank wasn't going to fire. At this range the bullet would dig up prairie a hundred yards off. Alerting Mackenzie served no purpose. Frank only imagined what he would do when they got close enough.

Means didn't much care who plugged Dewey Mackenzie. If he had to track him down across half of Texas, he didn't want to take him back alive to New Orleans. That'd be too much trouble for too little reward.

"Let's see what supplies we've got between us, boys," he said to the other bounty hunters. "We're in for a longer hunt than I intended. We don't want to get too hungry before we bring in Mackenzie." Under his breath he added, "And Hiram Flowers."

Chapter 6

"It gets harder," Hiram Flowers told Mac. "A damned sight harder. You won't be enjoying the trip near as much when we get to the Pecos River."

"Is the river swollen this time of year?" As he asked the question, Mac went about his work fixing lunch for the Circle Arrow hands. They'd been on the trail four days and he still had plenty of the things they liked best. When he started running out of eggs and other perishables, the real grumbling would start.

He worked the dough for his biscuits until it oozed between his fingers with just the right texture. Of everything he fixed, biscuits were what kept the men happiest. That had been true when he had worked for the Rolling J, and it had been true with the Circle Arrow. So far.

"It's all swole up like a son of a bitch. Swole up worse 'n a rattlesnake-bit hound dog. Flowing over its banks, waiting to drown the lot of us." Flowers spat into the fire and caused a fragrant sizzling. He locked eyes with Mac, daring him to say anything.

Ever since leaving the ranch, Flowers had been in a foul

mood. Mac thought much of that choler came from Desmond Sullivan being along. The trail boss had ignored the young rancher, but as he'd said, the going had been easy. Mac hoped the rest of the Goodnight-Loving Trail proved as smooth.

At this rate they'd be in Santa Fe before they knew it, though Flowers had been muttering about stopping at Fort Sumner to sell some beeves to the Army. If Mac was any judge, that would make the trip from the fort to Santa Fe all the easier. Fewer cattle meant fewer problems, and they had started with north of a thousand head.

Mac divided the dough and placed the lumps into the Dutch oven to get the first batch ready. The rest of the meal would go fast enough. The cowboys would eat their steaks raw. One had even complained that the steak he got for breakfast hadn't mooed loud enough to suit him when he cut a slice off. Mac had jabbed him with a fork, getting a cry of surprise from him that had kept the rest of the crew amused until they saddled up and went to get the ornery longhorns moving for the day.

"How much farther do you intend to get today?" Mac cleaned his utensils and sampled some of the peach cobbler left over from breakfast. The supply of fresh fruit was coming to an end, too.

"Another five miles," Flowers said. He took off his hat and ran a hand over his thinning hair. "I got a bad feeling about tonight."

Mac studied the sky. Clouds moved fast from the west like giant puffs of cotton. Not one of them showed an ugly gray underbelly that promised rain. He had never been trapped out on such flat land during one of the infamous Texas frog stranglers, but he had heard about them. The rain came down in buckets and had almost nowhere to go. Everything turned to mud, and deep ravines cut through the ground made travel by wagon hard. Getting a herd across those arroyos would be quite a job, too.

"It's not the weather that's worrying me," Flowers said. He

looked back along their trail. A dust cloud rose where the herd moved toward them.

"Trouble with the men? Anything you want me to do?"

Flowers shot him a cold look and shook his head.

"Not the men that's worrying me. It's the men trailing the herd."

"Rustlers?" Mac sucked in his breath and looked at his revolver hanging in a holster he had won from one of the drovers in a poker game. He still didn't have any ammunition for the .44.

"Might be cowboys looking to join our company," Flowers said.

"You don't believe that. Why not? How long have they been trailing us?"

"I spotted them a couple days back. From the way they tried to stay out of sight, we might have had their unwanted company since leaving the ranch."

"My gun's mighty hungry," Mac said. "It'd feel better if it had a belly full of cartridges."

"Tell Messerschmidt to give you a box or two from our stores. You're one of the first they'd try to rob, being out front of the herd most of the time and all by your lonesome."

Mac always followed Flowers as the trail boss scouted ahead for the entire herd. When he reached the spot the trail boss marked, he'd stop and prepare a meal, either midday or supper and breakfast where the herd bedded down for the night. As the cattle began their daily travels, he had to get after Flowers and repeat the routine, always leading and mostly on the trail alone unless he happened to find the trail boss.

"Much obliged."

Flowers fixed him with a steely, accusing look. "You can use that hog leg, can't you?"

Mac didn't answer. Anything he said would sound like bragging or worse. He might arouse Flowers's ire if he talked of the men he had shot down. Every last one of them had deserved it—and he was innocent of the one he was accused of killing in New Orleans. It hardly seemed fair. Whatever it was, Mac knew better than to talk about it.

"The men will get the herd here in another hour. I'm heading yonder." Flowers waved his hat toward a range of low hills in the distance. "Once everyone's chowed down, you skirt those hills to the south and then angle back toward me to the northwest."

"Is the going directly over the hills too rough for the chuckwagon?"

Flowers nodded, distracted. He swung into the saddle and headed out.

"You not eating?" Mac called after him.

"Not hungry." Flowers rubbed his belly. With that he trotted away, leaving Mac to wonder if the trail boss didn't like his food or if the man's stomach was hurting him. From the noises it made when he ate, his digestion was terrible.

Mac poked through the medicinal supplies he had, hunting for something that might ease belly pain. He found a bottle of Sal Hepatica and wondered if this might help Flowers. He had other nostrums that might serve a man better who spent his day in the saddle. Flowers might enjoy life more by seeing a doctor in one of the towns they passed along the trail, though many frontier sawbones tended to be as dim as an old buffalo trail.

Humming to himself, Mac finished the cooking just as the first of the cowboys came in. He served them up the last of the fresh food, then talked with Messerschmidt about getting a box of ammunition.

"You thinking on starting a range war, Mac?" The man rummaged through the supply wagon until he found a box of .44s. He passed them over.

"Thanks, Messy. Flowers suggested I keep my revolver loaded since he thinks we're . . . getting away from the towns," he finished lamely. Telling Messerschmidt or any of the others that

Flowers believed they were being followed by a gang of rustlers would spook them needlessly. While the cowboys ought to be on guard, worrying them over a few men who might just be heading in the same direction was pointless.

Besides, it was the trail boss's job to talk over such problems, not the cook's.

"How's he doing?" Mac didn't have to point out Desmond Sullivan. Messerschmidt knew right away who he meant.

"He does the work of five men."

"What?" This startled Mac. His eyebrows rose.

Messerschmidt laughed.

"What I mean, Mac, is that it takes five men to do his work after he makes a complete botch of it. He knows nothing about being a drover. He should ride along and do nothing. That would keep all of us happy, but he meddles and makes things bad." Messerschmidt shook his head. "Flowers should never have let him come along. We must take care of the herd and ourselves *and* him."

Mac didn't want to share what he had overheard back at the ranch and in Fort Worth. Flowers had struck the bargain of wet-nursing Desmond to keep Mercedes Sullivan from accompanying them. He wondered if he was the only one who saw how Flowers wore his heart on his sleeve for their boss lady. Flowers would walk through hell barefoot for her.

This image caused a smile to curve his lips. If Flowers did just that, the Devil would throw him out of hell because of the stink. None of them on the drive had a chance to bathe, and some didn't want to. In Hiram Flowers's case, it was almost a matter of pride that he smelled worse than a stepped-on skunk.

"Time to drive on and set up for this evening. You got any requests, Messy?" Mac held up the ammo box. "I owe you for these."

"You do a good job, Mac. Better than Cassidy ever did."

"By better you mean I haven't poisoned anyone yet."

"Yeah, that." Messerschmidt slapped him on the shoulder and went around to climb into the driver's box of the supply wagon. He rode with the herd to get the cowboys anything they might need during the day.

Mac finished cleaning the last of the utensils, pots and pans, packed his chuckwagon, and settled in for the drive Flowers had outlined for him. This wasn't the first time he had taken a different route from the man riding scout. Being on horseback allowed the scout to travel faster and find better vantage points to study the lay of the land for the herd. When he had been with the Rolling J crew along the Shawnee Trail he had doubled as cook and scout, learning firsthand how difficult it was to find the right trail for a large herd.

He whistled tunelessly as he drove his team down the slight incline and found a trail to rattle along that took him around the taller hills and finally brought him out on the far side.

As his team struggled to pull along in sandy ground, the hair on the back of his neck rose the way it always did when he sensed someone watching him. Without being too obvious, he reached back and caught the holster swinging gently behind him. The loaded gun slid free of the leather, then was tucked securely into the waistband of his trousers. The gun had just settled in place when a solitary Indian rose from behind a tall mesquite bush and blocked his way.

Mac drew back slowly on the reins to bring his wagon to a halt. One brave posed little threat. A quick study of the man convinced Mac he had come upon a hunter and not a war party.

But he knew the Comanche wasn't out on the prairie alone. He didn't carry enough gear behind him on the pony. That meant a camp somewhere nearby. A lone Comanche had no reason to pitch camp and ride around when he carried his entire wealth with him. There would be others, perhaps a dozen or more.

Not for the first time Mac wished he had eyes in the back of his head. He heard the horses coming up from behind where he couldn't see them. Turning and making a show of counting them lowered his status in their eyes.

"Howdy," he called. "How's hunting? I haven't seen anything the whole livelong day but a few scrawny rabbits." As if trying to find a more comfortable spot on the hard wooden bench seat, he moved his hand closer to the butt of his revolver.

From the soft thuds at least four rode up from behind. At least. He sucked in his breath when two more joined the Indian blocking his way.

The brave who had stopped him pointed to the rear of the chuckwagon. "You have food?"

"For the men riding herd. We are moving many hundreds of longhorns. Many, many hundreds."

They exchanged silent looks. The other four drew rein on either side and slightly behind him to make it harder for him to open fire on them should they attack. Seven braves, six rounds in his trusty .44? He was a good shot but even assuming every round found a target, that left one hunter unscathed.

He squinted a bit in the afternoon sun and again tried to read their painted faces. A few streaks meant decoration. And their horses lacked paint. Sometimes a war party put painted hand prints on their horses' rumps. These needed currying and, judging by their sunken flanks, decent fodder. But he saw no indication he had run afoul of a war party.

He let out a small self-deprecating chuckle. How stupid could he be? If they'd been a war party, they wouldn't stop to talk. They'd ambush him and take whatever was left.

"Cows?" the spokesman said.

Mac nodded. "Many, many cows. Perhaps my chief would be willing to give your chief a few beeves as a show of friendship."

"Many, many cows?"

"A few. In exchange for your friendship."

The three ahead whispered. The one speaking shook his head. Mac turned so his hand rested on the pistol. He'd go down shooting, if it came to that.

"We hungry now."

"Then on the behalf of my chief, let me extend friendship now with a meal. I've got some food left over from my noon meal . . . for many, many cowboys." It didn't hurt to keep reminding them that he was alone right now but a veritable army of cowboys came along behind.

"You feed?"

"I will." Mac pushed hard on the brake and looped the reins around it. As he got down from the driver's box, he slipped his pistol from his waistband and left it on the floor. No gun, no mistakes.

They were hungry and jumpy. Shooting his way out of a jam wasn't possible if they got worked up. He'd had some contact with Comanches back in Waco and respected their fighting and riding skills. Talk—and a dollop of food—was the best way to avoid trouble now.

"Step right up," he said. "I'll get a fire going to boil some coffee. That'll help wash down the food."

Dried cow chips sent up a long, thin tendril of smoke when he got a pile of them lighted. Whether this warned Flowers or anybody with the herd of trouble, he didn't know, but he needed the fire anyway to make the coffee. As it boiled, he set out slabs of jerky, a pot of beans, and leftover biscuits for the Indians. They held back until he sampled each in turn, then he held out the various items for them. The way they gobbled down what the cowboys would have turned up their noses at told him how hard life was for them out here.

He stoked the fire with a few more dried cow chips. A gust of stinking gray smoke rose and got whipped around not fifty feet in the air. He only had two tin cups, but he filled those and passed them out to the Indians, who took turns gulping down his brew. The cowboys told him it tasted like varnish. The only response he got from the Comanches was a loud belch. They were so appreciative he was glad he didn't bother putting sugar in the coffee. This served the purpose of keeping them nice and peaceable. No reason to waste a valuable commodity out here on the range when anything he gave them was considered a banquet.

"Many, many cows?" The only one who spoke stabbed his finger in Mac's direction.

"Many, many cowboys herding them," he said.

The Comanches whispered again, then their spokesman said, "Many, many horses?"

"Not many," he answered slowly. For the Indians, horses were mobile wealth. They couldn't eat or ride gold. A brave with a dozen horses was a rich man. The Circle Arrow remuda had more than fifty horses in it. Without a mount, a cowboy was worthless. Nobody walked alongside a herd of longhorns and kept up.

"Many. You lie!" The brave swung his rifle up and pointed it at Mac.

He remembered how he had originally considered shooting it out with them. He would die, probably get scalped, and the entire chuckwagon filled with supplies would be stolen, but a blazing six-gun would let them know they'd been in a fight. Now he stood unarmed and helpless.

Mac raised his hands and stood to face the Comanche. The Indian cocked the hammer on his rifle and took aim.

Chapter 7

"Nice rifle. It'd be a damned shame if it got dropped in the dirt when I put a bullet through your head."

Hiram Flowers stepped from behind a greasewood, his Winchester trained on the Comanche with his rifle leveled at Mackenzie.

The cook took everything in with a single sweep of his eyes across the tableau. The Indians were frozen in place, but the bore of the rifle pointed at his face looked big enough to reach down with his fist and grab the bullet.

"You have many, many cows?" the Comanche asked.

"That's a crazy thing to say when you're an inch away from having your head blowed off." Flowers took another half step to get a better shot. He let out a curt "Stop!" when two of the Indians went to lift their rifles. None of them had six-guns that Mac saw, but all had wickedly sharp hunting knifes. Not for the first time, he regretted leaving his gun back on the chuckwagon driver's box.

"No ammo. Empty gun." The Indian lifted the muzzle and pointed it at the sky. He squeezed the trigger. Mac winced as it fell on an empty chamber.

"That's a good thing, since you ate our food. It's not neighborly to eat our food and then shoot the cook." Flowers shifted his aim a bit lower but kept the rifle pointed in the general direction of the Indians across from the cooking fire.

"This one promise cows," the Comanche insisted. "Many, many cows."

Flowers snorted disgustedly. "This one doesn't have the sense God gave a goose."

Mac started to protest, then held his tongue. He knew negotiating when he heard it, even if he was made out to be a fool. Better to look like a fool than to be a clever corpse.

"I sell cattle, I don't give them away to just anybody. But you're friends, aren't you? All seven of you are our friends?"

Seven heads bobbed up and down.

"For friends, I might be willing to give a steer. As a way to let you know how much I think of you and your hunters."

"Ten cows. We let you pass over Comanche land for ten."

"Two steers feed a passel of your tribe. How hungry are your squaws?"

Mac saw Flowers hit the nail right on the head. Hunting was poor this year, and from the look of the Indians' horses, they were next to be served up for dinner. The Comanche families wouldn't be in any better shape. Two cows would feed plenty of them for a week, maybe longer.

"Five. You go great way across Comanche land." The Indian made a sweeping motion using his rifle. This provoked Flowers to take aim again.

Mac fought back a laugh when he saw the Comanche jerk his rifle down, knowing he had made a mistake. To his credit, Flowers made no mention of this. It was going to be an act of charity to give even two steers to the Indians for their families because the Circle Arrow drovers had the edge with numbers and firepower. If a hunter couldn't even load his rifle, that meant they went out to set traps and club unwary rabbits with rocks. Fighting a crew of cowboys armed to the teeth meant sure death.

"We friends with three cows," the spokesman bargained.

Flowers lowered his rifle and stepped up. He held out his hand to shake. The Comanche stared at it for a moment, then grasped Flowers's forearm. Both exchanged quick nods of agreement.

"We're plenty good friends now," Flowers said. "It's my pleasure to give my *friends* three cows."

"I've already given them food," Mac pointed out.

"Good idea giving them coffee." Flowers sniffed as he stared at the smoking fire. The cow chips weren't very dry.

"Where we get cows?" the Indian wanted to know.

"Don't go getting so all fired anxious. The herd will come to us. Two miles. An hour's ride." Flowers pointed over his shoulder. "The land gets choppy, and I decided to make this a quick travel day." This he directed at Mac.

"I can lead them to the spot," Mac said. "I need to set up for supper. Our friends might want to stay for more food."

He saw this met with almost as much approval as Flowers giving them the cattle to avoid being harassed as they made their way to the Pecos River. It was extortion pure and simple, but he reckoned the Circle Arrow got off cheap. A few stragglers in exchange for safe passage was a good deal since those cattle were going to be the first eaten by the cowboys anyway.

"Go with him. I'll make sure the herd gets to the rendezvous." Flowers shook hands again with the Indian, spun and walked away as if he didn't have a care in the world.

Mac saw the tenseness across the trail boss's shoulders and knew he relied on his cook to keep from getting shot in the back. The one rifle might not have been loaded. That said nothing about the other six, though Mac guessed they were empty, too. The brave doing the talking carried some authority and the others deferred to him. The Comanches elected a leader of the hunt, just as they elected a war chief, so the man had his position only as long as they trusted him.

It paid to butter him up so they'd keep the deal he made.

"You want more coffee before I pack up?" Mac passed around the tin cups again. He considered using sugar this time, but common sense prevailed. Nothing different to show he had held back before. Giving reason to go back on their deal was something only a greenhorn would do. He had been on another drive and had dealt with Shawnee Indians, who weren't that much different from the Comanche.

When his uninvited guests finished, he tossed the tin cups into the back of the chuckwagon and closed up. Washing the cups and utensils later seemed reasonable. Get the Indians on the trail with the promise of enough beef to feed their tribe for a week or two.

He clambered onto the driver's box, gathered the reins, and put his foot down on the revolver in the foot well to keep it from rattling around. It took him the better part of a half hour before he reached down and snared it, getting it back into the holster. He wished he had the holster belted on, but knowing the revolver was close enough for him to grab if the need arose made him happier. If it came to a shoot-out now, he knew those six rounds might go farther than expected because the Comanches had to rely only on their knives.

Finding a spot atop a low hill, he parked his wagon and began preparation for feeding the entire crew. The Indians stared at him with wide eyes. The amount of food he fixed would be enough to keep them and their families fed for the rest of the season.

He kept them occupied with more coffee until Messerschmidt came rattling up in the supply wagon. Mac saw the man wore his pistol strapped down. Beside him in the driver's box rode Klaus Kleingeld, fingering a double-barreled scattergun's triggers. Both men had been warned by the trail boss what they'd find.

Mac waved and considered going over to talk to them. Talking to Kleingeld did him no good since the Comanches understood him better—and he understood them better than he did the German. What Mac wanted to know was if Flowers had mentioned more than the Indians being in camp. Had he told anyone else about the men following the herd? The last thing they needed now with the Comanches here was a gang of rustlers stealing a sizable portion of the longhorns.

The confusion would open the door for the Indians to take plenty more than the three head that Flowers had promised them. So far, they hadn't lost but a few head to accidents. Two had stepped in prairie dog holes and broken their legs. They had furnished meals for almost a week. A few others turned sickly and had been shot and left for predators. All told, the Circle Arrow hadn't lost more than ten head.

Instead, he began cleaning up from the hasty midday meal he had provided. The Indians watched in silence as he did squaw's work and only showed life when Desmond Sullivan rode up. He galloped to within a half dozen feet of the Comanches, then pulled back so hard his horse dug in its hooves. A shower of dirt rose and covered the Indians.

"Watch what you're doing," Mac snapped. "You're getting dirt in the food."

"What're them redskins doing here? They got to clear out pronto. There's no way—"

"Mister Flowers said it was all right for them to wait. He's invited them to supper."

"Like hell! He can't do that. I own this damned herd, and I say who eats our food and who rides along."

"You don't own the herd," Mac said, his voice brittle. "Your ma does. Since she's not here, Mister Flowers is the one everyone takes orders from."

"I'm the owner." Desmond kicked free of the stirrups and dropped to the ground. The redhead was reaching for his revolver when Mac moved. Fast.

He dodged between Desmond and the Indians and got the young man's gun poked into his gut. The danger was high, but Mac didn't budge.

"Put down your gun," he told Desmond, tight-lipped with anger. "Unless you intend to plug me."

"I ought to. Who're you to meddle like this? I want them out of camp. I'm not eating food they eat."

"Then you'll get mighty hungry until breakfast." Mac reached down and pushed the pistol away. He breathed a sigh of relief when the muzzle pointed at the ground. "They'll get the three head of cattle Mister Flowers promised them, and they'll be on their way peaceably."

"What? He's giving away *my* beeves!"

Mac wasn't prepared for Desmond swinging the gun up and around in a wide arc. He felt the barrel collide with the side of his head. For an instant, he didn't think any damage had been done. Then his knees turned to butter, and he dropped to the ground, stunned. Not sure how he did it, as he fell he swung his nerveless arm around like a club. New pain lanced up into his shoulder, but he knocked the pistol out of Desmond's grasp.

This didn't stop the youth from barreling ahead, fists swinging. His clumsy blow caught one Indian in the middle of the face. Blood spurted from a broken nose. Desmond's second punch went wild and missed by a country mile. Mac fought to focus his eyes. He groaned and got to his feet, almost falling again until he got his balance back.

"Don't, no, don't!" he called out, and wasn't sure who he was ordering to stand down. Desmond was swinging like a windmill, but the Indians all drew their knives. The owner's son would be gutted and left for dead in a flash.

A distant roar filled Mac's ears. He thought it was thunder, then realized it was too close and the sky was clear of any storm clouds. A second blast solved the problem. Kleingeld had fired both barrels of his shotgun into the air.

The explosions startled Desmond, who half turned. The brave he had punched got in a good blow to his exposed belly. Desmond folded like a bad poker hand. But the other Indians all ran for their horses, getting astride and galloping away.

"They ride for the herd," Messerschmidt called. "They will steal our cows!"

Mac stepped over Desmond and grabbed the dangling reins to the young man's horse. It took most of his strength to pull himself up into the saddle. The horse was spooked by the shotgun and Mac used all of his skill as a rider to keep it from bucking him off.

He put his head down and clung to the horse's neck for dear life. The uneven gait jolted him and caused the world to spin. Slowly, his eyes focused and the ringing in his ears died down to a buzz. Ahead he saw the Indians fan out along a broad, wide ravine. The herd wasn't visible, but the lowing as they approached told the story. The Comanches readied for their theft of as many cattle as they could. Somewhere in the back of his head Mac thought they deserved whatever they could steal. Desmond had violated the uneasy truce with his impetuous attack.

Then Mac came to his senses. It was stealing Circle Arrow property. No matter what Desmond had done, the Indians were wrong taking more than the three Flowers had promised them. He saw the Indians swooping down. They cut at least thirty head from the main herd and tried to rush them through the gap. Only their scrawny horses kept them from succeeding.

"Stop! Those aren't yours," Mac shouted, but the sounds from the herd drowned out his orders. Mac slipped his revolver from its holster. Shooting the Indians would be akin to murder since he knew they were out of ammo. But if he didn't they would make off with three times as many cattle as they'd lost this far in the drive.

He fired at one Indian and instantly regretted it. The gunshot caused the lead steer to run. He had unintentionally started a stampede.

The Comanches tried to cut out a few of the cattle, but the tide of frightened gristle and immensely wide, long horns kept them from stealing any. Mac galloped alongside the herd as the steers scattered the Indians. In less than a minute the Comanches had vanished back onto the prairie—but Mac rode alongside tons of stampeding cattle.

His horse began to tire. He knew something had to be done fast, and he was the only one in position to do it. Before, on his previous trail drive, he had learned the dangers of a stampede, and how to stop it. Getting the beeves to mill was the only way to keep dozens or even hundreds of them from being run into the ground and killed. Turning the leaders was the answer. The cattle instinctively sought to gather rather than run out by themselves. Getting a few to turn and try to lose themselves in the middle of the herd would eventually rob them of leaders and get them spinning around and around rather than racing across the countryside.

Lather flecking its flanks, the horse's speed began to slacken. Mac fired his gun in the air and yelled until he was hoarse. Make the leaders run away from him, cross back in front of the rest of the herd, find a way to circle and begin to mill. It sounded easy. The longer his horse galloped, the more it faltered and the leaders of the stampede outdistanced him.

Then he caught a bit of luck. The herd shifted just a little in the right direction, forcing the leaders to run up a slope. This caused them to turn even more and definite milling began to occur. Mac fired until his revolver came up empty. The reports worked a miracle to force the cattle away from him.

The stampede was broken. And then his horse stepped into a prairie dog hole. The cannon bone snapping sounded louder than any of his gunshots. As the horse pitched forward on the broken leg, Mac sailed over the horse's head. He hit the ground hard enough to jolt him senseless, but in some distant part of his brain he knew the shaking ground beneath his back meant the herd was coming in his direction.

Moving was impossible. Staring up at the twilight sky, he saw a star. Irrationally, he began to make a wish on that first star of the night. He hoped for a quick death.

He didn't get it.

Chapter 8

Mac tried to call out when he heard a horse approaching rapidly. The air had been smashed from his lungs. Simply trying to suck in a breath sent knife stabs of pain throughout his chest. His legs kicked feebly. Trying to sit up caused more agony than he wanted. Ribs might be broken. Or worse. There had been a loud sound that might have been his spine snapping when he hit the ground.

His hand twitched. He tried to signal as the swift rataplan of hoofbeats came closer, but the rider didn't seem to notice him lying on the ground. Outlined against the stars, the man slowed his horse, turned in the saddle, and called out, "Frank? You see him?"

From a distance came the faint reply, "Son of a bitch ain't nowhere to be found."

Mac stopped his struggles and simply lay motionless, staring up at the sky. The voices weren't familiar.

"Quick Willy is scouting the far side of the herd. He's having a devil of a time avoiding those cowboys."

"We gotta meet up with him. We're not havin' any luck findin' the son of a bitch."

"It was the stampede that scattered everything. Horses, cattle, men."

"We done missed our best chance to nab him."

"Nab him, hell. I'll shoot the bastard down when I find him. I don't much care what Quick Willy says about a bonus reward for bringin' him back alive."

Mac's entire body quivered as his breathing began to return to normal. He fought down the loud gulping sound that tried to well up from his throat. His heart hammered so loudly in his ears the riders had to hear it. Frank. Quick Willy. Those names didn't belong to anyone on the drive. Bonus reward? These weren't Circle Arrow riders. They were bounty hunters after him.

After *him*.

The two men moved away, the thuds of their horses' hooves diminishing to nothing. Mac began rocking from side to side. Finally, he was able to roll over onto his belly. A huge effort brought him to his hands and knees. Only after a moment of dizziness did Mac get his feet under him to stumble to his horse.

The forward tumble had taken its toll on the animal. It had broken its neck right after its leg. Mac swallowed. This saved him a bullet—one he didn't have since he had emptied his gun turning the herd.

That thought made him turn in a full circle. Except for the dead horse, he stood alone on the range. The herd had vanished. Of the two riders hunting for him he saw not a trace. A deep breath hurt, but not as much as before, and settled his nerves.

At least three men were hunting for him. He knew two of their names. Quick Willy. Frank. Whoever Frank had been talking to earlier had been on the other side of a nearby rise. Taking a few more minutes to recover his strength, Mac got the tack off the horse, heaved it onto his shoulder, and hiked to the top of the hill where he believed the other bounty hunter had ridden.

Careful not to silhouette himself against the clear night sky, he looked around for the bounty hunters but didn't see them. In the distance he heard cattle lowing. That was where the herd had finished its stampede. Grunting with effort from the weight of the saddle, he began hiking.

Less than ten minutes later, a rider approached him. Mac touched the empty revolver in his holster, then jerked his head from side to side as he searched for a place to hide.

Too late. The rider homed in on him like an eagle swooping down on a rabbit.

He wished there had been a rifle in the saddle sheath, but Desmond hadn't carried one. Considering the boy's recklessness, Flowers had done well not letting him stick one in the scabbard before going on patrol. Mac dropped the saddle and widened his stance. A quick move pushed back his coat to get at the empty six-gun. Bluffing never worked for him as well as outright shooting, but he had no choice.

"That you, Mac?" called a voice with a familiar twang.

"Mister Flowers?" He relaxed his stance.

"Who'd you think it would be? Tarnation, Mac, you saved the herd from running itself into the ground. Three of the drovers said you turned it all by yourself. They were too far away to help, but they're singing your praises."

"Glad to hear they appreciate something other than my biscuits." Mac mulled over telling the trail boss about the men hunting him for the reward on his head back in New Orleans. There wasn't any reason to reveal that, he decided, since Hiram Flowers couldn't do anything about it.

"Desmond's not so fond of you right now. What happened to his horse?"

Mac explained about the horse's sad end. As he spoke, he rested his hand on the butt of his pistol. Flowers noticed.

"I didn't hear a gunshot, not after the herd came to rest."

"I was out of rounds," Mac said.

Flowers nodded grimly.

"Well, it's too damn bad. But I'll make it good with Desmond."

"The horse was his personal mount, not one from the remuda?"

"Climb on up behind me," Flowers said without answering Mac's question. "We'll get back to camp. You need to move the chuckwagon before breakfast."

"This is Desmond's tack."

"Leave it where it lays. I'll have him come out and get it himself." Flowers chuckled at this small punishment. He sobered quickly. "The way you lit out to turn the stampede—and he didn't—says a whole heap about the jobs you each do on the drive."

"I just wanted to choose which beeves I fed the crew. Having to cut up meat that's been trampled doesn't suit anybody."

"Hamburger," Flowers said.

"I don't know what you mean." Mac perched behind the trail boss's saddle and settled down as Flowers walked his horse back to camp.

"That's something Messerschmidt told me about. Ground beef made into a patty and then cooked. It's something he heard about from back in Germany."

"Do tell." Mac shook his head. "That'll never be popular, not if you can get a nice, juicy steak."

"I'd have to lose all my teeth before I'd want one of them hamburgers."

"China clippers," Mac said, laughing. "False teeth work just fine for chewing up a tender slab of beef, especially if it's one I fixed up just for you."

"Get your chuckwagon moved." The change in Flowers's tone caused Mac to jump down. They were within earshot of many drovers, and Flowers had to keep his reputation as being a hard case.

Mac stretched, which made every bone in his body hurt

again. Landing flat on the ground had taken more than the wind out of him. He winced as he touched a spot in the middle of his back. He found a long spine from a Spanish bayonet plant stuck in him. He was lucky. If it hadn't broken, the spine could have run all the way through him as surely as a knife blade. The more he moved around, the more aches and pains he discovered.

He tried to climb up into the driver's box and couldn't. His legs refused to lift him.

"Give me a boost, will you?" he called out into the dark as someone approached, not caring who knew how bad a shape he was in.

"Flowers just told me you killed my horse," Desmond said as he stalked up to the chuckwagon. "You stole my horse and gear and killed it. You killed my damned horse! I had that horse since he was a colt."

Mac sagged. He took a deep breath and regretted it as more pain stabbed through him. His ribs burned like liquid fire. A slow turn brought him face to face with Desmond Sullivan.

"I didn't want to hurt your horse," he said. "You trained him real good. Without his heart, I'd never have been able to turn the herd. He kept up and—"

Desmond launched a clumsy punch at Mac's face. Even in his debilitated condition, Mac had no trouble ducking the blow. As the knuckles slipped past his cheek, he stepped up and swung as hard as he could with his right fist. The punch landed smack in the middle of Desmond's belly. The young man gasped and backed off. He leaned forward and rubbed his belly, then spat. He doubled his fists.

"You sucker punched me."

"Better figure out what that really means." Mac ducked and weaved as Desmond came at him, flinging wild punches. "You weren't sucker punched. We were facing each other and you left your belly open. Like this!"

Mac let another punch slip past, then stepped up and drove his fist hard into Desmond's exposed midriff. His fist disappeared up to his wrist. The gush of air rushing from Desmond's lungs meant that the fight was over. Desmond folded up, fell to his knees, and then toppled onto his side.

Mac stepped over his opponent. Desmond struggled into a sitting position but couldn't maintain it. He fell onto his side and retched. When he finished losing his supper, Desmond tried to get back onto his feet. When he finally made it, he stumbled toward Mac.

"You can't . . ." he gasped out.

Mac pushed him away with just the tips of his fingers. Desmond lost his balance and sat down hard, back propped against the front wagon wheel. Tired, Mac sank down beside him and also leaned on the wheel.

"You've got quite a chip on your shoulder. More than that, you can't fight worth beans." He almost added that the young man's performance in the Fort Worth brothel probably rivaled his fighting skills, but he held that back. He had no reason to further inflame the boss's son.

"You'll pay," Desmond rasped. "I swear it. You're gonna pay." He turned to the side and leaned over to begin gagging again. However, this time he had nothing left in his stomach to lose.

"If you square off before launching a punch, you won't leave yourself open. Take your time, measure your opponent. And don't retreat. Stand your ground or advance." In a short, compact punch, Mac slammed his fist against a wheel spoke next to Desmond's head. "That's a lot more powerful than this." He duplicated the blow with his other hand, reaching a long way and keeping his elbow stiff when he hit.

"You're giving me boxing lessons?"

"Somebody has to. Didn't your pa ever show you anything about fighting?"

"Him?" Desmond snorted. "He was always doing something out on the range, with the damned cattle. When he did come home, he spent all his time with my ma."

"Can't blame him for that," Mac said. Desmond's sudden reaction made him add hurriedly, "Whoa! I meant your ma's a mighty fine-looking woman. And you're one ugly little sprout."

"Why, you—" Desmond tried to swing a roundhouse punch, but his position seated next to Mac kept him from even coming close with the blow. Mac batted it away.

"You don't know when somebody's joshing you. Learn how to recognize that. Learn, or your life's going to be a living hell."

"It already is hell because of Flowers and you and all the others." Desmond levered himself to his feet and staggered off, clutching his belly. Within seconds the dark swallowed him entirely.

Mac closed his eyes and wanted nothing more than to go to sleep right then and there under his wagon. But Hiram Flowers had told him to move the chuckwagon and be ready for breakfast. A glance at the stars told him it was still three or four hours until sunrise, when a passel of hungry drovers would ride up demanding to be fed.

Using the wheel for support, he pulled himself to his feet. Still not up to climbing onto the box, he made a circuit and checked the harness on the team. He tried to soothe them and convince the horses he wasn't any happier than they were about traveling in the middle of the night. Returning to the box, feeling up to the chore—maybe—he stepped first onto the yoke and then pulled himself the rest of the way onto the driver's seat. A snap of the reins got the team pulling.

The stars blazed down with an intensity that turned the prairie into an eerie world unlike the daytime of heat and sharp shadows. He wished he could ride into it and leave all the bounty hunters and the troubles of the past behind.

The sound of hoofbeats behind him brought him back to the

real world. He looped his reins around the brake and dived back into the wagon, fumbling in his gear for the box of cartridges Messerschmidt had given him. He should have already reloaded, he chided himself.

His fingers were numb and worked like giant sausages, but he slid fresh ammo into all six chambers. With a painful twist, he came to his knees and peered over the driver's seat, revolver cocked and ready.

The rider came up fast, slowed, and then halted just a few yards off. Mac tried to make out his face in the dark but couldn't.

"Where are you?"

The voice was familiar. Mac got his legs under him and climbed over the seat but kept the gun in his hand.

"What do you want, Desmond?"

"Not another whipping, that's for sure. Flowers sent me to help you, but he told me to pick up the gear you dropped after you killed my horse."

That wasn't the way Mac would have put it, but he lowered the hammer gently and tucked his pistol into his holster. Whatever threat dogged his steps, Desmond wasn't part of it. Not a deadly part, at least.

"About a quarter mile south of here. Follow the ground all cut up by the cattle. Where the ground's in good shape, look there."

"That's not much to go on." Desmond sounded skeptical. Mac didn't blame him since the directions were so vague. All he wanted was for the young man to leave him the hell alone.

"Go on. I've got to find where Mister Flowers wanted me to set up camp."

"I know that," Desmond said. He paused, as if thinking over something hard. "I'll help you if you show me where my saddle is."

"South," Mac said. Spending the rest of the night scouring the plains for the dropped gear wasn't in the cards. By the time he made it back to camp, the cowboys would be lining up for breakfast. An hour after they finished, he had to be back in the chuckwagon making his way to wherever Flowers wanted him to serve the midday meal.

Nowhere in that next twelve hours was there any time to sleep. He didn't need much, but he had to get a few hours to keep him from falling asleep while he drove.

"Which way's that?" Desmond asked.

Muttering in impatience at the young man's ignorance, Mac leaned forward, found the Big Dipper and the Pole Star, then ran his finger from it across the dome of stars to due south. He stabbed out with his forefinger in the proper direction.

"Go to hell, you son of a bitch." Desmond yanked on his horse's reins and trotted off.

"A pleasant good night to you, too," Mac said tiredly, too worn out to raise his voice enough for Desmond to hear the sarcastic rejoinder. With the reins resting in his hands, he snapped them until the team began pulling.

Tangling with bounty hunters suddenly seemed like the lesser of two evils. He had to put up with that annoying little son of a bitch Desmond Sullivan for the rest of the trail drive.

Chapter 9

"Had better." The cowboy licked his fingers to get the last crumb of biscuit and dollop of thick gravy. When his fingers were clean—cleaner than the rest of his hand—he looked up expectantly. "Got any more, Mac?"

Mac forked over a couple more. The cowboy snatched them before anyone else claimed them.

"When did you ever have better?" Mac challenged. "Your mama? If you say your mama's done better, I won't argue. Otherwise, you have to prove it."

"Naw, don't ever remember my ma fixin' anything this good. Nope, it was a little place in Wichita Falls. Just a stone's throw from Seventh and Ohio Streets." The cowboy gobbled down the last of the biscuits, then wiped his hand on his jeans. "A tiny little café called the Green Frog. The woman doin' the cookin', she was danged near the size of one of them longhorns. Big woman. Sampled her own cooking too much."

"And it was that good? Her biscuits were better?" Mac enjoyed joshing the men as much as he enjoyed a good-natured argument. It was about all they had to pass the time between back-breaking, long, tedious, dangerous days in the saddle.

"You know, my memory ain't so good these days. Gimme another and let me see if I can remember. Got to give you a fair trial, I reckon."

"All gone," Mac told him. "You'll have to wait until this evening."

"Not this afternoon?" The man sounded genuinely sad at the prospect of waiting that long for another biscuit.

"Got a pot of stew ready to heat up, so that will be dinner. Flowers said we've got to make up all the time we lost because of the herd stampeding the way it did."

"Yup," the cowboy said, standing, hitching up his trousers, and settling his hat just so before he set off to work. "We're gettin' near the Pecos. Mister Flowers he says that's always a dangerous crossing. Don't know why we don't stay on this side of the river till we get up into New Mexico Territory and cross there."

"The closer to the headwaters you get, the bigger the river," Mac said.

"You talk just like Mister Flowers. You and him share a brain?"

"Something like that," Mac said.

He began cleaning up as the last of the cowboys left to ride herd. Getting the chuckwagon ready for the trail took a mite longer than starting the cattle moving again, but once he got rolling, he would outpace the beeves. It would take the better part of an hour to set up for dinner. Fixing several kettles of stew at a time more than fed even the always-famished drovers. Having leftovers for a second meal sped things up for at least that one meal.

As he fastened the tailgate, Flowers rode up.

"You're too late for breakfast, but I can find something for you," Mac offered. He started to unlatch the tailgate but Flowers stopped him.

"Not necessary. We got to move the herd farther in the next couple days and get across the Pecos."

"You're worried about that?" Mac wondered why. He waited for the trail boss to get to the point.

"The Comanches are still out there. I saw traces of them when I rode around the herd this morning. They left their tracks on purpose."

Mac nodded. "If they wanted to be sneaky, you'd never find any sign. That means they still want a few dozen cattle."

"The cattle they can have, as long as they leave us alone. They want our horses. I've doubled the night guard on the remuda."

"I wondered where Kleingeld got off to last night."

"Him and a lot of others are drawing double duty, guarding the horses and then riding herd. I want you to do some double duty, too, Mac."

"What more do you want? I can only drive the wagon so fast." The way his body ached and the cuts he had suffered in the stampede wouldn't heal for another week, and that was if he was lucky.

"I'm telling Desmond to drive the wagon."

"That'll keep him out of trouble, I suppose," Mac said, wondering if he was lying to himself by thinking that. "What do you want me to do?"

"Scout. I saw how you can do that. You've got a good eye and a sense where the herd can travel easiest. The quicker we cross the river, the better I'll like it."

"Will the Comanches stay on this side of the Pecos?" Mac could tell something else was bothering the trail boss. If Flowers watched their back trail as closely as it seemed, he must know about the bounty hunters. But he wouldn't know *why* they were dogging the herd. Again Mac wrestled with telling the trail boss that the men were after him for the reward on his head back in New Orleans. But again he held his tongue.

"They go wherever they want, though they're not likely to follow us. The other side is Apache country. The Comanches and Apaches don't get on too well, stealing each other's squaws and using their children as slaves. I'm more worried about the weather. A good storm will send the Pecos over its banks and make fording it a chore, no matter where we cross."

Mac looked up at the blue sky. A few puffy white clouds meandered across it in a lazy way he wished he could copy. After everything he'd gone through the night before and the lack of sleep, he wanted to while away the day. Any chance of that was behind him before he ever signed on with the Circle Arrow crew.

"You don't see it up there. You don't even smell it, but I *feel* it in my bones. We've got a big storm coming at us."

"Should I leave the wagon here or drive it to wherever Desmond is?"

"He got back to camp just before sunrise." Flowers chuckled. "He spent the night hunting for his saddle. Not that I blame him. That's expensive tack. I wish he'd take better care of it."

Mac was glad he didn't have to lug it all the way back to camp, just to give it up to the boy.

"I tried to give him directions to where I left it. Might be I should have gone with him to speed up his hunt."

"Don't worry your head none over that, Mac. He's got to learn to do for himself. You get some of the spare gear and take a horse. Range out straight west, then curl on northward. I'm scouting straight to the northwest. If you come across a river, head straight on back and let me know. The Pecos winds all over the place. Even if I had a map, it wouldn't do me any good since the damned river is so cantankerous about keeping to its banks, year to year."

Mac nodded and started walking toward the remuda, wondering at how talkative the trail boss had become. Flowers kept to himself and seldom said much at the best of times. This sudden flood of words was a good indication of how worried he was about fording the Pecos.

Or was he worried about more than that? Mac shivered at what that might be.

He was out scouting within a half hour. As he left camp, he saw that Desmond had shown up and worked to hitch up the team. Mac considered helping him, then remembered what Flowers had said about the boss's son learning to do for himself. This chore wasn't anything Desmond hadn't done before. Driving the wagon could be difficult at times, especially over rough ground, but if Desmond got a move on, he'd be ahead of the herd and not have to drive through the prairie cut up by their hooves.

Settling into a rhythm as he rode, Mac tried to keep an eye out for the river and a route to it, but the swaying motion kept lulling him to sleep. Like most cowboys, he had learned to nap in the saddle, but this wasn't the right time.

Despite his best efforts, exhaustion caught up with him and he dozed off into a sound sleep. His horse shied and tried to bolt, causing him to snap awake. For a moment he panicked, unsure where he was or how long he had been asleep. The world around him looked different, as if he had ridden for months rather than—what?

A quick look at the sun's position in the sky showed he had been asleep for more than an hour. Shaking himself, he forced away some of the fuzzy feeling that stalked him.

To make sure he wasn't dreaming, he pulled out his pocket watch and studied it as if he had never seen its like before. The watch ran slow, but he had looked at it when he began preparing breakfast that morning. He had ridden more than two hours without realizing he had done so.

Grumbling, he tucked the watch back into his vest pocket. It was time to look around and do the job Flowers had given him. Finding a low rise, he gazed due west. No sign of the river. Nothing to the northwest, either. As his gaze slipped northward, he spotted several figures on horseback and caught his breath. Silhouetted on the hill like this, he made an easy target.

Backing his horse back over the crest, he got out of sight of the Comanches. Flowers had been right. The Indians hadn't moved on. The lure of so many beeves—and horses!—proved too powerful for them to let a stampede scatter them.

Mac took a better look around to fix the landmarks in his head. He had to let Flowers know right away that the Comanches lay in wait for the herd.

As he turned to go back eastward, a knot tightened in his belly. He drew rein and wished he had a spyglass to study the countryside spread out in front of him. For almost ten minutes he sat astride the increasingly restive horse, watching and waiting, before he decided that he hadn't seen anything suspicious after all. He patted the horse's neck and started to put his heels to the animal's flanks, his caution unnecessary.

He hadn't ridden a hundred yards when he stopped again. The sun burned hot on his back. And now it reflected from metal ahead of him. If he kept the sun behind him, he'd be harder to see. Not outlining himself against the sky almost assured he wouldn't be spotted by the men ahead of him. As he watched, this time with better knowledge of what to look for, he made out three men directly ahead blocking his route. A fourth rode to the north, probably scouting in that direction.

Indians behind him. Bounty hunters in front of him. The old saying about a rock and a hard place went through Mac's mind as he swallowed and tried to figure out his next move.

He was cut off from the herd by two gangs willing to kill him, though for different reasons. Humiliating the Comanches the way he had required them to lift his scalp to regain honor. The bounty hunters wanted only money for that scalp. More likely, they'd take his entire body to prove they had earned their reward. It didn't matter to him which of the two groups won. He was dead either way.

He turned toward the south, thinking to swing wide around the bounty hunters. The horse balked and began to snort and paw the ground. He struggled to control his mount. Something in this direction spooked the horse. He swung the animal around to quiet it.

Running away wasn't any answer. It he kept riding west, he could cross the Pecos and get to the Rio Grande. Cross that river and he could lose himself in Mexico within a week or two. All he had in the way of gear was stashed in the chuckwagon, but he had his gun and a coat pocket weighed down with a full box of ammunition. Taking the horse would make him a thief, and he didn't like the sound of that. Deep down, he was an honest man and had never stolen except in emergencies.

"Honest men don't run out on their jobs," he muttered to himself. Hiram Flowers had given him a job when he needed it. He had hired on to do that job. Sneaking away, stealing a horse, betraying Flowers's trust in him, none of that set well. In fact, it stuck in his craw, and he wouldn't do it.

Taking on the bounty hunters looked to be the worst trail to ride. They would open fire the instant they spotted him. The Indians, however, likely had no idea he was anywhere around. That gave him a small edge he had to use. How he was going to do that was something of a puzzle, but he turned due north and rode behind the ridge of sand hills in the direction where he had spotted the Comanches.

Staying in the shallow valley hid him from the bounty hunters, at least until he reached a point not a quarter mile from the Comanches. Careful observation told him that the bounty hunter riding to the north of his partners had spotted him and started for him. There wouldn't be any honor among men like that, who hunted others for money. If this one reached him first, they'd have to shoot it out. The bounty hunter intended to be the one to collect the entire reward on his head.

Mac picked up the gait and cantered more to the northwest

now, directly toward the Comanches. When he topped a rise, he saw six of them below. They had dismounted from their ponies and now squatted down around a small fire cooking a rabbit. The odor wafted up to him and made his mouth water. He had missed a meal today, while he was asleep in the saddle.

At the moment, all he wanted was to be alive for supper. Twisting around, he dragged out his revolver and waved it high over his head as he let out a loud holler and galloped downhill toward the Indians.

Disturbing their meal had been a stroke of luck. They fumbled for their weapons and lifted their rifles. His heart seized up for a moment, fear striking him that they had found ammunition for their weapons since the previous encounter. Comancheros roved these plains. The Indians might have traded a few skins for cartridges. When they dropped their rifles and picked up bows and arrows instead, he knew his luck was holding.

"Thank you," he whispered to Lady Luck. Surely, she rode on his shoulder. All he needed now was one more turn in his favor.

He galloped straight through the camp. His horse jumped the fire, dug in its hooves, and kicked up a cloud of dust. Wheeling around, Mac kept up his string of whoops and hoots to inflame the Comanches. When arrows began to fly in his direction, he bent low and used the horse as a shield. They wanted his horse alive as spoils of war as much as they wanted him dead. The arrows flew well over his head until he got out of range. He pulled himself upright in the saddle and slowed his headlong pace.

The Indians, bless their hearts, jumped onto their ponies and gave chase.

Judging distances and locations, Mac rode straight for the bounty hunter who wanted to bring him in and claim the whole reward. Mac burst over the crest of a sandy hill, saw the man not fifty yards away, and for the first time opened fire. At that range, on horseback, hitting the bounty hunter would have used up all his remaining luck. All he did was cause the man's horse to rear.

That was good enough. He veered slightly and forced the man to come after him . . . following him so he ended up between Mac and the pursuing Indians.

The Comanches caught up fast, and when the bounty hunter realized that, he twisted in his saddle and threw a few shots from his Winchester in their direction. Whether the Indians believed the bounty hunter to be Mac or simply didn't care, they shifted their attack from the fleeing cook to the man willing to use his rifle on them.

Mac's hastily formed plan was working so far, but he wasn't satisfied. He veered again, going to the southeast until he caught sight of the other three bounty hunters. A few more shots in their direction emptied his gun and brought them racing toward him.

Reloading on the gallop proved to be a challenge. He lost more than a few bullets as he fumbled in his pocket for cartridges to replace those spent already. When he got six more in the cylinder, he charged the bounty hunters, scattering them with a barrage of shots.

Now it was time to put the icing on the cake. He cut back again so the bounty hunters trailed him. Mac thundered up behind the Comanches and then veered sharply aside, behind one of the sand hills. The Indians never saw him, but they saw the three bounty hunters who seemed to be shooting at them, sure enough. Yipping frenziedly, they swung around and relaunched their attack in a different direction.

Arrows whistled through the air, met by the bounty hunters firing back. Mac halted and swung around, waiting for the three men to gallop past him. When they did, he opened fire in a flank attack, taking his time to aim and making every shot count. Whether he actually hit any of them wasn't the point.

He stopped them in their tracks, confusing them and forcing them to deal with the Indians whooping toward them from the front.

Mac's gun came up empty again, but the bounty hunters weren't going to chase him any longer. They were too busy. They'd jumped down to take refuge behind the scanty cover of bushes and rocks poking out of the sandy soil.

Mac changed direction again, riding for the herd. He didn't know what had happened to the first bounty hunter. The Comanches might have killed him. But even if he had escaped, he was out of the way for now.

A large dust cloud rose on the horizon. That had to be where Mac would find a couple of dozen revolvers willing to back him up if necessary. The Circle Arrow cowboys would fight for him because he was one of them, part of their trail family.

That, and he made the best damned biscuits they'd ever tasted, Green Frog Café or not.

Chapter 10

"You go scout, Johnston. We need to find a place to set up an ambush." Quick Willy Means glared at the gunman. Johnston thought he was better than the rest of them. Maybe he was, but as long as he rode with this gang, he would take orders like everybody else.

Arizona Johnston shook his head, picked up a stick, and began scratching in the dirt.

"There's no reason for us to split up, Willy. See here? This is where the herd is. The last we saw, Mackenzie was driving the chuckwagon. There are only so many places he can go with that wagon. We don't need to split up. We all stay together and swoop in when he heads in this direction."

"Why's that gonna work?" Frank Huffman scratched himself. "How do we know what direction he'll head in?"

"Because," Johnston said, as if explaining to a simpleton, "he's their cook. He stays ahead of the herd. They're following the Goodnight-Loving Trail, so we know the direction they're going already."

"Fort Sumner," Means said. "That's where they're most

likely going to sell them beeves to the Army. I don't know about the rest of you, but chasing Mackenzie over into New Mexico Territory isn't what I want to do for the next couple weeks." He pitched his voice lower so it carried a menace that hadn't been there before. "Find us a place to ambush him *before* we get to New Mexico."

"All I'm saying is that we stand a better chance if we stay together." Johnston crossed his arms over his chest and looked at Means with cool, barely concealed defiance. Quick Willy saw that he stood so his right hand rested near the pistol in the cross-draw holster. As much as Johnston wanted them to think he stood easy, he was tighter than a drum and ready to throw down on the lot of them.

"You're nuthin' but a coward," Charles Huffman said abruptly. "You don't want to go traipsin' off by your lonesome 'cause Mackenzie might shoot you." Huffman was stupid enough not to see how close Johnston was to exploding.

"We'll be following," Quick Willy said in one final effort to defuse the tense situation. "You find the place and we'll—"

"No."

Arizona Johnston's flat-voiced refusal hardened something inside Quick Willy Means. Nobody challenged him for leadership of this gang. Being a bounty hunter was tough enough. Keeping these yahoos corralled and riding in the proper direction was almost as difficult as being trail boss for a big herd. Sometimes he thought it was harder. All Hiram Flowers had to deal with were cranky steers. They weren't too bright, either alone or in a herd, and had only a few things they did instinctively. The Huffman brothers were as stupid as a longhorn but always managed to find new and different ways to blunder on.

However, they always followed his orders. Arizona Johnston was another matter. He had plans he wasn't sharing, and Quick Willy figured those plans didn't include him. Not alive, anyway.

"You can ride out any time you want, Arizona," he said softly. By the different pitch to his voice, he added a quiet menace. The Huffmans wouldn't be threatened if he did it to them, because they were too dumb to notice. Shouting got better results with them.

Johnston caught on to the threat right away. Smart fellow, Johnston. Too smart.

"I'm not forfeiting my share of the reward for Mackenzie, not after I've come this far."

"Then ride. We can be done by the end of the day. Find where he's going to park that chuckwagon for dinner. It'll take the herd hours to reach that point. By then we'll have him in custody."

"Or dead," Johnston said. "In custody or dead."

"Leclerc wants him to stand trial and will give us a hefty bonus if we take him to New Orleans alive."

"Easier if he's dead." Johnston never twitched a muscle. He kept his hand near the gun on his left hip.

Quick Willy Means considered what he could do. Slowly nodding, he agreed with the gunman.

"Or dead. It *is* easier that way. If you get him, Arizona, you get an extra share from the pot."

The spark that lit in the gunman's eyes was everything Means could hope for. Greed won out over the need to be leader. Or maybe it was a lust for killing. Whatever moved Arizona Johnston kept him in line. For the moment. He wasn't a man to let sleeping dogs lie. There would be trouble eventually, even as soon as when they brought down Dewey Mackenzie. Quick Willy had to be ready for it and never turn his back.

"Don't get all caught up in a stampede," Charles Huffman called as Johnston stepped up into the saddle.

Means rested his hand on his revolver. If looks could kill, Huffman would be dead and buried. Johnston flicked his eyes from Charles to his brother, then fixed on him. Means made a mocking salute to send Johnston on his way.

When the rebellious bounty hunter was out of earshot, Frank Huffman said, "That's one dangerous galoot. Like a rattler all coiled and ready to strike. Only he don't know what direction to sink in his fangs."

Quick Willy Means eyed Frank. The man was smarter than his brother. He might be smarter than Means had given him credit for up to now.

Arizona Johnston never tried very hard to hide his contempt for the lot of them. Their paths had crossed just outside Fort Worth when Means had needed another gun hand after Jimmy Huffman had been cut down. He knew nothing about the man, other than the few sparse details Johnston had doled out. On the run from a Tombstone marshal meant nothing to Means. From what he'd heard about Tombstone, eventually everyone crossed the law there, be it sheriff, local, or federal marshal. The town was that rough and tumble.

For all he knew, Johnston had come from back east or up north or who the hell knew.

"Who the hell cares?" The sentiment was mumbled, but Frank overheard.

"If he uses those revolvers of his as good as he talks, you're right. Who the hell cares?"

"We didn't find Mackenzie last night. It's time we ended this," Means said. "Johnston will find him."

"Why can't we go 'n find him, Quick Willy? You'd give us an extra share if we done it, right? Like you promised Arizona?"

Charles drummed his fingers on the butt of his Colt dangling at his side as he spoke. Quick Willy had never decided if the man thought he was fast or hoped he was. Either way he was wrong. Clumsy, banging around like a bull in a china shop, Charles Huffman was better suited for lying in ambush and shooting his quarry in the back. Facing them in a gunfight, he would chicken out, turn tail and run, if he bothered to show up at all. His brother was the same way, too, but only because Frank was enough smarter to know he was going to die if he did anything else.

"Mount up. We're going to end this today. I'm tired of sneaking around all night, trying to find Mackenzie amongst those damn drovers."

"You don't want to tangle with their trail boss, do you, Quick Willy?"

Means considered how easy it would be to simply remove Charles Huffman. A shot between the eyes . . . No, that wasn't the way to do it. Blowing out his brains was too hard a shot. The brain was too small.

He said nothing, turned, and stepped up into the saddle. Johnston was a smart one. He'd find Mackenzie. Let him take the risk of a gunfight with a man reputed to have shot down a dozen hombres, including Jimmy Huffman. Even if that reputation was puffed up, he had to be dangerous or a rich, powerful man like Pierre Leclerc wouldn't put out such a lucrative reward.

The sound of a shot came through the hot air.

"You hear that, Quick Willy?" Charles exclaimed as he leaned sharply forward in his saddle. "A gunshot! It's gotta be Johnston. He's done found Mackenzie already!"

Charles whipped his horse into a gallop, his brother only a second behind.

"Wait up!" Means called after them. "Don't go rushing into something when you don't know who's firing."

They ignored him. Means shook his head, then galloped after his men.

For a minute, he thought Johnston was on to something. A rider galloped toward them, low in the saddle as if avoiding the gunfire. Quick Willy's heart sped up when he recognized Dewey

Mackenzie. They must have Mackenzie caught in a vice, Means thought, with Johnston on one side and the rest of them on the other. He dragged out his rifle and levered a round into it. The time had come to end the manhunt.

But Mackenzie wasn't running. He was attacking, charging right into their midst as he threw lead. Quick Willy and the Huffman brothers had to scatter because of the bold, unexpected assault.

Then somehow, in the confusion, Mackenzie was headed back the other way. Quick Willy brought the rifle to his shoulder and squeezed the trigger, but the shot went wide.

Means slammed his boot heels against his horse's flanks. "Get that son of a bitch!" he shouted at the Huffman brothers as he galloped after Mackenzie.

Dust from all the flashing hooves roiled the air. Means could see his quarry up ahead, then suddenly Mackenzie was gone. Where in blazes had he gotten to? The sand hills in this region formed little tucks and folds in the landscape, and all Means could think of was that Mackenzie had ducked into one of them.

A bullet racketed through the air near Quick Willy's head. He had just realized it came from the side when Charles Huffman's horse suddenly screamed and bucked, its rump burned by another slug. Charles fought to get the animal under control while Means and Frank yanked their mounts to a halt and tried to figure out what was going on.

Out of the blue, an arrow almost skewered Quick Willy. He had ducked instinctively when he caught the blur of the arrow coming at him from off to one side, and that was the only thing that saved his life.

Quick Willy lived up to his name. Whipping around, he got off another shot, a killing shot. A Comanche fell from his horse and lay flat on his back. One threat gone. But a half dozen more thundered toward him.

Where the hell had *they* come from? And where was Johnston?

No time to worry about that now. "Get the hell out of here!" Means shouted to the brothers. "Mackenzie led us into a trap!"

He frantically hunted for their quarry, but Mackenzie was still nowhere to be seen. He was too smart to stick around to watch the massacre he had engineered.

Quick Willy winced as an arrow raked along his side, a shallow scratch that burned like hellfire. He pressed his hand into it. Wet heat oozed between his fingers, but he felt nothing more than the blood. He wasn't hurt bad, but he was madder than a wet hen. Fury rose. He lifted his rifle and got off a couple more shots. One took out a Comanche's horse and sent the brave tumbling to the ground. Means rode past without bothering to waste an extra bullet. The Indian was out of the fight and on foot. Better to find some cover.

Means dropped off his horse and clung to the reins with one hand while he rammed the rifle back in the saddle boot with the other. He knelt behind a rock and drew his revolver. A few yards away, the Huffman brothers were taking cover, too, Frank stretching out behind another rock while Charles knelt behind a scrubby bush. The growth wouldn't have stopped a bullet, but it might deflect an arrow.

Both of them had enough sense to hang on to their horses as they opened fire with their revolvers. Would wonders never cease? Quick Willy asked himself bitterly.

He fired three times and scared off a Comanche intent on sticking a knife into Charles Huffman. Charles never noticed either the attacker or how he had been rescued. A lot of arrows were flying around and shots rolled like thunder over the plains, but not much actual damage was being done.

"Get outta here. Now!"

The shout came from Arizona Johnston as the gunman galloped in from the north. A trickle of blood ran down his forehead, a sign that he had tangled with the Comanches, too. He swiped it away.

Quick Willy locked eyes with Johnston and saw nothing but his own fury reflected there. He waved Johnston on past. Unlike the Huffman boys, Johnston didn't need to be told twice. If anything, he had figured it out for himself that they were outnumbered.

They outgunned the Indians, but numbers would wear them down if the fight went on much longer.

Quick Willy Means snapped another shot at the savage, then vaulted into the saddle, bent low, and urged his horse up to the crest of a sandy hill. From here he saw that retreat wasn't just their best course of action. It was their only one. A dozen more Comanches were coming on swift ponies from the south. Where their camp might be, Means couldn't tell, but the number told him there was an entire village not too far away and the warriors there had heard the gunfire.

Means took one more look around for Dewey Mackenzie. The murdering son of a bitch had caused this, but he was nowhere to be seen. He had poked the hornet's nest and then gotten out of the way of the real trouble. In a way, Quick Willy admired that. It was downright sneaky and showed Mackenzie had a sharp mind. Facing two different enemies, he had set them fighting each other rather than tangling with either—or both.

A Comanche struggling up the hill on foot provided Quick Willy a last chance to vent his anger. His first shot missed. He cocked the gun and tried again, only to have the hammer fall on an expended round. By the time he pouched the iron and yanked out his rifle again, the Indian was almost on him. Means fired three times.

At this range he couldn't miss. A trio of crimson flowers blossomed over the man's heart. Despite that, the man came on, his face twisted with hate and his knife raised. Means fired a fourth time and finally sent the Comanche falling facedown on the ground. The Indian was still twitching when Quick Willy's panicky horse reared and came down with its hooves on the Comanche's head, crushing the skull with a sound like a dropped melon busting open.

Quick Willy watched him die without so much as a flicker of emotion. He reserved that for Dewey Mackenzie.

He sawed at the reins, regained control of the bucking horse, turned, and galloped from the new spate of Indians thinking to join the battle. How many of their tribe had been killed wasn't something he wanted to consider. If enough had died, they might pursue. Or, seeing they lacked ammunition versus men who were not only armed but deadly accurate with it, the Comanches might break off the fight. The worst that could happen was them coming after his men, intending to slit their throats in the night.

That was all the more reason to finish off Mackenzie and clear out of West Texas.

Quick Willy's plans for the day hadn't included fighting to the death, so he hadn't made any provision for a rendezvous after a battle. He just kept riding north until he spotted Frank Huffman. The man joined him.

"Where's your brother?" Means asked.

"Comin'. He took an arrow in the shoulder. You got scratched, too, didn't you, Willy?" Huffman pointed to the oozing wound just above Means's gun belt.

"Doesn't amount to a hill of beans." He touched the cut again and shuddered in pain. Sewing up the wound struck him as a good idea. In order to do that, they had to camp for a spell.

Ten minutes later Charles joined them. They kept riding north and finally saw Johnston ahead of them. He slowed and let them catch up. The group was back together, without too much damage done. Johnston had a few cuts. A knife wound along his calf showed he'd let an Indian get too close to him.

"Blood's filled up my boot," he said, pressing his hand down on the leaking wound. "Walking's going to be a chore for a while."

Means saw how Johnston sized up the others' wounds. The look of expectation on the man's face didn't set well with him. He planned something, and it wasn't going to be acceptable.

"Let's pitch camp. The Comanches won't come for us, not this soon, anyway," Quick Willy said. "We did enough damage they'll be licking their wounds for a while."

He rode down into an arroyo that provided some protection if he was wrong about the Indians' determination. Being lower than any attackers wasn't a smart move, but being able to shoot over the banks made for a better defense than being out in the open.

Within fifteen minutes, Frank had a small fire started. Means leaned back and pulled free his bloody shirt. As he had thought, the wound was hardly a scratch, but it bled furiously when he probed it. He used a burning twig from the fire to cauterize the wound. Sewing it up would have taken too long.

"You're gonna have one fine-lookin' scar there, Quick Willy. Somethin' to brag on to all the wimmen." Charles looked down with some admiration. He touched his own wound. "All I got for my trouble's a hole in my shoulder. That ain't gonna scar up good at all."

"Too bad the arrow didn't go through your damned skull," Means growled. He forced himself to sit up with his back against the dirt embankment.

Charles frowned, trying to figure out what his boss meant. Frank wore a disgusted look but said nothing. Arizona Johnston was another matter. The man limped over and towered above him.

"There's no point in keeping after Mackenzie," he said without preamble. "Admit it. We're on a hunt that's going to see us all killed."

"You let him go." Quick Willy worked his way to his feet. The pain subsided as he stood and stretched. "He came for you, and you let him slip through your fingers."

"If you didn't notice, he was in front of a tornado of Comanches. I got off one shot at him, then I was fighting the Indians for my life."

"Which way did Mackenzie go? Back to join the others driving that herd? We can sneak in there tonight and find him. I want to grab him and be gone by sunrise."

"You're a fool. Let this one go, Means. Sometimes it's easy as pie. Other times, nothing will ever go right. This is one of those times. We fought off the Indians. Do we have to fight off a couple dozen drovers, too?"

"So you want to give up?"

Johnston looked away. When he spoke again, it was to the Huffman brothers.

"You see how it is. Come with me. There're plenty of wanted men out there that aren't half as hard to find and take in for a reward. We work together real good."

"You trying to take my men, Johnston?"

"No, Means. I don't care if they come with me or not. But if they've got a lick of sense, they'll ride out, too. I've had it with you getting us into jams where we have to shoot our way out and not have anything to show for it but our own spilled blood." Arizona Johnston took a step. There was a liquid squishing sound from his boot as he moved.

"Go on. Clear out," Quick Willy said.

Johnston turned to mount his horse. Means drew his gun, cocked, aimed, and fired in one smooth motion. The bullet hit Johnston in the back of the skull. He fell forward into the sandy arroyo bottom. Means saw how the blood drained out of the man's boot and formed a puddle around it. If Means hadn't put him out of his misery, he would have died from blood loss.

"Bury him," he said. "No need to make the grave too deep."

"The coyotes will dig 'im up if we don't go down far enough," Charles said. He was a little wide-eyed with surprise from the sudden violence.

Means snorted.

"I hope they enjoy the meal." With that he sank back to the ground, hand pressed into the charred wound on his side. His brain spun in wild circles as he tried to figure out how to track down Dewey Mackenzie and bring him to the same justice he had just dished out to Arizona Johnston.

Chapter 11

"What do you think, Mac? Can we get across it?" Hiram Flowers asked as he stared across the wide expanse of the Pecos River.

This was the point along the Goodnight-Loving Trail Flowers worried about the most. Fording the river was dangerous at the best of times. Now it appeared swollen and several feet higher than the last time he and Zeke Sullivan had come this way with a herd.

When Mac didn't reply, he glanced over at the young man. For someone so young, Mac carried the weight of the world on his broad shoulders. Flowers wished Desmond Sullivan had the same dedication. Mac did the work of three men. He drove the chuckwagon and fixed meals, he scouted, and from what Flowers had seen, he wasn't half bad at being a drover, though he denied it. The only thing he was piss poor at was singing to the herd at night. He couldn't carry a tune in a bucket, and if he knew more than two songs, he kept it hidden real good.

"Mac?"

"Sorry, I was thinking."

"Think how long it'll take to get across this stretch of water. You reckon scouting some more will help us?"

"We can find a shallower crossing," Mac said. "If not shallower, since this is a fast-moving river, maybe a spot that's not quite so far. I can't throw a rock hard enough to land on the other bank."

"It's too late in the day to begin fording," Flowers said, as much to himself as to Mackenzie. "We bed down for the night, then cross at first light."

"Sounds like a good idea. It'll give the men a chance to rest up, too. And get a good enough meal. I can take my time." Mac looked hard at him. "Are you going to eat?"

"Not hungry," Flowers said. His belly rumbled, as if putting that to the lie. He knew that food—even Mac's, which was tasty going down—caused a minor earthquake deep in his gut. He hadn't been puking lately, but the unsettled feeling kept him from aggravating it into full-blown rebellion by eating a full meal.

"I can see what's in the medicinal stores. Mostly, I brought along medicine for the trots and the reverse. Doesn't do a man good to have every meal he's ever eaten all packed up tight inside."

"Not my problem. Either of them."

"My ma used to whip up a medicine to soothe upset stomachs. Me and my brother Jacob used to eat anything that didn't run away from us fast enough. Once, I double-dirty-dog dared him to eat a bug. He did. He won the bet but was sick for a week." Mac chuckled. "That meant I got his dessert for a week, and that was in the autumn when Ma had a whole basket of peaches." He smacked his lips. "That peach cobbler was the best."

"I'd eat some peach cobbler." Just saying it brought back memories Flowers tried to keep tamped down. Mercedes Sullivan had a cook and a housekeeper, but she did most of her own cooking. The sensation of smelling a pie cooling on the windowsill had been the moment Flowers realized how much he loved her.

That memory caused his belly to rebel. He let out a belch, wiped his mouth, and said, "Fix the men whatever they want tonight. Get the chuckwagon ready to cross. Have Desmond help."

"I've been meaning to talk to you about him."

Flowers sighed. Being trail boss shouldn't require more than getting the herd to market. Dealing with a young snot carrying a chip on his shoulder wasn't high on his list of things to do when he faced a dangerous river crossing.

"What's the problem?" He knew what Mac was going to say. That didn't make it any easier to hear.

"He's been drinking the whiskey I keep for medicinal purposes. He takes a swig or two, then fills the bottle back up with water so it's still full to the same level. That cuts the whiskey left, making it almost useless to kill the pain for the men who need it."

"You sure it's him? There's more'n one riding for us with a taste for rotgut."

"I smell it on his breath. He has to know, but he doesn't give two hoots. There's not a whale of a lot I can do since I'm not his boss."

"He doesn't think I am, either." Flowers sighed as he looked across the river. Tree trunks the size of a large wagon raced past, carried all the way from New Mexico. This year the Pecos ran high and fast. He found himself wishing he was not only on the other bank but in Fort Sumner with a pocketful of cash from selling the herd to the Army. He was getting too old for the trail.

"I know the deal you made. It was either Desmond or Miz Sullivan coming with us. You made the right choice, but—"

"Don't give me no 'buts,' Mac. I'll talk to him. I'll send him home with his tail between his legs, if I have to."

"That'd mean your job."

Hiram Flowers shrugged. That might be for the best. The Circle Arrow was a fine ranch, and the Sullivan family the best he ever worked for. Zeke had been a decent man, and Mercedes, well, he tormented himself over her. She was too fine a woman to ever team up with a lowlife cowboy like him. Removing himself from all that frustration might be a good thing and give his belly a chance to settle down.

He drew in a deep breath and let it out fast so that his nostrils flared. He repeated it and felt even more responsibility crushing down on him.

"We might try crossing now. Most of the herd'd get across before it was too dark."

"You can't be serious," Mac said. "You want to split the herd like that? Having a bunch on this side and the rest across the river? Why would you divvy them up like that?"

"You don't smell it, do you? The storm?"

"The sky's clear. There are some clouds, but they're not rain clouds."

Flowers pointed to the south.

"The storm's movin' in on us from the Gulf of Mexico. Have you ever seen the gulf, Mac?"

"Not really. As close as I ever got was New Orleans."

The way the young man turned cautious warned Flowers not to press him on the subject. What he knew of Mac's background could be chiseled on the head of a pin. He'd just mentioned a brother and before he told of how his ma and pa died of typhus. The S&W hanging at his side had belonged to his pa. Other than that, all Mac had spoken of were his experiences on a cattle drive up the Shawnee Trail. Even then he had been tight-lipped about it. Flowers wondered what had happened and who had died.

It wasn't his place to pry. Not when he had problems of his own.

"The air tastes different, smells different. Everything changes, if you pay attention."

"Well, Mister Flowers, I'll try to pay more attention, but right now I need to see if Desmond has left any liquor at all and what I need to do to whip up a good meal for the crew."

"Are they really going to have a bullwhip contest?" Flowers had to ask. He'd never approve of such a thing since it always came down to one man trying to snap a rock off another's shoulder or head, missing, taking off an ear or eye, and then the fights started.

Still, the men were expert with their twelve-foot whips. Using those to crack over horned heads moved the cattle easier than yelling at the beeves all day. He had seen the best of his cowboys crack straw from the lips of their friends, usually without taking off a nose in the process.

"If they are, I wouldn't be able to tell you. They know what you think of such foolishness."

"You ought to be a politician, Mac. You can give an answer without answering. Get on back to camp. I might just stop in and sample some of your vittles." He rubbed his belly. The pain wasn't too bad at all at the moment. Tempting fate with a decent steak would fortify him for the crossing in the morning.

"I'll fix a good meal especially for you. Don't disappoint me by letting it go to waste."

"What? Are we married? Are you nagging me? You're not that good at it. Get along, now." Flowers leaned over and smacked Mac's horse on the rump. It took off like a rocket, leaving him alone on the bank to stare across the river. If wishes were all it took, they'd already be across.

But he had to do more than wish. Another deep breath confirmed his suspicion that a big storm was on the way. They had to cross before it hit or be pinned down for several days. The sooner they got to Fort Sumner, the sooner he could push on up to Santa Fe and then return to the Circle Arrow.

Hiram Flowers snapped the reins and got his horse walking around the perimeter of the herd so he could estimate how long it'd take to cross the river.

The steak set well in his belly. When Flowers crawled out of his blankets before dawn the next morning and rubbed vigorously on his stomach, he expected the burning sensation inside to return. It didn't.

"Dang, Mac, you do serve a good meal," he said, even though the cook wasn't around at the moment. "Sorry I doubted you and ever tried to keep that drunkard Cassidy."

Keeping the wastrel around as long as he had had resulted in big trouble among the cowboys, but he had done it out of need. His sister's boy should have straightened up when he got a job. Instead, he used the money he earned to get drunker and drunker. That had never set well with Mercedes Sullivan and her temperance ways, but she had let him keep the boozehound on.

That made Flowers wonder why. She never meddled in how he ran the ranch, but everything about Cassidy went against her heartfelt beliefs. He had never been comfortable with her business associates, much less her social circle. He was a hired hand, not a ranch owner.

He snorted at that as he swung up into the saddle and rode out to check the river again. Without being too stuck on himself, he considered himself, Hiram Flowers, trail boss, to be a better man than Desmond Sullivan. He had a code of honor he followed as surely as Mercedes believed demon rum was evil.

A yawn almost cracked his jaw. He had set out only half the night riders on the herd that he usually posted, telling the rest to get a good night's sleep to prepare for the river crossing in the morning. He had told Mac to have breakfast ready an hour before sunrise so everyone would be tending the herd when the first light poked above the eastern horizon.

From the way the Pecos was swollen and flowing so fast, it

might take most of the day getting across. He wanted every second of that to be in sunlight. And he wanted them across before the storm hit. Another sniff at the air convinced him he was right about the coming storm. The only question was when it would arrive.

His horse left sucking hoofprints in the muddy riverbank as Flowers tried to find the exact right spot to cross. Unless he took another couple of days scouting both directions along the Pecos, he wasn't going to find a better place than this. He shook his head sadly. This year that meant no single spot was better than any other due to the flooding.

Getting across fast mattered. If the river flooded any more than it already was, fording might become impossible for days or even a week. Urging his horse up a low rise, he had a decent vantage point to look out over the herd. He caught his breath when he saw thousands of horns dancing with blue fox fire in the darkness. Tiny, fuzzy patches formed along the ten-foot spans and crept to the very tips. There the fox fire shimmered and sometimes jumped from one horn tip to another, causing the steers to complain restively. He had seen this curious fairyland display before.

It always meant an electrical storm was on its way. In this part of Texas that might well mean a tornado. From the feelings he had in his gut and increasingly in his aching joints, his bet lay on a thunderstorm rushing up from the Gulf of Mexico. More than once while he worked a ranch down near Corpus Christi, this sensation had built in him. A storm always followed within a day or two. The fox fire glimmering along the cattle horns lent more credence to his belief that they were in for a gully washer.

He cocked his head to one side, heard the beeves beginning to stir, and knew dawn was on its way. Not wasting any time, he rode down into camp, saw Mac was already serving up breakfast, and smiled. That boy was always on top of his work and helped out when needed with everyone else's chores. He started to tell Mac to get a horse and help with the herd crossing the river, then realized that would leave Desmond to ferry the chuckwagon over the Pecos. Losing the chuckwagon would be a catastrophe for the drive. Better for Mac to use his expertise driving the wagon.

But then a different thought came to Flowers. He rode to where Mac was serving the last of the food.

"Take Desmond with you when you cross," the trail boss said. "He can help. You have the floats ready?"

"All ready, Mister Flowers." Mac seemed to want to say something else.

"Spit it out. What's eatin' you?"

"I'd be fine getting the chuckwagon across on my own. I don't need Desmond to help out."

"Take him." Flowers spoke with such force that it left no question of his intention. Mac might resent being a wet nurse, but the cowboys couldn't afford to be distracted once the cattle entered the water.

Flowers rode around, made sure the crew was ready. Facing east, he waited for the first pink and gray fingers of a new day to claw at the sky.

"Get 'em movin'!" Flowers ordered when the time was right. "The sooner we get across the river, the sooner we can take another rest."

The promise of the opposite bank being as far as they had to go for the day spurred the cowboys to action. Some unlimbered their whips and sent them snaking out to crack above the lead steers' heads. This caused a ripple throughout the herd, a shrug, a stirring, then they began to move.

Flowers wheeled his mount around and led the way to the river. When the horse stopped, the water sloshing around its hooves, the morning light burned warm and inviting on Flowers's back. He took his time watching the river flow to be sure they weren't going to swim the cattle into submerged trees or other debris. As far as he could tell, submerged sandbars here and there provided the only impediment to crossing. With luck the cattle could rest on those sandbars before finishing their crossing, but he had to be sure they didn't get bogged down in mud. Suction on those sandbars could hold even a twelve-hundred-pound bull until it drowned.

So many problems to avoid, so many things to worry about. No wonder his belly hurt so often.

Hiram Flowers lifted an arm high over his head, then lowered it like a cavalry general ordering a full charge of his horse soldiers. The cowboys began shouting, using their whips and crowding the cattle on the edges of the herd toward a single spot on the bank. The cattle protested, then started a slow walk into the water.

The first of the beeves got caught by the rush of the current. Flowers wanted to go out and make sure they didn't take the easy route and let the water carry them off to drown. But the Circle Arrow crew knew their jobs. They worked to do what he could never do as a solitary rider.

Flowers watched the steady stream of cattle enter the Pecos and swim their way across the raging river. Runoff had been extreme this year. He was glad to cross here and not farther north near the headwaters. If he had been that far north in New Mexico Territory he would have passed Fort Sumner and headed for Santa Fe instead. The decision to try to sell part of the herd at Fort Sumner had come to him in a dream of starving soldiers and Indians, now departed from Bosque Redondo, begging for beef. The more head he sold to the Army, the fewer he had to drive northward another couple hundred miles.

Back and forth he rode, keeping the cattle moving, having cowboys double up when necessary. As Mac drove the chuckwagon forward, Flowers waved it on. Desmond sat beside Mac, glowering. Flowers ignored the boy and studied the floats tied on both sides of the wagon. They were needed to keep the wagon from sinking. Mac had used tarpaulins to waterproof the interior the best he could. While the chuckwagon wasn't a real boat, it came close enough for the time it would take to make the crossing.

A sudden protest from a cow nearby forced him to help get the animal into the water. Some weren't happy but went with the rest of the herd. The ones that panicked made the ford the most dangerous, not only for themselves but for the riders. It took Flowers a few minutes to get the balky cow moving. He followed it until it had to swim, then started to return to the bank to urge the remainder of the herd across.

That's when he heard a loud shout. He jerked around to see the chuckwagon listing heavily to the side, shipping water as a huge wave broke over it. He started into the swollen stream to help, then saw a more immediate worry. Mac had been washed over the side of the chuckwagon and was being swept downstream in the middle of the river.

Mac held his arm up and waved it around, showing he was still alive. And then another wave rose over him and pushed him underwater.

Chapter 12

"You can't make me go." Desmond Sullivan had crossed his arms and thrust out his chin defiantly as he faced Mac a short time earlier.

"What'd I tell you about leading with your chin? Tuck it in or I'll plant a right jab on the point, knock you out, load you in the wagon, and go."

"Come on, then. Let's duke it out." Desmond shifted his weight and put up his fists, ready to fight.

Mac looked around. The cowboys cracked their whips and got the herd moving. Flowers had told him to get across the Pecos as quickly as he could. From their scouting yesterday, Mac knew the floats on the side of the chuckwagon might not be enough to keep it bobbing on top of the water. He had used a tarp to line the bottom of the wagon bed, turning it into a boat.

At least, he hoped it would be watertight enough to serve as a boat. The trick would be to get over to the far bank as fast as possible and not tempt fate.

"I don't have time to play around," he told Desmond, ignoring the young man's pugilistic stance. He cinched the last of the belly straps on the team and went to climb onto the driver's box.

"I ain't playing. This is for real. You gonna fight me or not?"

"Look at that, will you?" Mac pointed into the air just behind Desmond. As the young man turned to look, Mac stepped up, grabbed his right wrist, and twisted back hard. Then he leaned into the grip until Desmond cried out in pain.

"Here are your choices," Mac said coldly. "I can break your arm and leave you behind to get home any way you can. Don't expect Flowers to give you a horse."

"You killed my horse!"

Mac ignored him, applied a little more pressure, and shut Desmond's mouth with a new jab of pain.

"You can go on home with a broken arm. Tell your ma whatever story you like. Make yourself out to be the hero. I don't care. Or you can head south and vanish into Mexico. There's plenty of opportunity down there, I hear." Desmond squirmed. Mac did not loosen his hold. "The last choice is the one I'd take, if I were you. What might that be? Do you know?"

"G-get onto the driver's box."

"You're not as dumb as you act." Mac released him. Desmond clutched his tortured wrist while Mac pulled himself up onto the seat.

"You busted a bone," Desmond accused him.

"No, I didn't, since nothing snapped. Come on up." Mac reached out to help his unwilling assistant climb onto the box. Desmond ignored the outstretched hand. That suited Mac just fine. He had work to do, and crossing the river required every bit of concentration he had.

Once Desmond was on the seat beside him, he snapped the reins and got the team moving. By the time he reached the river a quarter of the herd had dipped their noses in. He had to laugh at the sight of so many longhorns in the water.

"What's so damn funny?" Desmond asked sullenly.

"They look like a hundred rocking chairs floating across. I've never seen anything like that before." Mac drove a bit downriver from where the herd waded in.

This close, the sight of what he was facing made Mac swallow hard. The Pecos ran deep and swift. The strongest cattle led the way. The rest followed, too stupid to consider that they might never make it.

Mac, on the other hand, knew what the chances were. They were good because of the preparations. Bad because of the river's depth and the strength of its flow. He refrained from checking the floats on either side of the chuckwagon. Having Desmond riding with him didn't make him any braver, but it caused him to think about showing any concern. Besides, what more could he do to prepare for the crossing now?

He called out to the team and used the reins to drive the horses forward. They balked when they got chest deep in the river. Slapping the lines on their backs and shouting at the top of his lungs got them swimming.

The chuckwagon lurched as the current caught it sideways. He kept the horses pulling. This kept the wagon directly behind and held the force of the water at bay.

Everything went well until they were three-quarters of the way across. Then one of the wheels hit a sandbar. The chuckwagon canted to one side and let the water surge underneath, lifting it up.

"Pull! Keep going!" Mac jumped to his feet to better use the reins. As he stood the wagon tilted precariously.

He tried to take a step to keep his balance. His feet got tangled up together, forcing him to twist to the side. A wave hit the wagon and a giant watery hand lifted. Mac cried out as he flew through the air. The wet leather reins slid from his grip. He hit the edge of the driver's box, spun around because of the swirling water and then felt as if he had lost all weight. He was caught by the river and carried away from the chuckwagon.

"Get it on to shore!" he yelled at Desmond as he waved an arm. "The wagon. Get it—" He sputtered as he was pulled under.

The last thing he saw was the chuckwagon leaning precariously, Desmond shifting his weight in the other direction to counter it. Whether or not it capsized, he couldn't tell because muddy, filthy water filled his eyes and nose and mouth, blinding and choking him.

For a moment he fought the river's power, struggling so hard his arms went limp from the effort. But Mac refused to give up. To panic now meant certain death. He relaxed and let the current carry him along. He bobbed to the surface, sucked in a couple of quick breaths, and then was pulled back under.

He twisted and turned, prisoner to the river. Something banged against his arm. He grabbed it and hung on for dear life. The added buoyancy took him back to the surface where he saw he had seized a large tree limb. Using it as a float, he kicked hard and angled toward the shore. The tumult had scrambled his brains enough that he didn't know which side of the river was in front of him. Either promised safety.

He kicked and tried to swim but weakened fast. His wet clothes weighed him down. The revolver at his hip added another three pounds of iron he had to support. The wild notion of getting free of the gun belt flashed through his mind, but he rejected it immediately. His pa had given him that S&W. Lose it and he sacrificed the last thread connecting him to his family, to Missouri, to his life growing up. He kicked and dog paddled as hard as he could. The shore wasn't more than ten yards away. Close.

"I can make it. I can."

He couldn't. He surrendered more and more to the power of the river, and it wanted to sweep him downstream. Eventually he would wash up on the shore, but he would never know. He'd be dead.

"No, no, no," he spat out. His words bubbled as his head went underwater. He reached up.

A scream of pain ripped from his lips as it felt like his arm was being pulled out of joint. He fought, only to spin around and around, his arm the axle. The pain mounted in his shoulder until he quit fighting and let the new force drag him along. As he was pulled up facedown on the muddy bank, he saw the horsehair rope looped around his wrist. As he had reached up, someone had lassoed him and used this to pull him ashore.

"St-stop. You're d-draggin' me." He failed to get his feet under him and could hardly make a sound because of exhaustion and the mud coating his face. But his rescuer realized the danger from drowning was past and let the rope go slack.

The rope slid from his wrist. Forcing himself to sit up, he wiped mud from his eyes and saw about the prettiest sight he'd ever seen. Astride his horse sat Hiram Flowers.

"You make a lousy doggie, Mackenzie. Roping you was too easy. I don't even want to think about hog-tying and branding you."

"I'm not going back out there to give you a fight." Mac tried to stand. His legs refused. He sat back down and wiped more mud from his face.

"I saw you get washed out of the chuckwagon. That wave was twice the height of the wagon."

"Desmond! He was in the wagon. Where is he?" Concern powered Mac to his feet. He took a few tentative steps back toward the river. "I don't see him. There's no sign of Desmond or the chuckwagon."

"Can't tell if they got swept downriver. I was concentrating on getting you out of the drink."

"Give me a hand up." Mac reached up for Flowers to hoist him behind. The trail boss hesitated, then pulled him up.

"Damn, boy, but you're filthy from the river. I thought bathing was supposed to get you all clean."

"How'd you know?" Mac shot back. "You haven't had a bath in a month of Sundays."

"That's because I spend all my time around cattle. It's months past dipping time to get the ticks off them, so why bother sticking myself in water?"

"There!" Mac almost fell from the horse as he pointed. "That's a float from the wagon."

Flowers rode to where the crude pontoon was caught in some weeds. The rope holding it to the chuckwagon had been frayed, dragged repeatedly against the side of the wagon by the rise and fall of the river until it came free.

"There's no wreckage I can see." Flowers put his hand over his eyes as he peered into the rising sun.

"If the wagon went straight to the bottom, we might salvage it. If it got washed away, everything inside will be strewn along the river for miles and miles."

"We'll have to search," Flowers said.

"For Desmond's body," Mac finished. He felt beaten and battered by the river. Adding to that rose a sense of guilt. He should have taken better care of Desmond. The boy was a greenhorn on the trail, ornery and arrogant, but he never should have died the way he did. That was entirely Mac's fault. He should have looked after him better, and the chuckwagon with all their vittles, all their utensils—and maybe worst of all if there had been injuries—all their medical supplies.

"Kleingeld got across with the rest of the gear," Flowers said. "I see him waving."

"I should hunt for Desmond."

"You should stop blaming yourself. I told you to watch him. It's my fault he got into trouble out there. I knew he wasn't a trail hand. Hell, I should have made sure he had floats on him like the wagon. I don't even know if he could swim."

"Wouldn't matter much," Mac said. "The current's too powerful to fight for very long. If you hadn't roped me when you did, I'd be no better than one of those dead limbs sailing down the river."

"Shut your yap and save your strength. We've got the rest of the herd to get across the river. I knew it'd be tough goin'. I expected to lose upward of a quarter of the herd, but I hoped we wouldn't come up short because of men drowning." Flowers swallowed hard. Mac rode with his arms around the man's waist and felt him quaking. Losing Desmond hit him as hard as it did himself.

Flowers rode slowly up a rise to look down on the mud flats where the cattle filed past, wet and angry at being forced to endure such indignity. Kleingeld had parked his wagon a hundred yards inland from the river and worked to get what looked like half the river drained from the wagon bed. A couple of cowboys helped him.

Flowers suddenly reared back and almost knocked Mac from behind him.

"What is it?" Mac looked around the trail boss. His eyes went wide. He shook his head in disbelief and said, "That can't be. It just can't."

"Reckon you're wrong, Mac. It is." Flowers put his heels to his horse's flanks and galloped down to the riverbank, dodging cattle the entire way.

Chapter 13

"It's hardly dawn," Desmond had complained as the river crossing got underway. "There's no reason to ford the river this early."

Beside Desmond on the box, Mac had never twitched, never showed any sign he heard. Desmond started to poke him, then decided against it and settled down in a pile of dejection. Nothing ever went his way. The world kicked him in the teeth at every turn. Nothing he did was right or good enough. Flowers rode him constantly, and his ma ignored him, but at least she was better than his pa. Everybody worshipped the old man like he was some kind of saint. Desmond knew different. Zeke Sullivan had poked fun at him every chance he got.

Desmond yelped when the chuckwagon hit a rock and almost sent him sailing from the driver's box.

"You did that on purpose," Desmond protested, his accusation falling on deaf ears. Mac looked straight ahead. The roar of the river, its putrid, decaying smell, spray rising up to reach inland, occupied him more than answering the complaint. Nobody ever listened to Desmond. Nobody, and especially not a lowly cook, should boss him around like that.

"Hang on. We're going across."

"I don't want to go," Desmond said, staring at the choppy water of the Pecos. Logs the size of the chuckwagon tumbled in the dark, churning water. To ford here was crazy. It was sure death.

"Hop off if you want. This is your last chance. But I can use the help getting across."

"What? How?" Desmond looked at the cook, sure he was poking cruel fun at him.

"I'm going to be driving and won't be able to shift around to keep the chuckwagon from capsizing. You need to stand up, move your weight in the direction opposite that caused by the river. Keep us from turning over. Can you do that?"

"I . . . yes." Desmond doubted this was actually any kind of a job. It sounded stupid.

Then the team began pulling and got caught by the rush of the powerful current. Mac kept them moving with the wagon directly behind the horses. Desmond saw that the river wanted to spin the wagon around the tongue. If that happened the team would break free, and the wagon would be swept away, powerless against the flood.

He let out a yelp as the wagon tipped. The floats on the downriver side submerged and the upriver ones rose from the water. Desmond realized this was what Mac wanted from him. He jumped up and grabbed the brace immediately behind the driver's bench. Applying all his strength, he leaned into it. He thought he wasn't having any effect.

"That's the ticket. You're doing just fine," Mac shouted over the roar of the river.

Desmond thought he was taunting him. Mac never passed up a chance at sarcasm. Then Desmond felt the wagon tipping back. The floats on both sides dipped down into the water. He'd righted the wagon.

"We're halfway across. We're going to make it." Mac bent back, tugging hard on the reins to turn the horses toward a spot on the far bank off at an angle. They tired fast, fighting the current. He aimed them for a spot they could reach without exerting themselves as much.

Desmond had to jump up and lean into the wagon again. It righted fast, almost throwing him out into the river. He collapsed to the seat. His clothing clung to his body, as wet from the river spray as from sweat. Exerting every ounce of energy was taking it out of him. He saw that Mac's face was pale and drawn with strain. The cook fought the team every inch of the way, and it drained him.

A smirk came to Desmond's lips. So the great Dewey Mackenzie wasn't so great after all. He got tired and scared like everybody else.

"Help me. Take the reins. My hands are cramped up." Mac held out the leather straps. Desmond took them without realizing he did so.

The sudden jerk almost tore his arms from his shoulder joints. He shoved out his feet against sodden wood and pulled for all he was worth. The team began to move in the right direction, at an angle, through the river.

Mac took back the reins after flexing his hands for a minute or so. Desmond gave them back, glad to be freed of the responsibility but at the same time surly because Mac hadn't told him he'd done a good job.

Then a powerful invisible hand lifted the wagon straight into the air and dropped it down with a thud as if it hit solid ground.

"What do you think about that?" Desmond shouted over the roar of the water. It took him a moment to realize he was alone in the wagon. "Mackenzie? Mackenzie! Where'd you go?"

Frantic, he hunted for the cook. Mac was nowhere to be

seen. He had been washed over the side of the wagon and carried away by the dark river. This startled Desmond so much, he almost didn't think to grab the wet reins that lay at his feet.

But those reins represented his only chance for survival, he realized. He knew he would die if he followed Mac into the river. His only chance to keep on living lay ahead. He had to get the team to pull him from the Pecos.

Desmond snatched up the reins and drove in a half crouch, controlling the team as he had never done before and using his shifting weight to counter the roll of the wagon. After an eternity, he realized the force of the river had diminished against the wagon because all four wheels were miring down in river bottom mud as he neared the shore.

"Pull, damn you! Keep going!" He whipped the tired horses. They saw dry land ahead and struggled to pull forward to reach it. Before he fully grasped what was happening, the horses were dragging the chuckwagon over dry ground and up an incline near the river.

Out of the river!

He stomped on the brake and set it, using the reins to hold it in place. Standing, he let out a wild whoop of glee. Then he collapsed to the bench seat, his legs the consistency of stewed okra. His insides were liquid and weak. Not a muscle worked right for him. He shook all over as if he had the ague.

Desmond sat up when he heard the rattle of another wagon.

"Mac!" a guttural voice called. "You made it, Mac! We celebrate, eh?"

He peered around the side of the wagon and saw Kleingeld driving up in the supply wagon. Their eyes locked. The German's faced melted into horror.

"Where is he? Where is Mac?"

"He got washed overboard," Desmond said. "Served him right. He was showing off. I had to drive the wagon the rest of the way."

"He is in the river? We must find him."

"You mean you're going to hunt for his body. As fast as the current is, he'll be halfway across Texas by now."

"Go. You go and hunt for him! I will tell the others!"

"What do they care? They have the cattle to tend. That's all that's important. The damned longhorns." Desmond let his bitterness gush forth. Kleingeld and the others would never have mounted a search if he had been the one dumped into the river. More than likely, they would have celebrated. He knew it because they all hated him so. Hiram Flowers would be the one doing the most cheering over his death.

Desmond jumped down and walked slowly around the wagon. He blinked in surprise when he saw one of the floats had been ripped off. He had never noticed. Working with fingers that felt five times too big, he untied the remaining floats and tossed them into the back of the wagon.

As he stared inside, his mouth turned dry. He poked around and found the crate with the whiskey in it. Mac had been such a spoilsport about using it for anything but medicine. He picked up the bottle and held it.

His shaking went away at the touch of the smooth, cool glass against his palm. He pulled out the cork and let the fumes drift up to his nose. His nostrils flared, and his mouth turned drier than the Chihuahuan Desert. A single sip. That's all. He had sneaked a few drinks and Mac had never known. Now that the cook was gone, he had the bottle all to himself. Lifting it to his lips, he paused. Another deep whiff. Then he put the cork back in and carefully packed the bottle in its crate again.

"Later," he muttered to himself. He'd sample the whiskey later, to celebrate.

He finished bailing out the water inside the wagon, mopping up what he could. By now the sun had risen a good way and made it easier to hang out cloth and get the tarps hung up to dry. The sound of the herd kept him company. Nobody else came by, nobody else cared.

"I'll show them. I'm as good as any of them."

Those words had barely left his lips when he heard a loud hoot of glee. He turned and saw Hiram Flowers riding in his direction. For a moment, it didn't penetrate to Desmond's fatigue-dulled brain that someone came up alongside the trail boss, on foot.

Mackenzie. A broad grin stretched across the cook's muddy face.

"Desmond!" Mac shouted. "You saved the chuckwagon!"

"Of course I did," he said. Had there ever been any doubt?

"I knew you could do it." Mac thrust out his hand. Desmond started to shake, then pulled back.

"Like hell you did. Why'd you leave me stranded in the middle of the river?"

Mac shot a look at Flowers, who shook his head.

"I've got a herd to bed down. There's a storm coming, mark my words." The trail boss put his heels to his horse's flanks and trotted off.

"Him and his weather sense," Mac said. "He's for certain sure we're in for a storm." He looked around. "I don't see it."

"You don't see much of anything," Desmond snapped.

Mac's lips thinned, but he held back any sharp words.

"Thanks for tending the wagon."

"It's still there."

Mac frowned slightly. "What's still there? I know we lost a float, but that doesn't matter. There aren't any more big rivers to cross like this."

"The whiskey, damn it. I didn't touch a drop of your precious whiskey." Desmond spun and stalked off. Mac said something, but he didn't try to understand. The cook had it in for him and would lie about the liquor. He'd probably drink it himself, then claim Desmond had drunk it.

He should have gone ahead and taken the whole damned bottle. Stomping to the top of a hill, he looked back over the river. If the Pecos wanted to really mock him, it would be all calm now.

The swollen river still sloshed against its banks, at flood level. He marveled at how he had driven the chuckwagon across such swollen, racing water and lived to tell about it. A thought crossed his mind that he ought to ask if everyone else had made it. Mac had, in spite of being washed out of the wagon.

Then Desmond decided it didn't matter one whit. If any of the cowboys had drowned, nothing would bring him back. And if they had all made it just fine, what did he care? They didn't like him. Why should he bother about them?

"Hey, Desmond!"

He saw Flowers waving to him. Reluctantly, he hiked down the hill to see what the trail boss wanted.

"Grab a horse and go out to the north side of the herd. Keep 'em all together. When the storm comes, it'll be a whopper. Get a slicker. Everybody's gonna get mighty wet before we hit the trail again."

"You putting everybody out riding herd or just me?"

"Doesn't concern you what anyone else is doing, but the answer's simple. I'm sending as many out as I can because the storm's going to break before sundown. Now get your ass on a horse and get to work."

Desmond watched him ride off, shouting orders to others. So much for gratitude, for saving the Circle Arrow's chow, utensils, everything that kept the drovers fed and happy. No matter what he did, they never appreciated it. No matter what.

He found a decent horse, saddled, and went out. At least being alone kept the others from mocking him all the time.

Desmond nodded off as he rode, then jerked awake. It wasn't right keeping him out here this long. Flowers had given him a break to eat supper and sent him back out without any sleep. Crossing the river had been enough for any given day, but riding herd the rest of the day while the cattle milled around irked him. They could have made another couple of miles, but Flowers insisted on bedding down not a quarter mile from the river.

He drifted off to sleep again, only to be awakened by a sharp crack. He thought someone was shooting at him. The cattle began making noises like they were afraid. Singing to them to soothe the stupid animals was beneath his dignity, but he worried that calming them wasn't possible any other way.

A new rumble caused him to look at the sky. The sunset had been spectacular, but what did he care about that? Clouds. Lots of them. But these coming up from the southeast now were dark, their leaden bottoms filled with flashes. The lightning in those storm clouds was still miles off, but the rain promised a long, wet night.

"Wet again." Desmond sighed. "Just when I dried out from getting across the river."

A single heavy, cold raindrop spattered against his hat brim. He turned his face up and caught another drop just under the right eye. He flinched. Flowers had doomed him for another terrible night. Licking his lips, he almost tasted the whiskey he had put back. The bottle would have gotten him through this miserable night.

The cattle moaned and began to stir as even louder thunder rolled over the land. The promise of more rain made Desmond twist around and fumble in his saddlebags for the slicker Flowers had told him to bring. That wouldn't make the night any better, but it kept him drier than he would have been without it.

As he kicked one foot from the stirrup to get a better reach, a lightning bolt tore through the sky directly overhead, well ahead of the storm as such things sometimes were. The violent electrical display startled him and terrified his horse. The animal bucked, hit hard, then reared. In his contorted position, Desmond couldn't keep his seat. He grabbed for the saddlebags to stay astride. The horse bucked again, sending him flying through the air. Desmond landed with a hard whack.

The fall stunned him for a moment. He climbed to his feet, every bone in his skeleton aching from being thrown. In his hand he clutched the yellow slicker.

"I may walk back to camp, but I won't get too wet," he grumbled as the horse tore off into the distance, thoroughly spooked. As he started to slip into the slicker, he felt the ground under his feet quiver and shake. He looked up and saw the dark mass of the herd shift. The cattle began to move.

"Oh, sweet Jesus, no!" Desmond turned and ran away from them, but the storm had spooked the biggest steers along the edge of the herd. They began to run. The others followed.

Stampede.

Heart pounding crazily, Desmond staggered along, his legs not working right. The herd snorted and let out a terrible sound that chilled him all the way to the soul. There was nowhere to run. Flowers had bedded the herd down in a shallow bowl away from the river. Desmond wished the cattle had stampeded toward the Pecos. Let them all drown. They came toward him instead, running away from the riverbank.

"Hang on, I'm coming!"

He looked over his shoulder, trying to see who called to him. The sun had set. Twilight should have let him see better than this, but already the onrushing storm had turned the evening pitch black. He tried to keep running. Whatever he heard might have been his imagination.

Then he saw the flashing hooves of a horse rush past him. The rider spun around and blocked his way, reaching down to help him up.

"Mackenzie!"

"We've got to get out of the way. Those cows aren't going to stop running for a month of Sundays. That's how scared they are."

Desmond started to reach up but held back. Mac would never let him hear the end of this, how he had pulled his fat from the fire, how he had saved the boss's son just like he had plucked him from a Fort Worth whorehouse.

"Damn it, get up here!" Mac looked behind Desmond. "Too late."

Desmond's heart threatened to explode. He saw the cook was right. The charging herd was too close to them. They couldn't get clear. In seconds they'd be goners.

Mac leaped off the horse. "What are you doing?" Desmond demanded. For a second he thought Mac had dismounted to give him the horse, but then the cook yanked the yellow slicker from his hand.

He began waving it around. The motion drew the herd's attention. The deadly cattle changed direction, but not much. Then Mac did something that confused Desmond. He yanked on his horse's reins, stuffed the slicker under the saddle and gave the horse a solid whack on the rump. Its eyes were rimmed in white with fear from the stampede. It galloped away, the slicker flapping behind.

"What are you doing?"

Mac didn't answer. He grabbed Desmond and threw both of them to the ground.

"Stay down. Keep your head down. These rocks might not be enough to protect us, even if the cattle chase after the horse."

Desmond looked up. The horse frantically tried to escape the cattle as it galloped away. It quickly became evident the race was not to the swift but to the frightened.

He heard the horse die. He couldn't see it because of the rippling mass of beef between him and the doomed animal.

Mac grabbed his collar and held him down. Desmond thrashed

around, trying to get away, then stopped. The cook was right. They huddled behind rocks poking up from the ground. Not more than a couple of feet high, but enough. Maybe enough.

The stampede broke over their heads, deadly hooves whistling through the air only inches away.

Chapter 14

"Get up," Dewey Mackenzie said after what seemed like an eternity of being surrounded by roaring, pounding, certain death. "We've got to get away. There are still longhorns out there willing to trample us."

He grabbed Desmond by the coat collar and lifted. The young man's legs buckled. Mac supported him until he stood upright under his own power. If he hadn't realized the trouble they were still in, Mac would have felt the same. The closeness of death frightened anyone with an ounce of sense.

"You're bleeding." Desmond reached out and touched Mac's arm.

"A hoof caught me. Just missed my head." He took off his battered black hat and looked at it. Part of the crown had just vanished as the longhorn kicked past. "If it rains much more, I'll drown if I wear this."

Desmond snickered. Then he laughed harder. Hysteria hit him, and he doubled over guffawing at the bad joke. Mac didn't begrudge him this, either. They both knew how close they'd come to being killed. Finally as the paroxysms of laughter died down, Desmond straightened and stared at him.

"You saved my life. You didn't have to do that. You could have let me die."

"No way would I do such a thing," Mac said, shaking his head and regretting it as pain jabbed into him. That hoof hadn't just kicked away part of his hat. It must have grazed his skull. He pressed his fingers into the top of his head. They came away sticky with blood. "Flowers would never let me forget it. He might even dock my pay."

"We lost a horse," Desmond said.

"Two. And you lost your slicker."

That set Desmond off again, but the laughter died faster this time. Mac took him by the arm and guided him away from the herd and up a hillside. From here they had a better look at how the cattle had stampeded away from the river. In that, Flowers had had a touch of luck, but most of the longhorns were still running as the rain pelted down on them and lightning stabbed across the sky, jumping from cloud to cloud. If it ever flashed downward to blast apart a tree or even a cow, there'd be no stopping the stampede.

"How long can they run?" Desmond's voice sounded small, subdued.

"As long as they're scared. I heard tell of a stampede along the Chisholm Trail that lasted a week. They had to chase the beeves more than a hundred miles before they wore themselves out. What you have to do is get the leaders to turn back toward the center of the herd, get them to mill, to spiral around. That breaks their forward run." Mac heaved a sigh. "Of course, that causes other problems."

"They trample each other."

Mac looked at Desmond. He hadn't expected an answer. His own fear was running out like sand through an hourglass, but he babbled rather than laughed.

"Not only that, they generate so damned much heat pressing together that it'll burn a cowboy riding close by."

"You're joshing me. That's not so."

"God's truth," Mac insisted. "They get all bunched together. Animals that big and frightened generate a lot of heat. Then there's the hooves pounding on the ground, hitting rocks. Never heard of a cowboy who got blisters from being too close by, but it's as bad as being out in the desert sun. Hotter than hell."

"You want me to put a tourniquet on your arm?"

Desmond stared at the steady flow of blood down Mac's left arm. It was a deep wound, but not as bad as it looked. Mac bunched up his coat and pressed it down hard. The blood turned sluggish and soon stopped flowing as it clotted over. It was his head hurting like a thousand wasps had built a nest in it that bothered him more.

"You two, are you all right?" The urgent shout came from down the slope.

"Up here, Mister Flowers," Mac called. "Me and Desmond. We dodged the worst of the stampede."

"Son of a bitch, Desmond, you got yourself caught in it," the trail boss said as he rode up the hill toward them. "I bet Mac here had to pull you out. Isn't that so?"

"I—"

"We lost two horses, Mister Flowers," Mac cut in. "It was a small price to pay for both of us getting away. I had to fasten his slicker to my horse and let it lead the cattle away from us."

"You're hurt. You two get back to the supply wagon." Flowers jerked a thumb over his shoulder. "Messy can patch you up. He's handy with needle and thread, if you have cuts needin' stitches. He said that he'd worked for a tailor when he was a young sprout."

"Thanks."

"Son of a bitch," Flowers grumbled under his breath as he turned his horse, but loud enough for both men to hear. "He's bound and determined to get himself killed. Mercedes would blame me for sure." He rode away to rally the cowboys and get the herd under control.

"He blames me," Desmond said bitterly. "He blames me for everything! Probably even for the storm!"

"Not that as much as he's blaming himself if anything were to happen to you."

"What's he care?" Desmond stormed away before Mac could explain. Maybe he didn't know how Hiram Flowers felt about his ma. Or maybe he did and that caused the bad blood between them, not that he saw Flowers as unnecessarily riding Desmond. The kid was pretty dumb when it came to most things, but he'd never had a chance to be on his own and learn.

Mac trailed him to the supply wagon, where Messerschmidt was already fixing up a couple of other cowboys. Mac sat on the tailgate. Messy had retrieved a bottle of whiskey from the chuckwagon and used it liberally on the men's open cuts. Mac picked it up, looked at it a moment, then called, "Desmond. Heads up!"

He tossed the half-full bottle. Desmond caught it. He stared at it, then looked up to Mackenzie.

"Go on, take a swig. It's for medicinal purposes."

Desmond pulled the cork, lifted it to his lips, then paused. He lowered the bottle and recorked it. He tossed it back.

"Not interested." He spun around and stalked off.

"What's that all about?" Messy took the bottle from Mac. "You're not seein' me pass up a chance to take a long pull." He expertly plucked out the cork with thumb and forefinger and, using the same hand to hold the bottle, upended it. A good inch of amber fluid disappeared down his gullet. He let out a sigh and recorked the bottle.

Messerschmidt held it out to Mac, who shook his head and said, "No thanks."

"You and the kid got a pact to see who can be more mule headed?"

"Something like that." Mac had to wonder at Desmond turning down the whiskey. Deciding if that was a good sign or bad gave him something to ponder.

"Better get everything packed up and ready for the trail," Mac went on. "Flowers never said, but since the herd stampeded in the direction he intended to go, there's a meal to be fixed before long, and I had better be ready."

"I wouldn't go more 'n three miles, not in this rain. There's still a passel of men to patch up, and I don't want to leave with them leakin' blood everywhere."

"See you at dinner, Messy." Mac waved as he walked off and added over his shoulder, "Obliged for the patching up!"

He trudged back to the chuckwagon, his head hurting worse than ever. He made a quick check and saw that Desmond had cleaned up the wagon enough to press on. The rain wasn't pelting down as hard as before and might stop soon. From the crash of thunder, the storm center had moved to the north and they were traveling northwest now. Let the rain swell the Pecos even more. They were across it.

"Desmond!" He climbed onto the driver's box and looked around. "Desmond, you riding with me?" No answer. "I'm pulling out. You'll have to catch up." As Mac sat, the world spun a little before settling down. He blinked hard. Having Desmond with him to be sure he wasn't seeing double would have been a boon, but the youngster had gone off somewhere to lick his wounds and be mad at the world.

The team moved, but they were difficult to control. The sporadic rain kept them shying one way and the other, but the distant sound of the running herd worried the horses the most. They were smarter than he was, Mac reflected. They knew better than to get in the way of a stampede.

After a few minutes, the team settled down and dutifully pulled the chuckwagon along the muddy track that passed for a road. Commerce came this way, wagons and mules and men driving stagecoaches. He hunted for traces that they actually followed the Goodnight-Loving Trail and found nothing. The rain had erased such obvious marks, leaving behind only the dual ruts baked into the ground by the sun most days of the year. Mac turned up his collar to keep the cold raindrops from running down his neck.

The rain was more of a fine mist now, but he had driven through worse. His mind drifted away from driving and went to fixing a meal for the hungry cowboys. They deserved something special for all the work they'd put in this day, from getting the herd across the river to stemming the raging tide of a full-out stampede.

At the thought of the mindlessly running cattle, he reached up and touched his tender scalp. He was lucky the hoof hadn't caught him a half inch lower or it would have split open his head.

If Mac was lucky, then Desmond Sullivan was even luckier that someone had come by just as he fell off his horse. There wouldn't have been more than a trampled, bloody corpse if Mac hadn't decoyed the steers away and forced Desmond to stay low behind the rocks. As it was, they had both come close to ending their days.

"Ingrate," Mac muttered. "I saved his life, and he seems to blame me."

As he ranted and raved on, he began gesturing with one hand and then the other. Switching the reins from one hand to the other proved easy for a man used to driving the wagon. But the horses balked when they came to a steep hill. The road was muddy, and getting up to the summit required a running start.

He applied the reins, snapping them and shouting to the horses to keep them pulling. The chuckwagon worked its way up the hill, sideslipping now and then in the slick mud. Mac let out one last hoarse shout to get the team to the top. From up there it would be easy to find a spot to set up camp and feed the men.

The chuckwagon began sliding. Mac tried to get the horses to pull faster. That was the only way he had of keeping the wagon from tilting precariously. The horses simply stopped. The wagon slid faster, sideways down the hill. A last effort to have the team pull him out of his predicament failed. He heard the wagon tongue snap as the wagon tilted far on its side. Freed of their burden, the team bolted. The wagon slammed back down on all four wheels, but it was completely out of control now.

Mac screamed as the wagon slid. He tried to stand and jump off, but the speed was too great. When the chuckwagon wheels hit a rock, the world went spinning. The wagon landed on its side and kept sliding down toward the bottom of the hill.

Mac had to hang on for dear life because he was on the wrong side of the runaway. If he jumped off, the chuckwagon would go over him and crush him. The mud lubricated the way until wagon and cook fetched up hard against a rocky patch. It felt like a giant fist had slammed down on them, stopping them.

Mac tried to move but couldn't. Looking down, he saw his legs were pinned under part of the wagon. The weight felt as if it increased with every passing second. Mac realized he was weakening from the fight to get free. He sagged, taking a moment to gather his strength. When he was again aware of the world, he realized he had passed out. The rain came down harder now. The gully between hills began to fill with runoff.

And Mac was held down as the water rose around him. It would take a lot more rain for him to drown, but gully washers out on the prairie dumped inches of rain at a time. That might be more than enough. He fought to pull his legs free, and again he failed.

Flopping back down, he tried to figure out how to escape. There had to be a way, but his head hurt worse than ever. Still, that was better than what he felt from the waist down—nothing. There wasn't any feeling at all in his hips and legs.

"Help!" he called out, but his voice was weak. He had

turned hoarse shouting at the horses to keep them moving in the mud.

He wasn't sure how long he lay there, half aware of the world, but finally a new sound drifted to his ears over the constant pounding of the rain. A horse was approaching.

Mac used his arms to force his body up like a snake ready to strike. In this position he saw the rider coming through the sheets of rain.

"Here. Over here!"

His heart leaped when the rider turned and rode toward him.

"Desmond, get me out from under here. The chuckwagon flipped and . . ."

Mac lost all strength, all hope, as Desmond Sullivan turned his horse's face and rode off without saying a word.

Chapter 15

The rain washed dirt off Mac's face and out of his eyes, allowing him to see the full extent of his problems. Wiggling around, he began scooping at the soft earth in an attempt to free his legs from under the chuckwagon. His fingers quickly turned raw and his strength faded. He lay back, gasping, letting the rain hammer down on him.

The cold water renewed his determination, if not his strength. Muscles screaming in agony, he returned to burrowing under the wagon. He finally dug a tunnel to his right leg.

He ran his fingers along his leg. No sensation. Panic rose, then anger replaced it. He should have driven better. And Desmond Sullivan should have tried to help. Instead he had ridden away, leaving him to die. Fury filled him. Mac pinched his leg and yelped as pain lanced all the way down into his foot. For a second he let that build, then he realized what the pain meant. His legs were still good, only pressed down into the mud under the weight of the chuckwagon.

Another five minutes of digging furiously exhausted him completely. He gasped for breath and tried to think of another way to get free. Nothing came to him.

"You need help?"

The voice came from far off. Mac knew it had to be a hallucination. But what did he have to lose? He answered.

"Whatever you can do would be mightily appreciated. I don't know what more I can do for myself."

"You done good, moving that much dirt with nothing but your hands."

"What choice did I have?"

"You're a mite hoarse from shouting, but you could have called for help. Hang on."

Mac closed his eyes and smiled. He had such good hallucinations. He even thought he heard wood creaking and the pressure on his legs vanishing. A yelp escaped his lips as strong hands gripped his arms and pulled him hard and fast.

"That's got him free. Let the wagon down real gentle. I don't want it more banged up than it already is."

"We ought to push it back onto its wheels, but it'll be easier if we turn it so the front end is pointing downhill."

Mac blinked. His eyes were filled with rainwater and tears. More blinking cleared them. Hiram Flowers stood over him. The trail boss had pulled him from under the wagon. Near the chuckwagon Messerschmidt and Kleingeld held a long pole they had used to lever it up.

Walking around from the rear came Desmond Sullivan.

"It's all set to move," Desmond said. He glanced at Mac.

"You went for help," Mac said in a choked voice.

"You thought I abandoned you. Figures."

"Thank you."

"Enough of this yammering," barked Flowers. "Messy, get him back to your wagon and fix him up the best you can. You get back to riding the herd, Desmond. You, too, Kleingeld. The stampede's over, but the rain is still spooking the beeves."

Mac looked up at the trail boss. Words didn't come. His throat felt as if someone were strangling him.

"Desmond came straight to me," Flowers said. "He saved you. Nobody would have missed you until they didn't get fed."

"Nice to be needed," Mac croaked. He closed his eyes and let them move him around. It felt good to be out from under the wagon. It felt even better knowing Desmond had had a hand in saving him.

"Some folks back east would kill to get steak every day," Desmond said. "I'd kill to have a fruit pie." He cut the steaks into strips, readying them for Mac to fry.

"Fruit pie?" Mac perked up. He hobbled as he went from one kettle to another, stirring the midday meal. His legs worked but were still stiff and sore, days after the mishap with the chuckwagon.

The savory smell from the kettles made his mouth water. It took all his willpower not to sample everything every time he stirred or checked. That was how cooks got to weigh twice what any cowboy did.

"That's one thing I remember," Desmond said. "My ma fixing peach pie. Or apple. Sometimes chokeberry. It'd depend on what she could find. She'd let the pie cool on the windowsill. I'd sneak over and sit underneath, just sniffing like I was a hound dog hunting down a rabbit." Desmond let out a sigh as the memory pushed away his darker moments.

"We don't have any fruit." Mac checked the larder to be sure. They were too long into the drive for any fresh fruit to remain uneaten. Even the dried fruit had run out before they crossed the Pecos. In the week since then, since he had been trapped under the wagon, they had worked northward but kept away from towns where he might trade a cow or two for more supplies. This stretch of New Mexico was sparsely populated desert.

"I know, but having a full belly isn't the same as pleasing your taste buds."

They finished preparations for the meal, Mac's mind racing.

Desmond had settled down after rescuing him and had dutifully done whatever he was told. Some resentment still simmered in the young man. That was obvious by the narrowed eyes and the facial twitches, but he had been almost bearable.

"Are you riding herd this afternoon?"

"That's what Flowers said." Some antagonism sneaked into Desmond's answer.

"I won't need your help anymore," Mac said. "I'm getting around just fine now."

"You're still limping."

"Thanks for working as my cooking wrangler. It helped having someone to lean on rather than doing it all myself."

Desmond looked at him, expression unreadable. He shrugged and went back to his work.

He had come a ways from the way he acted before they crossed the river. A powerful lot of responsibility had been dropped on his shoulders, and he had stepped up to take it on. He had saved the chuckwagon in the middle of the river after Mac had been washed over the side. The lapse riding herd where he had almost been trampled was something that could have happened to any of the cowboys. It had been an exhausting trip across the Pecos and the entire crew had been faced with a powerful thunderstorm immediately after. If Desmond hadn't been the one falling from his horse, another could have just as easily. Mac was glad he rode by when he had to save him.

Whether Desmond had saved him out of common decency or thought of it as evening the score worried Mac. On the trail they all depended on each other. This wasn't a poker game where the winner stacked the most chips in front of him on the table. He thought back on his own experience with the Rolling J crew and how that trail boss had fared. Patrick Flagg had saved more than one of the cowboys when they got into trouble, Mac included, only to lose all his chips at the end of the trail.

Some gave, some took, everyone worked together. Where Desmond fit into the Circle Arrow cattle drive remained to be seen. But that didn't mean Mac couldn't show some gratitude for what he had done.

Humming to himself, he packed up the last of the kettles and other utensils, checked to be sure the wagon tongue repair held, then got the wagon rolling toward the spot three miles north where Hiram Flowers decided to spend the night with the herd. As he drove along, Mac kept a sharp eye out for cactus. He saw a few barrel cactus and cholla everywhere, but they wouldn't suit his needs.

An hour along the trail, he halted, secured the reins, and jumped down. His leg threatened to give way under him, then strengthened.

With a smooth move he drew his knife. Spreading his bandana on the ground, he began cutting off the seedy fruit from a prickly pear cactus. Half a hillside was covered in the spiny plant and hundreds of purple-red bulbs poked out. A quick slash with his knife separated the fruit from the spiny, succulent pad. In less than five minutes he had a couple pounds of prickly pear fruit.

He tied the corners of his bandana together and put the precious package into the back of the wagon. The next two hours passed slowly as he thought about how to fix a special dessert for Desmond to thank him and maybe to win him over from his hostile ways.

Hiram Flowers stood near a clump of cottonwoods and waved to him. Mac veered over and came to a rattling halt.

"This where you want to set up camp for the night?" Mac secured the reins and climbed down, careful not to show any injury to the trail boss.

"Exactly right. You feeling up to fixing a full meal for those hungry drovers? I can get Desmond to help."

"He's been handy but use him how you want, especially if he's needed with the herd."

"He is," Flowers said. He chewed on his lower lip, then locked eyes with Mac. "You see anybody on our back trail?"

"The men who tangled with the Comanches? I haven't seen them since that dustup." Mac hesitated to say more. Flowers would fire him if he thought for an instant that bounty hunters were after him or if he ever learned that the wanted poster was legally issued, even if Mac had been framed for a murder he would never have committed under any circumstances.

"That's what I'm thinking." Flowers broke off, stared at his boots, and said in a voice almost too low to hear, "They're after me, I think. I tangled with one of them a year back. He didn't come out of the fight ever wanting to be partners, that's for sure."

Mac's eyebrows rose. It never occurred to him that the bounty hunters were after anyone but him.

"A guilty man flees when no one pursues," Mac muttered.

"Not sure how guilty I am, if I'm right about the man leading them. He's a snake in the grass. You keep your eye peeled for them, and let me know if you see anything out of the ordinary."

"I'll do that," Mac said.

"You're the most responsible man I've got here, Mac. Thanks."

Before Mac could reply, Flowers vaulted into the saddle and trotted away. Mac watched the trail boss go, his head buzzing again. Being kicked in the head by a longhorn hadn't done him any good. It had led to him rolling the wagon down a hill and now it kept him from thinking this through. In a way he hoped Flowers was right about their pursuers being after him to settle an old score. But the night he had overheard two of them talking led him to believe they wanted to collect a reward—from New Orleans.

He looked around and found a decent spot to set up his wagon near a pond. Lugging water caused his already bruised body to complain. Painful or not, after getting what he needed for cooking, he refilled the water barrels. They were entering harder desert and water might be impossible to find unless they turned into Apaches. The chances of that were small.

"What Apache likes fruit pie?" Mac laughed as he began working on the pie for Desmond.

Taking out the prickly pear fruit, he began skinning them. He split each open. The juicy, sticky interior was mostly seeds. He worked to get them out, then tried one of the pieces. Biting down on it produced a curious taste. Slightly bitter, but he knew ways of making it taste better. He cleaned the rest of the prickly pear fruit of spines and skins, then worked to make a crust using his biscuit mix.

He popped the entire completed pie into a Dutch oven and turned his attention to preparing the meal for a herd of hungry cowboys. By the time he finished fixing the first batch of boiled greens and a few pounds of steak, the men began riding in.

He joked with them as he served their food. He was nearing the end of the meal when Desmond rode up and dismounted. The young man's nose wrinkled, and he looked around.

"What's wrong?" Mac asked.

"I thought I smelled a pie baking."

"Just for you." Mac popped it from the Dutch oven. "It'll take a spell to cool."

"What do you mean it's for me?"

"I appreciate you getting help to pull me from under the wagon. It was a damned stupid thing I did and you saved my life."

"Hey, I want a piece of that," one of the men spoke up.

"Me too!" called another.

The cry went up from the rest of the cowboys. They crowded around and reached out with their filthy hands, but Mac whacked their knuckles with his wooden cooking spoon.

"If Desmond wants to share, he can," Mac declared. "It's his reward."

"I'll save you. Go on, try to drown yourself in that pond," Messerschmidt said. "I will wade in and save you for a piece of this pie."

The jokes made the circuit, but Mac held firm. When the pie had cooled enough he gave it to Desmond. He dug into it, ate in silence, then spat some of the seeds out.

"Pie isn't supposed to be chewy. Here, you can divvy it up." He handed the plate to Messy, who began spooning out a tiny bit to every cowboy who wanted some.

"Desmond is right," the German said. "This is terrible, Mac. You got any more?"

This set off a new round of jokes. Mac took it good-naturedly, but he watched Desmond. For all his complaint about the pie, he had eaten a fair amount. Passing it on, saying it tasted terrible, might have been his way of sharing. He had never learned to do that gracefully.

"Help me clean up, will you, Desmond?"

"I knew it was too good to be true. You bribed me to do extra duty."

Despite the griping, Desmond threw himself into the work, and Mac finished a half hour early. The others sat around a fire, swapping lies about their love lives and how much whiskey they could drink and still shoot the eye out of a flying eagle at a hundred yards.

Desmond moved as if he was on a spring, edging away and then hesitantly returning. He wanted company—and he didn't.

"You know how to use that revolver on your hip?" Mac asked.

"What?" Desmond perked up like a prairie dog on guard duty. "You calling me out?"

"I'm asking if you know how to use it, that's all. Before I went on my first trail drive, I had my pa's revolver and no idea how dangerous I was with it. The trail boss showed me how to draw. I can tell you what all he taught me."

"Why would you do that?" Desmond turned suspicious.

"You need to know things like that, or you'll end up in a world of trouble." Mac half turned and drew. He had the Smith & Wesson out, cocked and aimed, before Desmond blinked.

"You're as fast as anyone I ever saw."

"If the only ones you ever saw throw down were drunk cowboys in Hell's Half Acre, that's not much of a compliment. Wait. Watch this." Mac turned so he faced away from Desmond and drew the S&W again, this time slowly. "See all that I did?"

"No, I was watching how you stood."

"That's good, Desmond. It's important to keep your balance. Here's how to clear leather and not shoot your own foot off."

They worked for a half hour until Mac's shoulder began to hurt.

"You practice some, and you'll be good enough," Mac said.

"Good enough for what?" Desmond demanded.

"Good enough to stay alive. Take the cartridges out when you practice the draw."

"Why?" He got bristly. "Think I'll shoot myself?"

"You need to practice getting that smoke wagon out, cocked, and then fired. Do that a hundred times, and you've wasted a wagonload of ammo."

Desmond stared at him, a poker face betraying no emotion. "Why?"

"I told you. You can practice the draw. When you get good, we can try some target practice, though too much shooting's likely to scare the cattle."

"No, not that. Why are you doing this?"

Mac hesitated, then said, "You remind me of somebody."

"Who's that?" Desmond pressed the matter.

Mac laughed harshly as he answered, "Me. You remind me of me. Now get your ass out on night herd. Flowers will chew us both out if you're late."

Desmond went off without another word, leaving Mac with a good feeling. He saw glimmerings of a real man inside the boy. All it took to bring it out was someone treating him as an equal. At least, he hoped that was true. It'd be hell teaching Desmond to use his gun, only to have him shoot down the first cowboy who crossed him.

Chapter 16

Quick Willy Means couldn't see ten feet in front of him. The rain came down in sheets that might as well have been shrouds. He kept his face turned down so most of the rain pelted hard against his hat and ran off the brim, but even so he got water in his eyes and had to wipe it away to see anything.

"We got to take cover, Quick Willy," Charles Huffman said. "Ain't possible to get wetter, but we might not get any more miserable."

"Shut up." Means spoke without malice. He worried over the potential for catching up with the herd and cutting out Dewey Mackenzie. Every passing minute made it less likely.

"He's right, Willy. There's no call to go blunderin' on in this rain. It's pure hell out here. I can't tell if it's day or night." Frank Huffman stood up for his brother, which was to be expected. But the edge in his voice surprised Means. After Quick Willy had cut down Arizona Johnston, the two men had been docile enough and willing to follow his every order. Now the rain had washed that compliance out of them.

"Find a place where it's dry. I dare you," he said.

"We're close to the river. I hear it roarin' to beat the band." Frank cupped his hand behind his ear. "That's the bad boy. I know it. Them drovers have already crossed by now."

Means looked at his pocket watch, trying to determine what time it was. The heavy clouds and driving rain obscured any sunlight trying to filter through. It could be noon or midnight for all he knew. The watch face beaded right away with water. He wiped it against his vest, then tucked the watch away. Ten o'clock. He knew it had to be morning. By now Hiram Flowers had his herd across the river, but the rain would keep him from covering any real distance once he got bogged down in the mud.

Hiram damn Flowers, Means thought. He spat. He'd fix Flowers good and proper, but only after they snared Mackenzie. Business first, then pleasure.

"Trees over yonder. I can hear the leaves snappin' in the wind." Frank pointed.

Means turned and walked his horse in that direction. Huffman probably heard the sound of blood pumping in his own ears. How could anybody hear wind in tree limbs in this weather?

His horse veered suddenly, avoiding a tree. He looked up and saw a small grove of salt cedar holding back the worst of the wind and rain. It was hardly calm or dry in the middle of the grove, but it was better than being exposed on the flatlands.

"See, Quick Willy?" Charles said. "Frank was right. He's always right."

Means dismounted and scouted the area for an even drier section. The best he found was a tiny nest between four trees growing almost trunk to trunk. He tethered his horse in the lee of another large-boled tree, took his gear, and settled down with his back to the wind.

"What're we gonna do, Quick Willy? We can't get close enough to Mackenzie to nab him. I say we shoot the son of a bitch. They'll bury him, then we dig him up and take the body back." Charles sounded pleased with his gruesome plan.

"I'm not a grave robber," Means said glumly. "Doing it that way might get their whole crew on our trail."

"They'd never abandon a drive. I've heard about their trail boss. A mean one, he is. But determined. We kill Mackenzie and he'd keep right on herding his cattle toward Fort Sumner." Frank had it all worked out, too. Neither plan suited Means.

He wanted Mackenzie alive to collect the bonus from Leclerc. And he wanted Hiram Flowers dead. They had tangled in Abilene, and Flowers had pistol-whipped him until he passed out. The man's temper then meant his death now. No one did that to Quick Willy Means. No one, especially not a decrepit old drover who never took a bath.

"The rain's lettin' up," Charles called. "Lookee there. I see sunlight. The storm's danged near blowed itself out."

"We wait a spell," Means said. They had talked him into getting off the trail and out of the rain. He'd damned well enjoy a rest. Crossing the Pecos after a rain like this would be dangerous, and resting up before they tried it would increase their chances of reaching the other side. Their numbers were too diminished to lose any more.

He'd had to shoot Johnston. The man had challenged him for leadership. But Means missed Jimmy Huffman something fierce. He had been the smartest of the Huffman boys, even though that wasn't saying much.

How Jimmy had gotten himself gunned down in Fort Worth by Mackenzie was something he wished he had seen. Mackenzie would have died on the spot. Chances were good Frank and Charles had had something to do with their brother's death and lied about what had happened.

Hat pulled down to protect his face from the rain, Quick Willy drifted off to sleep. Sounds normally brought him awake. This time it was the rain stopping. It no longer pattered against his hat to drip off onto the ground. He sat up, stretched, then shook all over like a dog getting rid of water drops.

"We hit the trail. You men rested?"

"Ready to go, Willy." Frank kicked his brother to get him moving. For two cents, Means would have kicked them both just to vent some of his frustration. Tracking down Mackenzie had been a hell of a lot harder than he'd anticipated.

He would never give up, never stop hunting until he brought the murdering son of a bitch back. Preferably alive and hobbled in shackles, but if Mackenzie had to catch a few ounces of lead, Means wouldn't shed any tears over that, either.

They rode to the banks of the raging Pecos River. The turbulence looked worse than he expected. Means rode up and down the river for a quarter of a mile, hunting for an easier way across. In spite of the heavy rain, he saw tracks where Flowers had driven his herd across the river. From what he could tell, Flowers was a capable enough trail boss. He had been along this trail before and had to know the best spots to camp and to cross.

"This is it," Means said.

"I dunno, Quick Willy," Charles said, his voice slow and betraying a touch of fear. "That there river's runnin' mighty fast. We get caught in the current and we're goners. If the horse tires, we're goners, too."

"You don't start now, and you're a goner." Means rested his hand on the butt of his revolver. Even a dimwit like Charles Huffman got the message. Pulling his hat down until it mashed into his ears, Huffman let out a rebel yell and got his horse running as fast as he could into the water.

Means doubted this was a smart thing to do, then he saw how Huffman plunged a dozen yards into the swiftly flowing river. The horse tried to balk, but by then it was too late. All the horse could do was swim for the far bank. Huffman yelled and tried to put his spurs to the horse's flanks, but underwater that goad didn't amount to much.

"Can't let little brother have all the fun," Frank Huffman said. He duplicated Charles's plunge into the water and soon only his horse's head and everything above his own shoulders were visible.

Determined not to let his men show him up, Quick Willy Means rode to the edge of the water. He rushed in as they had worked, but he got his horse into the river gradually. Twice the horse denied him, then finally committed itself to the swift current. Means fought the river, in spite of it carrying him across at an angle. After what seemed an eternity, his horse found solid ground and pulled them onto the far bank. Both of the Huffman brothers already waited for him, shaking water off.

"Flowers got across without ending up this far downstream," Means said. He found deep, water-filled ruts left by a wagon. Whether this was the chuckwagon with its quarry or the supply wagon driven by one of the cowboys, he couldn't tell.

And it didn't matter. Both would follow the herd. Means only had to follow one set of tracks and Mackenzie would miraculously appear, the pot of gold at the end of the rainbow.

"They're makin' good time," Frank observed. "They crossed this morning, rode out the storm, and then pushed on. I don't see hide nor hair of them around."

"North," Means said. "If we ride hard we can overtake them before they set up camp for the evening. I want Mackenzie. That'll be the best time to grab him, before he's surrounded by all the cowboys as they chow down."

"Ground's kinda muddy, Willy. We ain't gonna make much speed in this slop. You got a plan to snatch him after the cowboys are fed?" Charles wrung out his bandana and mopped at his forehead. Water leaked out from under the hatband.

He turned away from the gunman and picked out the details of the trail they had to follow. Keeping tabs on his men wasted his time and annoyed them. More than once he had given perfectly good advice, only to have the recipient consider it an insult and call him out for it.

Means's fight was with Mackenzie—and Hiram Flowers. Let Huffman drown himself by inches or all at once if he pulled off his hat.

It turned dark again as new storm clouds blew in. It was after sundown before he sighted the Circle Arrow camp. Anger welled up inside Means. Mackenzie had cleaned up and sat at a campfire with a half dozen cowboys. Even if he crawled into his bedroll under the chuckwagon, the number of drovers nearby would be difficult to avoid. The smallest disturbance—and they were all on edge, constantly listening for any threat to the herd—and they'd be up, revolvers ready. Anyway, creeping into camp would make him and the Huffmans look like sneak thieves, and Means wouldn't stand for that.

"We can wait for him to feed the sorry lot of 'em, then grab him when he heads off on his own in the morning." Frank picked at his teeth with the tip of a big knife.

Means knew that was the smart thing to do. But he was at the end of his tether. Chasing Mackenzie for so long had built up frustration that boiled over.

"We're not waiting," he said. "I want him as quick as possible."

"If Jimmy and Arizona was still with us, we could hurrah their camp, then you could sneak in and snatch Mackenzie." Frank Huffman finished cleaning his teeth and slipped the knife back into a sheath at his left side.

"We're shorthanded, that's for certain sure," Charles said, agreeing with his brother. "What are we gonna do, Quick Willy?"

"That one, the kid with the red hair and strut in the way he walks. Him and Mackenzie spent a long time together at the campfire."

"So?"

"So they must be friends," Means said. "The red-haired kid

is saddling up to ride night herd. We'll take him prisoner and use him as bait in a trap. A note will let Mackenzie know what he's up against, and if he tells any of the others, we'll kill his partner."

"That's a hell of a lot to put into a note. You reckon he can read?" Frank scratched himself.

"You're right about that, Frank," his brother said. "Can you write, Willy?"

Means glared at the two of them. Insulting his education was no more than he expected from them, but Charles had posed an actual problem. What if Mackenzie couldn't read?

"To hell with that. We'll take on an army, if we have to. We take the kid prisoner, find a spot to lay our ambush, and it won't matter if only Mackenzie or Mackenzie and the rest of the cowboys fall into the trap."

"Either way, we got Mackenzie," Frank said, nodding slowly.

Means found an old wanted poster and a pencil in his saddlebags. Chewing his tongue, he wrote the note that would lure Mackenzie away from the Circle Arrow and into shackles all the way back to New Orleans. He finished and studied his handiwork.

"This will do. Now all we need to do is nab the redheaded kid."

"I'm up for it." Charles grinned.

"Me, too," his brother added, but with less enthusiasm. Frank thought a moment, then asked, "Where're we gonna lay the ambush? Should we find a place and then kidnap him?"

"I know Flowers. He'll insist on keeping the herd moving. It doesn't matter if we have the perfect spot. Anywhere will do."

Frank Huffman looked skeptical, but Means didn't care. His patience was at an end. The time had come to grab Mackenzie, get the reward, and move on. As he rode to skirt the camp on his way to take the redheaded cowboy prisoner, he considered his alliance with the Huffman brothers. They weren't what he looked for in a partner anymore. Their brother had been the reason he teamed up with them. Once Jimmy took the bullet in his heart, Charles's and Frank's usefulness died with him.

"This is gonna be easy. He's doin' exactly what we want." Charles let out a whoop that drew the rider's attention.

Charles Huffman didn't have the sense God gave a goose. Now Means had to act too soon, too close to the camp.

The red-haired rider looked around but didn't reach for his revolver. That was a good sign. Means waved all friendly-like and trotted over to him.

"Howdy, mister. This the Circle Arrow herd?"

The cowboy got a sullen look and answered, "What's it to you?"

"I'm looking for a gent named Mackenzie. Dewey Mackenzie. You know him?" Mean rode closer so they were knee to knee.

"He's the cook. If you got any quarrel with him, you got to go through me first."

"Friends, are you? Good friends?" Before the cowboy answered, Quick Willy Means showed how he got the moniker. He drew his pistol left-handed and swung it in a wide arc that landed across the kid's nose.

The redhead threw up his hands to his broken, bleeding nose. Means drew with his right and jammed that pistol into the cowboy's exposed gut.

"You're coming with us. First, we got to leave a message for your good friend Dewey Mackenzie." He slipped his left pistol back into its holster so he could grab the cowboy's hat, put the note inside, and then yank the knife from the boy's belt. With a show of dexterity he rammed the knife through the hat crown and tossed, backhanded, hat and knife toward a tree. The blade dug deep, leaving the hat hanging as a signpost.

"He'll come for you. He's good with a gun." The cowboy

used the end of his bandana stuffed up his nose to slow the bleeding.

"Yeah, he killed our brother. I want a piece of him." Charles Huffman rode over and tried to cuff the prisoner. The boy ducked so Charles missed and almost fell from his horse. "You little—"

"Enough of that," Means snapped. "We need to finish up. Our plan. We need to finish our plan." Means wondered if he had to repeat it a third time for Charles to get the idea that staying this close to the herd abusing one of the cowboys was a bad idea.

He motioned with his drawn gun for the boy to ride west. Seeing how his prisoner tensed and looked around furtively made him cock his revolver to emphasize the futility of trying to escape.

"You're holding me for ransom? Flowers won't give so much as a cow chip for me. He hates me."

"If you don't shut up, I'll take to hating you, too. You wouldn't like that. Faster." Means galloped hard when the captive lit out. If he thought to escape by outrunning his captors, he was wrong.

Means considered whether to make the young man dead wrong about that. A hostage added to complications he wanted to avoid. Most often he walked up to the fugitive he wanted to take in and shoved a gun in their gut. Using a hostage to get to Mackenzie was a hitch in an otherwise simple plan.

The three bounty hunters caught up to the redhead. The Huffman brothers flanked him while Means brought up the rear.

"Up there, Willy." Charles stood in his stirrups as he rode and gestured wildly. "That's a good spot."

Means took in what Huffman claimed about the terrain. For once, the idiot had it right.

"You and Frank get up on the hillside behind those rocks,"

Means ordered. "They don't give much cover, but you shouldn't need much. Take your rifles. If anything goes wrong, open fire and kill as many of them as you can."

This order caused Charles to grin from ear to ear. He and Frank galloped off to find decent spots to command the hollow where Means intended to stake out the cowboy to lure Mackenzie.

"Get off your horse," he ordered.

The redhead reluctantly obeyed. He had a truculent look that belied his position. Two men with rifles covered him, and Quick Willy Means could draw and fire twelve times before the youngster could even touch the butt of his revolver. Means staked out his horse and the cowboy's mount to one side and pointed to a rock exposed to anyone following the trail they had laid out.

"You didn't try to cover your tracks," the boy said. "You want to make it easy to find me. Well, nobody's gonna come. They don't like me. Flowers downright hates me because—"

"Shut up. Yammering the way you do bores me." Means drew and pointed his gun at the prisoner's head when he started to protest more. "Another word and I blow your brains out. I'll prop you up so from a distance nobody can tell you're dead."

The boy sucked in breath to protest, then let it out slowly when he realized Quick Willy Means didn't bluff. He meant what he said. The youngster sank to the rock and slumped forward, eyes on the ground as he muttered to himself.

Means walked around to find a better angle to shoot Mackenzie, if it came to that. He settled down behind another rock and considered what to do about the hostage. Letting him go free after they nabbed Mackenzie made no sense. Even if they tied him up and left him for the cowboys to find, he could identify them later. Means didn't care if he spilled his guts to a federal marshal and identified the Huffmans. Having the law breathing down *his* neck was another matter.

"You really don't think they'll come for you? That's a shame. If they don't, this is where you'll die." Means prodded his captive to see what response he got.

"He made me a fruit pie."

"What? What are you talking about?" Means perked up. The words showed how loco everyone working for the Circle Arrow ranch was.

"A pie. He didn't have to do that, but he did. Mac will come for me."

"That's what I'm counting on. I just don't want to wait forever. I get mighty impatient."

"Willy! Willy!"

Means looked up to where Charles stood, waving his arm frantically to get his attention. Before he shouted for the man to get back into hiding, he took a hard look along their back trail. A smile slowly curled his lips. The wait had been brief.

And it was over now. His hunt was over. Dewey Mackenzie made his way along the trail, eyes on the ground as he followed the hoofprints in the soft dirt. If he failed to look up in another minute, he would be in the middle of a firing squad of two rifles and both of Means's guns.

Quick Willy Means settled his mind and held his hands relaxed and ready over each holster. The moment of truth was at hand.

Chapter 17

Mac forced himself to keep his eyes on the ground. The tracks of at least four riders showed where Desmond had been taken. The difference in horseshoes made it obvious that Desmond rode flanked by the others. Mac's hand twitched, moving toward the gun holstered at his side, but he covered the action by scratching his belly.

He knew perfectly well where the gang that had kidnapped Desmond was. He had to pretend he didn't and that he was riding heedlessly into their ambush.

Mac slowed and finally stopped, as if confused about the trail. The earth, soft from the rains, took the prints well. He needed to play for time. He swung down from the saddle and continued pretending to study the tracks.

Then ignoring the outlaws was no longer possible. One of them stood up from behind a rock and called out to him.

Mac looked up. He tried to make it seem like he was taken by surprise.

"Come on over, or I'll put a bullet in his head." The man held a pistol to Desmond's temple. He thumbed back the hammer with an ominous sound.

For his part, Desmond showed great courage. He didn't flinch.

"There's no call for you to shoot him," Mac said. "What do you want in the way of ransom?"

"Ransom?" The man laughed harshly. "What'll you give me for him?"

"Five hundred head of cattle. That's half of what we have left."

Mac knew who he dealt with by the way the gunman jerked around and eyed his prisoner in surprise.

The reaction told Mac they had kidnapped Desmond to get him to surrender and had no idea who they held. He recognized the man from Fort Worth and later as the leader of the bounty hunters on his trail.

"Why so much for this kid? It's you we want, Mackenzie."

"I reckoned so," Mac said, slowly walking closer. He hunted for the others in the gang. At least two more lurked somewhere nearby, maybe three. He wished he had read sign better.

"Why's he worth so much?" The gunman moved around, standing half behind Desmond now, making a shot more difficult.

"You're bounty hunters. You want me. Let him go and take me."

"Who we got here?" the man insisted. "Is he wanted, too? If you wanted to buy me off with that many head, he must be somebody important. He's too young to be the rancher who owns that herd."

"I'm not that young," Desmond blurted. "My ma'd never give over that many beeves as ransom."

"Your ma?" the gunman laughed harshly. "This is my lucky day. I got me a fugitive from the law *and* a sprout who can get me half of that great, big herd."

Desmond should have kept his mouth shut when the bounty hunter revealed he had no idea who he had kidnapped. Mac couldn't blame the boy too much. He had planted that seed himself, trying to make sure these men were the bounty hunters who had been pursuing him.

His presence on the drive had been a fuse burning down to a keg of giant powder. When he learned that the bounty hunters were still on his trail, he should have left the Circle Arrow crew and hightailed it as far away from the drovers as possible. He respected Hiram Flowers and liked the others working for Mercedes Sullivan. Bringing down the wrath of these bounty killers on them was a great disservice.

"This is between us," Mac said loudly. "You don't want him."

Desmond struggled as the gunman circled his neck with a strong arm. The bounty hunter used him as a shield now.

"Drop your gun, murderer. Now!"

Mac looked around, trying to find the rest of the bounty hunters. No sign of them. His heart beat faster as he suddenly stepped behind the horse and used the animal as a shield just as Means used Desmond.

When he disappeared, he flushed out two more men. They popped up from the rocks higher on the hill, rifles in their hands. One had the stock snugged to his shoulder, ready to shoot. The other held his Winchester slanted across his chest.

Mac was done talking. His hand flashed to his gun. He felt like a machine, a smoothly oiled machine built to draw the Smith & Wesson, aim, cock, and fire. The first round sailed uphill to the bounty hunter with the rifle to his shoulder and knocked him back a half step.

Letting the momentum of his draw spin him around, Mac got off a shot at the second bounty hunter, the one lackadaisically holding his rifle. This shot went wide. He whirled in a complete circle and dropped to a knee, ignoring the men on the hill because the leader slugged Desmond with the revolver, then opened fire.

Mac had counted on the man's greed keeping him from putting a bullet through Desmond's head, and so far that hunch was right.

Mac got off a couple more shots as slugs whined over his

head. To his surprise, the leader stood his ground. The man pulled his second gun and blazed away, right, left, right, left. His marksmanship was off, and that saved Mac. But at least one slug hit his horse and caused it to rear and paw at the air with its hooves.

Dodging the flying hooves as well as the bounty hunter's increasingly accurate fire sent Mac diving forward to skid along in the mud on his belly. Trying to aim as he slid proved impossible. All he could do was throw enough lead in the leader's direction to make him take cover behind a rock.

One round remained in the S&W's cylinder, but Mac reloaded as he wiggled his way to a shallow ditch. Rainwater stood a couple inches deep. Partly submerged, he aimed in the leader's direction but conserved his ammunition.

"Throw down that six-gun, Mackenzie. Give up now or I'll plug your friend. What is he? Heir to the ranch? What's his ma gonna think if you get away alive and her son's caught a bullet in the head? Any more menfolk left to inherit?"

Mac's bile rose. He held it down because he knew the man intended to rile him, make him mad enough to show himself. The best he could do was cover Desmond, but the bounty hunter had a clear shot at him from behind the rock.

"I got him, Willy. I got him in my sights!"

The shrill shout made Mac shift his attention back uphill. The bounty hunter he had driven back readied his rifle, but he was aiming at Desmond. Resting the butt of his pistol on the ground to steady it, Mac drew back the trigger. Again he missed. The range was too great for a handgun.

"I'm gonna kill that little son of a bitch!"

As the man stepped up to put his foot on a rock, a shot echoed through the draw. Mac winced. He thought the bounty hunter had fired. Then he saw the man jerk around. A second shot took the man's legs from under him. Flailing, he began sliding down the hill. When he came to a halt at the bottom of the slope, he lay unmoving.

"Charles!" the other man hidden in the rocks cried. "You killed my brother, you bastard! You killed Jimmy and now you killed my little brother!"

The man showed himself and charged down the hill in blind rage. This time Mac began firing steady, sending his lead dead on target, then aiming a little left, a little right, and back to center. His hammer fell on an empty chamber with the last shot.

But he had hit his man at least twice and maybe three times. The bounty hunter sat down, out of sight, but no further cries of revenge came from him.

Reloading again, Mac wiggled forward in the shallow water. The sounds alerted the remaining bounty hunter, the leader of the bunch.

"Enough. You killed my men. You don't give up right now, I'll kill this one." The bounty hunter hauled Desmond half upright and shoved a gun into his spine. "Out where I can see you. Now. Do it now or I swear he dies."

"Don't give up, Mac," Desmond said as he thrashed about weakly. His captor shook him hard to make him stop trying to get away.

Mac called out, "Don't shoot him. I'm surrendering."

"No, no, Mac!"

"Let him go and—"

"Toss out your gun or I start shooting," the bounty hunter rasped. "Maybe only a bullet to his legs. He won't walk again. He won't ever ride one of his mama's horses or brand another of her calves. Throw down your gun!"

Mac slid his revolver into his holster and stepped out.

"You can hide behind him all you want, but if you shoot Desmond, I'll kill you."

"You want to face me down?"

"I think I heard you called Quick Willy. You really quick or are you just good at telling people you are?"

The man shoved Desmond out in front of him. Mac looked for an opening, but the bounty hunter was too clever to expose much. Drawing and shooting at a patch of shoulder or an exposed leg wouldn't work. Rather than rush it, Mac waited. It was the hardest thing he had ever done, but he bided his time because he knew the man would make a mistake.

He had to if Desmond and a cook wanted for murder in New Orleans were going to escape alive.

"I'm faster than you," the bounty hunter said, "but I'm not stupid enough to try your hand. You're a killer, and I am entrusted to bring you in."

"So you're not that quick."

"I don't get mad, either. I'm too smart for that."

Desmond moved without warning. Instead of jerking away, he drove his elbow hard into his captor's belly. The bounty hunter's gun roared. Desmond groaned and Mac's hand flashed for his revolver.

The bounty hunter jerked as Mac's bullet sent his hat flying. He started firing the gun in his right hand as his left whipped out the other pistol. Mac found himself standing in a windstorm of lead. He crouched low and triggered again, but nothing happened. He knew he wasn't empty, so the cartridge must have misfired.

The bounty hunter yelled in triumph. Mac thumbed the hammer and got off another shot but missed. As he fired again, he knew there wouldn't be another chance.

The man grunted and took a step back.

"Damnation," he said. He clutched his right side.

Mac saw the hole in the bounty hunter's body begin to bleed. He shook off his shock and fanned the rest of his cylinder as he came to his feet. His wild fusillade joined another as a rifle high up behind him began firing.

The bounty hunter kept firing as he backed away and fell behind a rock. Rifle bullets spanged off it. In spite of the chance he would catch a ricochet, Mac ran forward and grabbed Desmond's arm. Digging in his heels, he pulled the young man out of the line of fire. They flopped back into the shallow muddy ditch.

"Are you hurt?" Mac hunted in his coat pocket for more cartridges. He found only three more rounds. With a snap, he broke open the S&W and ejected the spent brass. Working methodically, he inserted the three cartridges and snapped it shut.

"I don't think so. You risked your life to save me." Desmond stared at Mac as if he had grown another head.

"Not just me. That's Flowers with the rifle."

"He came to get me, too?"

Mac started to give a bad-tempered reply to that, but he held back. The threat remained. The bounty hunter was still dangerous. Until he saw the man's body, Mac couldn't let his guard down for an instant.

"Stay here."

"I can help," Desmond insisted.

"You'll get hurt. Stay put." Mac waved and from out of nowhere Hiram Flowers came huffing and puffing, his rifle pointed ahead of him.

"Did I get the varmint?"

"That's the man you were talking about? Quick Willy?"

"Quick Willy Means. We crossed paths before. He didn't come out so good." Flowers stared hard at Mac. "He's after you, even if he knows me. He didn't want Desmond for ransom."

"Until Desmond told him, Means didn't even know who he was. And yeah, he's after me."

"The son of a bitch." Flowers checked his rifle to be sure the magazine was full. "Let's go get him."

"He's a bounty hunter and he and his gang have been after me."

"What? Can't hear you, Mac."

"I said—"

Abruptly, Mac shut his mouth. He realized that Flowers wanted to hear nothing of his past. It was enough that Flowers hunted Means for other reasons, for whatever had happened when they met before, for kidnapping Desmond. An attempt to take his cook back to New Orleans to stand trial wasn't necessary to add to the list of reasons Means had to die.

The bounty hunter was gone from behind the rocks, but he had left a trail of blood drops. With Flowers behind him, Mac began hunting for Means in earnest. Every step felt like his last. He knew Means intended to ambush him. "Dead or alive," read the wanted poster. A man willing to use Desmond as bait hardly cared about the condition of his quarry.

As he moved around the hillside, it occurred to Mac that the bounty hunter, although wounded, might check to see if either of his henchmen were alive. Revolver at the ready, Mac headed for the bodies while Flowers continued searching farther along the slope.

Both men were dead, and there was no sign of Means. Mac looked down at what appeared to be the older of the two brothers and shook his head. This one, Frank Huffman from the papers in his jacket pocket Mac pulled out, looked to be the twin of the man he had shot back in Fort Worth.

"Mac, over here," Flowers called. "I found the trail."

Mac hurried to join him. The trail boss knelt on the rocky ground and pointed out a blood smear. Means had bled enough to form a puddle and then carelessly stepped in it. Flowers pointed ahead to a sandy ravine.

"I'll go," Mac said. "Back me up."

"I'm not letting you have all the fun of killing that varmint."

Mac had no time to argue. The messy footprint had to be a trap. If it wasn't, Means had bled more freely than Mac expected from a wound through his side.

Flowers moved five yards away, and they advanced together. They reached the bank of the arroyo and poked their heads over the rim at the same time. Mac saw immediately that they were too late. Judging by the piles of dung, four horses had been staked out here. The one Desmond had taken from the remuda, a swayback mare long past its prime, stood beside a better quality horse.

"He got on his horse and took a spare. Catching him's going

to be a full-time job." Flowers looked at Mackenzie. "That a job you intend on taking?"

Mac considered all the things he could do. Quick Willy Means was wounded, perhaps fatally. But if he wasn't, he might decide to stay on Mac's trail. That meant he should be tracked down and taken care of.

"We've got a herd to drive north."

"To Fort Sumner?"

"To Fort Sumner," Mac said. He looked down the sandy arroyo and hoped he was doing the right thing by letting Means get away. They would be at the Army post in another few days and the drive would be over. Disappearing would be easier with a pocketful of money he had earned.

Chapter 18

Dewey Mackenzie kept looking over his shoulder. Every bump in the trail made him sure he was going to slide down an embankment and be pinned under the wagon. Every strange noise caused him to reach for his revolver. He was driving himself loco.

"It'll be over soon. We're almost to Fort Sumner," he said over and over. It had been a week since he and Flowers had rescued Desmond from the bounty hunters. Two of the killers had become worm food. Burying the brothers seemed like a kindness they did not deserve, but Mac, Desmond, and Flowers had clawed out a shallow grave for one of them. The other's body was missing, likely dragged away by coyotes. Neither Mac nor Flowers had been willing to spend more time hunting for it. None of the bounty hunters deserved that kind of consideration.

He hadn't even wanted to say words over it, but Flowers had insisted. But the trail boss drew the line at putting a grave marker of any kind over the body. They deserved to be anonymous. Mac didn't even want a casual traveler to look over and wonder who was buried in the grave. He wanted them wiped from all human memory or thought.

A second grave would have been satisfying, but a third grave for Quick Willy Means would have satisfied him most. But with the bounty hunter escaped and on his own, that small pleasure had been denied him. As Mac drove, he made a gun out of thumb and forefinger and relived the fight that had freed Desmond. Moving to one side, he could have plugged Means. Or if Desmond had acted sooner. Or . . .

"Bang." He curled his thumb in mock firing. "He should have been a dead man."

There was no changing the fight. Desmond was safe. Two of the bounty hunters had gotten what they deserved. And the herd was within a day of Fort Sumner. The end of the drive, if they sold the beeves to the Army. Otherwise, it was on to Santa Fe or even Denver.

This journey had been entirely different from his drive to Abilene. The dangers changed, and the dread of a bounty hunter breathing down his neck caused him to be jumpy. But they hadn't lost near as many cattle as on his other drive, in spite of the dangerous Pecos crossing and the storm and stampede afterward. The Comanches hadn't made off with many cattle, and there had been few towns along the way to demand tribute in exchange for passage. Texas was wide open and lonely country, as was this part of New Mexico Territory.

Mac liked that.

He jerked around, his revolver out and ready as he heard a galloping horse closing on the chuckwagon from behind. When he saw Hiram Flowers, he slipped the pistol back into the holster.

"No call to be that jumpy, Mac. If Means didn't bleed to death a hundred miles behind us, he gave up."

"Means didn't have the look of a man who would give up. And we never found the other brother's body."

"Is that why every night you take a horse and ride back along the trail? Looking for any trace of him?"

Mac changed the subject by asking, "What's ahead? I've never been to Fort Sumner before."

He felt uneasy talking about the bounty hunters they had cut down. He realized he was turning into a belt-and-suspenders man, never feeling quite secure enough. Seeing the bullet-riddled bodies of his enemies would have smoothed his ruffled feathers.

"The only time I was there was with Desmond's pa," Flowers said in answer to Mac's question about their destination. "The post is an important one for the Army, and they like to keep it well supplied, but that's not saying too much. Their paymaster up at Fort Union, north of Santa Fe, sorta forgets about frontier outposts now and again. They might be flush with money to buy beef or they might not have two nickels to rub together. Since they closed Bosque Redondo and let the Navajos and Mescaleros go back to their reservations, there's not much going on at the post. We're going to put the herd to pasture to fatten them up for a week or so while me and you go on into the post to palaver with the quartermaster."

"Why not bring Desmond along?" Mac suggested. "This is his herd, more or less."

Flowers rubbed his stubbled chin and nodded.

"Good idea, Mac. You've got a head on your shoulders. I hope you'll consider stayin' with the Circle Arrow after the drive. Most of them cowboys will head for other jobs. I'd appreciate it if you considered staying on permanent-like."

Mac had been afraid Flowers would ask him to do this very thing. Only willpower kept him from glancing back again, just to be sure Means wasn't catching up. Or some other bounty hunter Pierre Leclerc had set on his trail. Returning to the Circle Arrow outside Fort Worth would give him a permanent address and make it easier for anyone hunting for him to find him. But he liked Flowers. Hell, he even liked Desmond, just a little.

And his curiosity was eating him alive about Flowers and Mercedes Sullivan. How would that romance turn out, even if Flowers was down in the mouth about even saying more than "Good morning, ma'am" to the lovely ranch owner?

"Is this all open range? We just find a patch of grass and let the cattle graze?"

"That's about it. Most of the countryside is Spanish land grant. The king of Spain deeded it to his loyal soldiers and financial backers more'n a hundred years ago. Parts are open. New ranchers have moved in, but they don't have much claim to the land, unless they buy it from the Spanish. Then the Mexicans have come up with their herds and ways in the past ten or fifteen years. In spite of so many folks crowding in, there's plenty of land for us to use."

Mac looked into the hazy distance to the west where purple mountains rose. The Sacramento Mountains, he had been told. It was quite a ways over there. And the land between was prime grassland, perfect for fattening cattle. The Circle Arrow beeves would appreciate it.

"You going right on into town?" Mac tried to settle down. Losing himself in the middle of a crowd, even if the town was as small as Fort Sumner, pleased him. A drink or two would go down the gullet smooth and warm after being on the trail so long.

"Park the chuckwagon and let's go. And it's a good idea to take Desmond with us." Flowers added dryly, "You can look after him."

Mac bristled, then saw Flowers was joking. He smiled ruefully.

It took the better part of an hour to get the wagon set up and the team tended to before he joined Flowers and Desmond. Both were antsy about getting into town.

"Sure are a lot of cattle around here," Desmond said. "Can we get a fair price?"

"Doesn't matter that much," Flowers said. "If they won't

buy our beeves, we'll push on to Santa Fe or even Denver and sell them there. The railroad can ship them west, and we'll see a handsome profit."

"That's another six hundred miles," Mac said. Staying with the Circle Arrow outfit that much longer worried him. Then he decided Denver was as good a place to part company as Fort Sumner. It added another month of pay to his poke, and the company wasn't all that bad.

"There's the Army purchasing office. Let's get business out of the way," Flowers said.

The town looked like any other sleepy southwestern settlement. Mac guessed the Army post lay somewhere to the north. Places like this were peaceable enough, especially after the Navajos had been sent packing from Bosque Redondo. The Apaches who had been on the reservation with them trickled back to their homes in the Sacramento Mountains and beyond. Yes, sir, this was a quiet enough place now.

"Do I have to go? Business bores me."

Both Mac and Flowers glared at Desmond. He reluctantly dismounted and followed the trail boss into the cramped office.

Inside was cool because of the thick adobe walls and small windows. A few maps provided the only wall decorations. A lieutenant sat behind the battered desk poring over a ledger. His uniform was crisp and he looked hardly old enough to have graduated from West Point, although the heavy ring on his finger told a different story. His rumpled blond hair showed he had worn his hat recently and had not bothered to comb the mop. That told Mac the officer had arrived just ahead of them. From his expression when he saw who walked into his office, Mac doubted they'd be in Fort Sumner longer than it took to let the cattle rest and graze.

He was both right and wrong.

"What's the Army's need for cattle? We got a herd of prime longhorns waiting to be bought and et by hungry soldiers," Flowers said.

"The Army's got quite a need for fresh meat, sir." The lieutenant pointed to a single chair. Flowers took it while Mac stood to one side and Desmond prowled about the sparse office, bored.

"Then we can do business. I—"

"Wait. Before you go on, let me inform you about our . . . situation."

"There's no situation we can't handle," Flowers said with some confidence.

"Our operating funds have been held up for another few weeks. In truth, I am not sure when the funds will arrive. They are being sent down from Fort Union."

"Fort Union's up north," Mac said. "On the trail to Denver. Maybe we can drive the herd up that direction and sell there."

"I am sure they would appreciate such a gesture, though Union is the central supply depot for all of New Mexico Territory. They, of all the posts, will have adequate supplies." The lieutenant got a sour look. "Unlike here. We struggle in the midst of plenty."

"Plenty of cattle, you mean?"

The lieutenant nodded.

"Our problem is keeping a cork tamped into a bottle full of animosity here. The ranchers engage in what amounts to war between one another, and—" He stopped suddenly, took a breath, and let it out slowly. "That is none of your concern. If you wait a week, we will dicker for your cattle, or at least some of them, depending on how many you offer."

"Got close to nine hundred head," Flowers said.

"More than we need, but we can use two hundred head immediately."

"Fork over some money and you've got a deal."

"You weren't listening, Mister Flowers," Mac said, eyeing the officer carefully. "They don't have one red cent."

"Not right now. I can issue an IOU guaranteed by the U.S. Army, to be paid when our disbursement funds arrive."

"But you don't know when that'll be?"

The answer was written on the lieutenant's face. Not only did he not know, there was a chance the money would never arrive.

"I have to pay my hands. Giving them a piece of paper with a mark on it promising pay at some future time isn't going to set well with any of them. It don't with me, either."

"Then, sir, I suggest you find other markets for your beef. As much as the military's need for it is great, you must either sell elsewhere or wait."

"Reckon that settles the matter. We'll wait." Flowers cleared his throat. "We'll wait and find some other market."

Mac wondered how often the lieutenant had heard those very words. The young man closed the ledger and leaned forward, elbows on the desk. It wobbled a little because one leg was shorter than the others. The lieutenant adjusted unconsciously, used to it.

"Selling around here might be more difficult than you realize. I do, however, wish you luck. Good day."

Dismissed, they left and stepped out into the bright New Mexico sun. Mac pulled his hat brim down to shield his eyes. The hat almost fell to pieces. The crown had been kicked out by a cow, and a couple of bullet holes in the brim had grown until they were the size of a two-bit piece. If he'd received his trail pay, he would have gone hunting for a new hat.

"I need to ask around about selling some of the cattle. If I get enough, we'll have money to buy supplies to get us to Denver." Flowers shook his head. "I'd prefer to sell here to the Army. What do you think the chances are of them seeing any money soon?"

Mac had no idea. Desmond said, "Hanging around for a while isn't going to hurt us. I'm not looking forward to another drive, this time all the way up to Denver."

"You can always go back to Fort Worth," Mac said. He had

a sour taste in his mouth from hearing the lieutenant's tale of woe and why the Army wasn't in the market for cattle right now. Getting what was owed him wasn't possible. He knew how low on cash Flowers was. Without the cattle being sold, nobody on the drive would get paid.

"Trying to get rid of me? Because you're embarrassed at baking such a terrible fruit pie? You ought to be. I've still got seeds stuck between my teeth."

Mac started to snap back, then realized this was the first time Desmond had made any kind of a joke. Desmond was funning him when all he had done until now was gripe his fool head off. That was real progress.

"Go on, find a window and sit under it so you can smell a cooling pie and tell me mine wasn't better."

"The only way it'd be better is that I can't afford to buy even a slice, no matter what it's made from," Desmond said.

"Here, you two. I've got almost fifty cents. Go get yourselves some pie." Flowers looked disgusted. "Real men would buy a drink, but no, I got a cook and a drover who want *pie*. Get on along now. I have to do some business so we can all get a shot of real rotgut."

The trail boss stalked off, leaving Mac and Desmond on their own.

"There's a restaurant that looks like it sells pie." Mac pointed to a hole-in-the-wall adobe building down the street. A buggy parked to the side gave the only hint that the place was open for business.

They went in and looked around the cool, dim dining room. Both men froze when they saw the lone customer.

Mac forced himself to let out the breath he unconsciously held. He had seen prettier women in his day, but right now he couldn't remember where or when.

The young woman at the back table eating with precise bites wore a Mexican-style dress, bright and cheerful and matching her looks perfectly. She glanced up and smiled almost shyly. Mac thought the sun had come out. Her dark eyes and delicate face, high cheekbones, and carefully plucked eyebrows showed both intelligence and genteel upbringing.

"I want what she's having," Desmond said.

"Sit down and let's order. We've got no call to bother her while she's eating." Mac's mind raced trying to find such a reason to introduce himself. If he had known the women in Fort Sumner looked this lovely, he wouldn't have complained at all about the trail drive. The destination was worthy of shooting his way through murderous bounty hunters and crossing swollen rivers.

"What'll you gents like?" The waiter gave them a quick once-over and said, "You're likely sick of steak. Got good fried chicken."

"Pie," Desmond said. "What kind of pie do you have?"

"I knew it. You're straight off the trail and haven't seen any fruit in a spell. Well, you're in luck. We got peach and we got apple."

"All right," Mac said.

"Which will it be?" The waiter grinned. "Both? A slice of each for both of you?"

"That'll be so close to heaven that I am speechless," Desmond said.

"If you knew him, you'd know how unusual that is." Mac enjoyed being able to joke with Desmond. All it took to break through his arrogance was saving him from a stampede, rescuing him from being kidnapped, and serving up a prickly pear pie that was hardly fit for consumption by man or beast.

The pie came. Both men tucked into it. Mac started with the peach, Desmond the apple. It looked like a race to the last crumb when they each finished. They leaned back and eyed the spotless plates in front of them.

"I could eat the whole damned pie," Desmond said. He hastily looked at the woman, worried he might have been overheard and his language offended her.

Mac hoped it had so he could apologize to her. He swung around in the chair and hesitated. The waiter was speaking in low tones to the woman. She looked distraught and he wasn't pleased.

With a surge, Mac was out of the chair. Desmond was right behind as they went to see what the trouble was. The woman looked up, stricken.

"Please, Señor Weatherby. I did not do this on purpose."

"Miss Abragon, I know that, but I can't just *give* you the meal."

"Is there a problem?" Mac planted his feet and gave the impression of a solid, dependable rock.

"No, *por favor*, please." She fidgeted, her hands turning over and over on her small clutch purse.

"She can't pay. I'm not the mercantile or the dress shop. I don't run a tab."

"I forgot my money. I promise to pay."

Mac saw the waiter—also the owner from the way he spoke—wasn't going along with that. He wondered why. In a town the size of Fort Sumner, everyone ought to know and trust everyone else. Unless something was going on he hadn't heard about.

Before he could say anything, Desmond spoke up. "I'll be happy to cover the lady's meal. How much is it?"

"Forty cents," Weatherby said.

"Give him the money, Mac." Desmond prodded him to fish out the four bits Flowers had given them. Desmond snatched the coins from his grip and handed both of them to the restaurant owner. "No need for change. The dime's a tip."

"Much obliged. You gents want anything more? Another piece of pie? Coffee?"

"I'll escort Miss Abragon out, then we'll see," Desmond said, offering her his arm.

Mac tried to get in on the action but Weatherby took his arm, and it wasn't to escort him out. The man's fingers cut into his biceps.

"You owe me forty cents, ten cents for each slice of pie. No need to give me a tip."

Mac felt a sinking feeling. Flowers had given him the fifty cents because he didn't have a penny to his name and wouldn't until he got his trail wages. Desmond wasn't any better heeled. But Mac had been in similar straits before, back in Waco, and knew what to do.

"I can work it off. I'm the best damned cook you're going to find, and I don't mind cleaning and doing fix-up jobs around here."

"My big business starts in an hour. You sure you can cook and not poison anyone?"

"You'll have them coming back wanting more," Mac promised.

"Ten cents an hour, four hours and we're even." Weatherby thrust out his hand.

Mac wasted no time shaking. Four hours doing what he enjoyed wasn't any punishment . . . but what he would do to Desmond for leaving with the lovely Miss Abragon would be.

Chapter 19

Luther Wardell sat astride his black stallion, taking in the herd grazing on the section of land below him.

"Are those damned beeves on our land, Joe?" Wardell asked.

His foreman, Joe Ransom, pursed his lips and finally said, "Can't tell, Mister Wardell. I'd say they are on open range, maybe a couple miles from your property."

"Doesn't make no never mind to me. Those longhorns came all the way up from Texas. Whoever headed the drive did a good job."

"Why do you say that, sir?"

Wardell brushed dust from his fancy frock coat, then tended the accumulation of brown grit on his expensive Stetson with the hammered silver and turquoise hat band. He made sure every last speck was gone. He disliked the constant dust in the air in this part of New Mexico Territory, but the potential for wealth was greater here than up north where the Spanish controlled every inch of land.

Down here in the southeast section, the desert was more open and the land deeds always in contention. The Spanish king's surveyor had been drunk most of the time—that was Wardell's guess for such sloppy work. In places, the property lines were off by as much as five miles.

A clever man took advantage of such discrepancies. Luther Wardell was a very clever man and one itching to become another rancher of the stature of Richard King and Gideon Lewis. Their ranch in South Texas stretched over six counties and thirteen hundred sections. Lincoln County was going to be his. Lincoln and the surrounding land. De Baca and more.

He settled his hat back squarely on his head and poked his glossy black hair up under the band. Moving the coattails away, he rested his hand on the ivory butt of his Colt .44. That ivory had come all the way from Africa and some monster elephant. His one regret in paying so much for the ivory was not being able to shoot the beast himself so he personally harvested the ivory. He'd have to be content to take on anything—or anyone—charging straight at him right here in Fort Sumner.

After he owned all the land fair and square, he considered how traveling to Africa and bagging some big game himself would be the perfect reward. Maybe he'd bring a few of them back and let them roam the desert—his desert, his land, his empire. After all, Jeff Davis had put African camels down at the Texas fort bearing his name. Why shouldn't Luther Wardell do the same with elephants and lions?

"You hear any more about the Army's budgetary allotment arriving?"

"You mean their grubstake from Fort Union? The gossip says it won't be sent for another couple weeks. Maybe later."

"Maybe later," Wardell mused. He rubbed his clean-shaven chin, then the billowy muttonchops. The bushy facial hair belied his whipcord thin body. A man had once told him it made him look like a mushroom, with a scrawny stem and puffy head.

The authorities never looked much for that loudmouth, but

even if they had the marshal would never have found the body. Ever.

"You want me to run them drovers off? Me and some of the boys can do it and never break a sweat."

"No, Joe. I have other plans for that herd. What's the ranch?"

"Circle Arrow by the brand. I can send José down to be sure."

"Knowing the Circle Arrow brand is fine." Wardell turned toward town. He had a lieutenant in the quartermaster corps to speak to—after he located the trail boss for the herd.

He trotted along, thinking how best to proceed. Joe Ransom kept pace a few yards to his right.

"Joe?" His foreman rode closer. "Did Don Jaime come to town this morning?"

"That's what I heard. I didn't see him with my own eyes, but a couple of the outriders saw him riding up from his rancho like his ass was on fire."

"He heard that the Circle Arrow drovers arrived. That's what's got him so riled."

"He thinks the Circle Arrow boys will sell to the Army and cut him out of the military market?"

"That's part of it. I spoke with the banker a few days ago. Don Jaime is falling behind on his payments."

"A place like that," Ransom said, a touch of glee in his tone, "can cost a man dearly. An arm and a leg."

"It won't come to that." Wardell glanced at his bloodthirsty foreman. Ransom enjoyed killing a little too much. "His claim that he controls a Spanish land grant is on shaky legal grounds."

"You saw to that, Mister Wardell."

"I did, Joe, I did."

Wardell rode the rest of the way into Fort Sumner, going over his plan in his head. Try as he might, he saw no downside to any part of it. Before the end of the month, he would own twice the land that his Big W now covered. Another year and the King ranch would be small potatoes in comparison.

"He's there, Mister Wardell," Ransom said as they rode along the street and approached the lieutenant's office. "Don Jaime. That's his horse tied outside, the one with the fancy Mexican saddle."

"So it is. Let's not bother him and his palaver with the lieutenant. I don't think it will last long when the lieutenant makes it clear he has no money for Mexican cattle. If you were the Circle Arrow trail boss, where would you be?"

"In a saloon. There's plenty around. Bob Hargrove's saloon is right over there and Beaver Smith's is—"

"No, that's not where you would go if you brought so many longhorns all the way along the Goodnight-Loving Trail."

"It ain't? There're some more saloons over a few streets, out by the fort."

"You find that the Army isn't buying your cattle because they don't have the funds. You look for someone else to buy your longhorns." Wardell suppressed the irritation he felt at having to explain such a simple matter to his foreman. Ransom had his uses, many of them in fact, but deep thinking was not one of them.

Wardell kept moving down the street and halted in front of the grain and feed store. He dismounted, smoothed wrinkles from his frock coat, and rubbed the toes of his boots on the backs of his pants legs to get them all nice and shiny.

Only then did he march into the store and look around. A slow smile came to his thin lips. Three men sat at the table near the back of the store. He knew Garton, the store owner, and Maxwell, a newcomer to the county and potential rival. A quick snort dismissed them as he focused on the third man, the stranger. His time on the trail was cut into every line in his forehead. Hands tanned tougher than leather by sun and holding reins rested on the table, palms down as he leaned forward earnestly.

This was the man Wardell wanted to see.

"Good afternoon, gentlemen."

"What do you want, Wardell?" Maxwell asked curtly. He recognized Wardell as a rival for control of the area and instinctively got his back up.

Wardell ignored him. He thrust out his hand in the drover's direction.

"I'm Luther Wardell, and you must be the trail boss for the Circle Arrow herd grazing outside town."

"Pleased to make your acquaintance," the man said. "At least I think I am. That's not your land my longhorns are chewing up grass on, is it?"

"No, sir, it's not."

"Then I'm the trail boss, Hiram Flowers."

"Pleased to make your acquaintance as well, Mister Flowers." Wardell gestured. Joe Ransom fetched a chair and had it under him as he sat between the drover and Maxwell, effectively blocking any chance the rancher had to continue his talk.

"I was dickering with these gentlemen. I'll be happy to talk to you when I'm done."

"Well, Mister Flowers, Maxwell wants a bull and a few heifers to improve his chance of raising a good herd in a few years. And Mister Garton is thinking on selling you grain to fatten up your prime animals, possibly the ones Maxwell is most interested in." Wardell took a cigar from his vest pocket. "Is that correct?"

"What's your game, Mister Wardell?"

Maxwell said something obscene under his breath. Wardell moved his chair around a little more to cut off any chance of Maxwell speaking with the Circle Arrow trail boss.

Leaving the cigar unlit, he gestured with it to emphasize his words as he said, "I want to buy some of your herd, sir."

"Some?"

"Three hundred head."

"Well, now, that's something we can discuss. Since you're not making an offer for the entire herd, I'd have to say . . ."

Hiram Flowers considered how much to ask. Wardell knew it would be high. "A hundred dollars a head."

"Very well, sir, that is a fair price. Let's get the bill of sale drawn up. I think Mister Garton has a blank or two we can use."

Flowers stared, his mouth hanging open. He closed it, then held out his hand. "We got a deal."

Maxwell stood, kicked over his chair, and stormed out of the grain store. Wardell moved his chair around the table, reached into his pocket, and pulled out a thick, tooled leather wallet. He put the cigar in the corner of his mouth, then laid the wallet open on the table and began counting out the bills.

Wardell enjoyed the look of surprise on the drover's face. Hiram Flowers might never have seen so much cash in one pile in all his born days. The act of dumbfounding the ignorant cowboy made him feel just a little bigger.

"There you are. Do you have the bill of sale, Mister Garton?"

"Right here." The store owner dropped the paper on the table, then placed pen and ink beside it. "You want me to fill it out?"

"If you would be so kind. I hate getting ink on my fingers." Wardell wiggled them in front of his eyes, staring between them at Flowers.

"You want them for what you claimed Maxwell did? Breeding stock?" Flowers asked.

"Not at all, sir. I want them for their meat."

"Here? In Fort Sumner?"

Wardell enjoyed seeing how confused the drover was. That added to his overall enjoyment of the transaction.

"I intend to make a tidy profit, sir." Wardell got Flowers to sign, then added his name, blew on the wet ink until it dried, and tucked the paper into his pocket. "I need to conclude my business now. Thank you, sir."

"Any more you want, let me know," Flowers said, his eyes on the stack of greenbacks and not on the man who had bought his cattle.

"Three will be sufficient for my purposes."

He left, Joe Ransom trailing. His foreman knew better than to ask what he intended. Wardell paused outside to light the cigar and puff on it in great satisfaction with both the fine tobacco . . . and himself.

They rode back to the quartermaster's office. Don Jaime was still there. This made Wardell's triumph all the more joyful—for him. He went in, removed his Stetson, and held it in front of him, waiting for the officer to notice him.

It took only a second. Don Jaime had bent the lieutenant's ear long enough about his troubles and he undoubtedly sought relief. He found it in Luther Wardell.

"Today's the day for cattlemen to come calling," the officer said. "I'd've thought you heard there's no money yet to buy cattle, Mister Wardell. I don't know when there will be."

"I have heard, Lieutenant." He nodded in Don Jaime's direction. The Mexican rancher turned a little pale, or so it seemed. That added to Wardell's enjoyment.

"I offered the Army my cattle at fifty dollars a head," Don Jaime said.

"But, as I told you repeatedly, as much as we need the beeves, I don't have enough money to buy even ten head from you at that price. And you won't let us have the cattle on a promissory note."

"I must be paid immediately, Lieutenant. Being paid at some time in the future that none of us know will not do."

"Three hundred head of prime Texas longhorns," Wardell said. He took the bill of sale from his pocket and laid it on the officer's desk. "You can send your soldiers out to pick which of the cattle you want."

"Mister Wardell, I—"

"I consider it my civic duty to let you have the cattle on consignment." Wardell waved the cigar he held between the first two fingers of his left hand. "You can pay when you receive your funds."

"That's all well and good, but even then I won't have enough to cover three hundred head. Not at a price where you'd make a profit." The lieutenant pressed his finger down on the bill of sale next to the total amount. "You'd do well to keep the cattle for breeding and—"

"I said I wanted to do my civic duty. Don Jaime's price was fifty a head?"

"That is so," the Mexican said. "It is a rock bottom offer, but I need the money now. Cash on the barrelhead, as you say." The rancher crossed his arms over his chest. He wore a colorful vaquero jacket with intricate embroidered patterns. At his hip, a revolver rode high in a holster. Tight dark pants with the legs tucked into his tooled boots and silver spurs with large Spanish rowels completed the image of a successful Mexican rancher.

"Civic duty," Wardell said again. "The Army protects us from the Mescaleros and the Lipans."

"What's your point, Mister Wardell?" The lieutenant began to look uneasy.

"Ten dollars. When you get the money from Fort Union."

"What's that?" The lieutenant sat bolt upright. His eyes narrowed. "What exactly are you offering?"

"Three hundred head at ten dollars each, payable whenever you have adequate funds."

"What if I don't get as much as three thousand dollars to pay you? You know how appropriations go." The lieutenant's face flushed, and his breathing became strained.

Wardell hoped the man would not die of a heart attack when he finally realized this was not a joke. He was being given a deal no one else in the territory would ever hear.

"You cannot give away those cattle!" Don Jaime began to fume. "This is not right! You cannot make a profit. This bill of sale says you will lose ninety dollars a head. Why are you doing this?"

"As I said, my civic duty commands me to help the Army in whatever way I can. They need meat. This is an excellent chance for me to show my gratitude for all they do."

"You do this to prevent me from selling my cattle to them!" Don Jaime accused.

"Not at all. You already turned down their offer." Wardell looked over at the lieutenant, who had started quickly scribbling the terms onto a contract. "Be sure to leave the final payment date open."

"Whenever we get adequate money, yes, thank you, Mister Wardell." The officer wrote even faster, as if afraid that Wardell would change his mind.

That was the last thing in the world Wardell wanted. When the contract was signed, he would have cut off any chance for Don Jaime to sell enough cattle to pay the mortgage on his ranch. The land would be foreclosed soon and put up for auction by the bank. Wardell would see his ranch more than double in size, all for little more than the price of the Circle Arrow cattle. Who wouldn't pay less than a dollar an acre for prime ranch land? Don Jaime would never sell under any circumstances.

It was a sweet deal for Hiram Flowers—and the new king of the ranchers in New Mexico Territory, Luther Wardell.

Chapter 20

Don Jaime Abragon stood, his horse nervously pawing the ground beside him, and looked out over his rancho. He had inherited it from his uncle, a Spanish don, a man of great importance to the king. To lose a land grant would be the ultimate shame. All he needed was a little more time to pay the loan he had taken out the year before from the bank to double the size of his herd.

How was he to know the Army would stop buying beeves because they had no money? That hardly seemed possible, the government with so much money from far-off Washington. He had so many cattle, and no place to sell them. Because of Luther Wardell he could never sell to the Army this year.

"How did he sell for so little?" He chewed on his lower lip as he considered what the upstart rancher had done. Bit by bit he pieced together the scheme. Without realizing it, he drew his pistol and cocked it. If Wardell had been in front of him just then, the man would have died with six bullets in his worthless, black heart. The loss he sustained buying the Texan longhorns and virtually giving them to the Army mattered little since it allowed him to bid for the rancho, the hacienda, everything that Don Jaime saw stretching to the very horizon.

"The land is worth hundreds of thousands of dollars, and he will buy it for pennies, because I cannot sell my cattle to pay the bank." The unfairness struck him hard. More than this, he saw no way around what was being done to him because of his heritage, his legacy, his beloved rancho.

He let out a heartfelt bellow of rage and fired into the air. The report caused his horse to rear. Strong hands jerked its reins to hold it down. His fury mounted. Killing Wardell would solve some of his problems, but how would he pay off the bank? The debt was real, the debt was owed. No Abragon defaulted on such an obligation. He had asked for the money of his own free will, and now he must find a way to repay it.

Lowering the pistol, Don Jaime watched the last curls of white smoke wreath from the barrel.

"I am no highwayman. I cannot rob those in stagecoaches or banks or trains. I am descended from nobility. The king of Spain honored my family with this land for their bravery and loyalty to the throne. How can I disgrace such a legacy?" He hung his head in shame that such an idea had ever occurred to him. "I cannot. I, Don Jaime Abragon y Suarez, will not descend to acts of the common criminal, an outlaw who should be hanged for his misdeeds. But then what am I to do?"

No one was there to answer. He was alone as he gazed out over his imperiled domain.

He slipped his revolver back into the high, soft leather holster, mounted, and rode the still skittish stallion across the pastures where his cattle grazed. No finer cattle were to be had in all of New Mexico Territory, but he could not sell them because of Luther Wardell. Because of the Army turning him away when he needed their patronage the most.

Because of the Texas longhorns.

He turned toward the hacienda but drew rein when a cloud of dust popped up along the road leading from town. A tiny smile crept to his lips. He put his heels to his horse, tapping the rowels to get the most speed possible. The stallion rocketed away to intercept Don Jaime's daughter as she drove her buggy.

The closer he got, the more he frowned. Something was wrong. A horse had been tied to the back of the buggy. Someone rode with her. A man. Don Jaime bent over and let his horse race at full speed. He had told her to have nothing to do with the men in Fort Sumner. They were all beneath her station. When the time came for her to marry, he would find a ranchero of property and breeding.

She slowed and pulled the buggy to a halt as he skidded past. The horse had been trained to follow darting cattle during branding and closed back in as if she were nothing more than a calf. His hand went to the pistol at his side.

"Whoa," the man seated beside his daughter said. He handed her the reins and put his hands up to show he had no weapon.

Don Jaime came close to squeezing off a round anyway. This was not the kind of man his daughter should consort with. This was not only a cowboy; he was one of the Texas drovers. They were worse than those of the nearby ranches.

"Don't get an itchy trigger finger," the young, redheaded man said. "I'm Desmond Sullivan, with the Circle Arrow. You might say that's my brand since my ma owns the spread outside Fort Worth. That's in Texas."

"I know where it is," Don Jaime said as he trained his revolver on the young man. His lips curled with hostility under the thin mustache.

"Wait, don't shoot!" Desmond whipped off his hat and let it dangle behind him, his bright red hair shining like spun gold in the sun. "I was only escorting your lovely daughter home. She got into some trouble back in town, and I helped her out."

"Papa, please," Estella said. "Put down your gun. Mister

Sullivan has been nothing but a gentleman, and what he says is true."

"You were in trouble? What happened? If Wardell did anything—"

"No, not *him*." Estella spat the word out. Her opinion and Don Jaime's were the same of the upstart rancher and his ways. He had tried to court her, but Don Jaime had run him off. Estella would have sent him on his way with his horse's tail ablaze to make certain he did not slow down as he left the rancho.

"Who's this Wardell hombre?" Desmond asked. "If he's giving you any grief, Miss Abragon, I'll take care of him."

"This is not your concern, Tejano," Don Jaime snapped.

"Sir, we got off on the wrong foot. I worried that your daughter had to drive all the way from Fort Sumner by herself. Escorting her has been my honor and privilege."

"I invited him for dinner, Papa."

"No!"

"That's all right, Miss Abragon. I have to be getting on back to the outfit. The trail boss will have the entire crew out hunting for me."

"Go. Go now," Don Jaime said. He slowly holstered his revolver when he saw the brightly haired man climb down from the buggy. Desmond settled his hat on his head, politely touched the brim in Estella's direction. Then he said something to her that made her smile, look down, and blush.

Don Jaime started to pull his gun again.

Estella shot a hot, dark stare in his direction. How she looked like her *madre* in that moment, rest her soul. She was easily as beautiful—and headstrong.

He shoved his pistol back firmly into the holster as the cowboy mounted.

"Have a good day, sir." He cast one last look at Estella, turned and trotted away.

"What did he do?" Don Jaime demanded. "What is this little trouble that he rescued you from?"

"Oh, Papa, I feel like such a fool. I forgot to take any money in my purse. I ate a small meal and could not pay for it. Desmond—Mister Sullivan—paid for it since I could not. Mister Weatherby refused to give me credit. I don't know what I would have done if Mister Sullivan had not been there." She heaved a deep sigh. "Perhaps I would have been forced to sweep and wash dishes until the debt was paid."

"If only it were that easy," Don Jaime muttered, thinking of the bank loan.

"What, Papa? I did not hear you."

"He did not try to take advantage of you? Not even a little?" He studied her for any hint that she lied. Estella was a fine girl of good morals, but she was increasingly feisty since her mother died. How he wished she were here to speak to their daughter and convince her not to run off with the first wild cowboy who smiled at her and told her tempting lies.

"Not at all. He was a gentleman, unlike so many in this town." She looked a little bitter. "Unlike some who work for you."

"The vaqueros are not cultured. I shall send you to Spain for a proper education. You might find a husband there of your station."

"Or I might find one of those dashing Italians I hear about. The handsome ones, the suave ones who cheat on their wives. I could be his mistress with a villa on the Costa del Sol."

"Do not say such things. Do not even joke of that!"

"But why not? I enjoy seeing you squirm about like a flea on a hot griddle. You are so cute when you sputter and turn red in the face."

"Estella!"

"Oh, very well, Papa. I will be the sour old woman you want

me to be, never having any fun." She looked straight ahead, snapped the reins, and got the buggy horse moving.

Don Jaime trotted alongside, wondering what he should do with her. Sending her to Spain for finishing school was a possibility, but she needed a chaperone. Her sainted *madre* had died more than a year ago of a fall from her horse.

He involuntarily looked toward a stand of oak trees where the solitary grave with its elaborate marble marker lay. Burying her in the town cemetery had been possible. The priest had been reluctant to bury anyone outside the church graveyard. Either would have been sanctified ground, but he had wanted her nearby. Fray Esteban had argued with him about his choice but finally acceded to his wishes for the burial site.

Not a day passed that Don Jaime didn't go to his beloved's grave, kneel, say a quiet prayer for her soul, then begin the work demanded of him by the rancho, the work that would give Estella the life they both had wanted for her.

It was certainly not a life that included a cowboy. A Tejano cowboy, at that.

"Who is that riding so hard?" Estella looked over her shoulder as a swift rataplan of hoofbeats sounded behind them. "Do you think Mister Sullivan returns so soon?"

"Estella!"

"Papa, *un chiste. Nada más. Canto un chiste.*"

"You tell a joke." He felt like shouting, not laughing. He rested his hand on his pistol as the dust cloud hiding the galloping rider came closer. Don Jaime relaxed when he saw that his foreman caused the small storm.

"I have it, I have the telegram!" Fernando waved a flimsy yellow sheet about, as if displaying a flag in a parade.

"What telegram is this?" Estella looked hard at her father. "Your expression is . . . strange. You fear what is in the telegram?"

"I fear nothing. Nothing that concerns you." He swung his horse around so he could take the telegram from his foreman.

The dust kicked up by Fernando's horse swirled around both riders and the buggy.

"What do we do, Don Jaime?"

"You've read this?" He saw that Fernando had. Hastily unfolding the paper, he scanned it. Estella had been right. He feared what he read, but he also felt immense relief. That relief turned to anger, but he muted that. Too many conflicting emotions threatened to swamp him.

"Do we go?" The foreman looked expectant.

Don Jaime's mind raced.

"We have no choice. Prepare for the journey."

"All?"

"All the cattle, Fernando, and as many of the men as will volunteer. I know some cannot return and respect that." He smiled grimly. "Some must stay on the rancho to defend it while we are gone."

"Where are you going?" Estella asked. "A trail drive, Papa?"

He took a deep breath and nodded.

Estella's beautiful dark eyes widened. "No, Papa. Say you are not selling the cattle to Don Pedro. He is a hateful man."

"He is my bitterest enemy, but no one other than Don Pedro Escobar will buy my cattle."

"All of them? You sell them all? What will we do for next year and the year after?"

"The price he agreed to will barely pay off the bank debt. I will find ways to replenish the herd—after I have saved the rancho."

"You're driving the cattle into Mexico?"

"Some of the men are wanted for crimes there." Don Jaime shrugged. "We will have enough for the drive without them."

"Only ten vaqueros, Don Jaime," Fernando said. "That is not so many for such a large herd. It will be difficult."

"So be it. We begin the drive at dawn."

"So soon?" Estella said. She took a deep breath and let it out in a gust. "Then I have little time to pack."

"Pack? What are you saying?"

"I'm going with you." Estella Abragon spoke in a way that brooked no argument. For a heart-stopping moment, he almost told his foreman to forget the trail drive to keep his daughter safe.

"Very well," he said, giving in to the inevitable. "Dawn."

"Of course, Papa. I will be ready." Estella snapped the reins and drove to the hacienda to begin preparations for the long trip across New Mexico Territory and far into Chihuahua.

Chapter 21

"This is more money than I expected to see any time soon," Dewey Mackenzie said, riffling through the wad of greenbacks. "And most of the herd's still to be sold."

"Do you think the gent who bought the three hundred head will buy the rest?" Desmond rubbed his fingers over the bills he had received as his due for the work done on the drive to Fort Sumner. Some of the ink smeared and left colored marks on his thumb. The greenbacks he spent so freely at Fort Worth saloons and brothels didn't smear like this, but these were genuine U.S. Government bills. The banker vouched for these poorly printed bills and so did the Army quartermaster when Flowers had asked him to verify they were legit. Watching the lieutenant count out each and every bill, examining each in turn as if they were his and he spent them personally, had been amusing. With both men authenticating the money, Flowers had agreed to let Wardell cut out whichever cattle he wanted from the Circle Arrow herd.

Desmond wondered what the rancher's real interest was. He sent his men into the herd, not to find the fattest, healthiest cattle but to cut out the nearest three hundred. Even then his count was off by a few in the Circle Arrow ranch's favor. Mac had wanted to speak up about it, but Flowers shushed him. The more that remained, the more money they made. If a man didn't claim what was rightfully his, that wasn't anyone else's business.

"He wanted the cattle for some reason that had nothing to do with quality, that's for sure," Mac said. "From what Flowers said, he just about gave them to the Army to keep another rancher from selling his stock."

Desmond shifted his weight from foot to foot and looked around nervously.

"You got a bug up your ass? Settle down. Whenever Flowers decides what to do will be plenty soon enough to get antsy. My guess is that he'll push on to Denver. He sent a couple of telegrams and found out that the market there will take seven hundred cattle, maybe more, but at nowhere near as good a price as we got from Wardell. And that the Santa Fe market's as soft as the one here in Fort Sumner."

"How much can he get in Denver?"

"Might be as low as fifty a head, but we got the time to drive them a thousand more miles and let them graze along the way. Up near Las Vegas is supposed to be wide open grassland, about the best place to spend a week or so before pushing over Raton Pass and on up to Denver."

"But prime beef would sell for more than fifty dollars a head in Denver?"

"Could be as much as eighty. You know the business. If we get there during a lull, we might get paid well. If a half dozen other outfits show up when we do, it'll be a bidding war." Mac lounged back in the shade of the chuckwagon. "What's the difference? You suddenly taking an interest in your ma's profits?"

Desmond held back a sharp reply. He tucked his wages into his vest pocket, spun, and stalked off without a word. Mac had no call to say things like that. The horse Desmond had been riding came to him at the side of the corral and nickered. A quick pat, then he climbed over the makeshift fence and saddled up. Business in town called his name, and he wasn't going to keep her waiting.

The buggy he had driven for Estella was parked outside the restaurant where he had rescued her the day before. Its springs were depressed from the heavy boxes piled into it, leaving only a small space for her to drive. He hitched his horse to the back of the buggy and went into the cool, dim interior.

It took a few seconds for his eyes to adjust from the bright sun. As far as he was concerned, the smile that spread across her face when she saw him was brighter than the sun and more welcome. He went to the table, touched the brim of his hat politely, and said, "Miss Abragon. I'd hoped to see you again. May I sit down?"

Desmond didn't wait for her answer. Nothing she said would drive him off, manners or not. Besides, she had told him she would be here today before her pa had galloped up, waving his revolver as if he intended to fight off bandidos. She wouldn't have said a word if she hadn't wanted to see him again.

"You are very forward, sir."

"I will leave if you ask." He saw her pixie smile and knew she preferred that he stay. He moved the chair closer to the table to better look at her.

"You ordering a meal?" a voice asked. "One that you can pay for?"

Desmond looked up. The restaurant owner towered over him.

"I have plenty of money." He put his entire pay on the table. "All I want is a cup of coffee." He fixed his eyes on Estella Abragon. "Anything the lady wants, she can have."

"Why, thank you, Señor Sullivan, but I am content with what I have."

"You eat like a bird," he said, "and sound like a nightingale."

"You want anything but coffee?" Weatherby cleared his throat.

"Truth to tell, I was hoping you'd order and not be able to pay again."

Desmond stared at him.

"What do you mean?"

"For the price of a couple pieces of pie, I got about the best danged cook I ever did see workin' his butt off for four hours. Anytime that friend of yours wants a full-time job, and not shoveling food to a bunch of smelly cowboys, he's got a job here. A fine cook. Danged fine."

"Coffee," Desmond repeated.

Weatherby went off, mumbling to himself about how good a worker Dewey Mackenzie had proven to be.

"You paid for my food yesterday but couldn't pay for your own? I own you a debt of gratitude," Estella said. "Here. Forty cents, I believe."

Desmond pushed it back in her direction.

"My friend wanted to work here. You heard the waiter. Mac breaks into people's houses and cooks a meal, then sneaks out."

"No!"

"It's true. He's a prince of a fellow and my best friend."

"He is quite handsome." Estella smiled.

"Nowhere near as good-looking as me," Desmond said. "And certainly not in your class. You stand out like the brightest star at night, the shiningest rainbow during the day, you're—"

"Here's your coffee," Weatherby interrupted. "Sure you don't want anything else? Pie? Got some huckleberry pie."

"Nothing more," Desmond said, "from you." He leaned on the table, eyes only on Estella. She blushed just a little under his appreciative stare.

"You come on strong, sir," she told him.

"In this life, a man has to if he's going to get what he wants."

"Oh? What is it you want? Me?" She slid back in her chair and crossed her arms over her breasts.

"To buy you another meal," he said, slipping a dollar bill from his stack. "To please you."

"Nothing more?"

"Everything more, but in time," he said. This confounded her. She blushed more vividly and sipped at her coffee to cover her reaction. "What plans do you have for the rest of the day? I'm thinking there must be somewhere we could go with a picnic basket and watch the world go by."

"Sit by a stock pond?" She laughed at this. "I do so enjoy sitting on a lake shore, but water is difficult to come by."

"Except in the Pecos." Desmond launched into a description of fording the river and how he had saved the chuckwagon from certain destruction. He embellished his role in saving Mac because he saw how wide-eyed she got at his tale of braving the dangerous water and coming through with the herd intact.

"You are very brave. But your friend Mac seems to be, also. To ride beside you requires great courage."

Desmond almost told her of how he'd been kidnapped and held for ransom because the bounty hunters wanted Mac, but he realized no one came out sounding brave in that story.

"A picnic doesn't have to be near water, though that can be very . . . romantic. Where else can we go?"

"Why, nowhere, Mister Sullivan. I came to town to get supplies and must return immediately."

"I can ride with you again, but what's the hurry?" Desmond worried she was trying to brush him off. Mention of getting back to her hacienda turned her distant, as if her thoughts were there rather than on him.

"We leave in the morning. At dawn. We were supposed to leave this morning but supplies were necessary that we did not have. We have them now."

Desmond sat speechless. He wasn't going to lose her so soon after he had found her.

"Where are you going?" he asked when he found his voice again.

"Back to Mexico. Oh, don't look so forlorn. I will return after Papa sells our cattle there. That horrible Luther Wardell made certain we couldn't sell any cattle to the Army, so we must find other markets."

"There's Denver," he said. "The Circle Arrow is moving out what's left of our herd in a few days. We could combine our herds. That'd be safer for all of us and make it easier to handle the cattle."

"You have longhorns. They do not mix well with our breed. And no, it is too far, too long on the trail, for us to sell in Denver. Mexico is closer. Besides, Papa has received a telegram assuring him of a sale." She made a face.

"To someone you don't like? Maybe I can convince Mister Flowers to buy your cattle."

"Does he have more money than that which Wardell gave him for the three hundred head? We need more than that to . . . We need more than that." She covered her lack of forthrightness by taking one long, last sip of coffee. "Now I must go."

"You're riding along with the herd? You can stay here in Fort Sumner."

"I bullied Papa into letting me go. He would never permit me to stay now. I cannot go back on my word to help, either. We have too few vaqueros for the size of our herd. I will help however I can."

"You can ride night herd? I bet you've got a great singing voice."

"Oh, you. Thank you, Mister Sullivan, for your kindness. I must go. Really." Estella Abragon stood.

Desmond shot to his feet.

"How many more hands do you need on the drive?"

"We have ten. My Papa, me. That makes twelve. I can do many things. I am not what you call a hothouse flower."

"But you are as beautiful as one." Desmond took her hand, tugged a little until she yielded, then kissed it in what he hoped was a gallant, courtly fashion. Estella should be in high society and not riding along a dusty trail with hundreds of beeves threatening to stampede at every turn.

"Please, sir, return my hand to me." She tugged it free, then graced him with one of her sunshiny smiles. With that she left.

But he had to grin when she paused at the door and glanced back at him before leaving. If she had rushed out without a backward look, it would have left him disconsolate. That look meant she cared as much for him as he did for her.

So why did they have to go their separate ways? By the time she returned from Mexico, he would be on the trail and almost in Denver, a thousand miles to the north. He'd sparked many women and had even more he paid for, but none of them held a candle to Estella Abragon. Not a single one.

"I'm not letting you go, not alone," he said.

"You sure you don't want some pie?" came the ringing question. The restaurant owner leaned against the door leading to the kitchen, arms crossed and looking smugly satisfied. How much he had seen, Desmond didn't know. It wouldn't take much to guess what was going on, him making dewy cow eyes at such a beautiful woman and she playing coy.

"When we get back. Both of us will have a piece." Desmond rushed from the restaurant. Estella's heavily laden buggy was gone. She had moved his mount's reins from the back wheel to an iron ring set up high on the restaurant wall for the purpose of tethering horses. He should have looked at what she carried, though he had no reason to doubt she had purchased supplies for the trail drive, as she claimed.

She couldn't get far or drive very fast with so much cargo. He started after her, then drew rein. All he could do was ride alongside, then watch her leave him behind. A dozen excuses rattled around in his head, but he realized none would hold water with Hiram Flowers. The best way for him to proceed was both sneaky and straightforward.

Asking Flowers for permission to leave the drive would be

futile. He might as well hammer nails into his own skull. Flowers hadn't wanted to let him come in the first place but agreed to wet-nurse him to keep his ma from riding along.

He smiled crookedly. Estella Abragon and his ma had a lot in common. Fear didn't make up any part of their personality.

Galloping hard got him back to the Circle Arrow camp just as Mac had supper ready. Desmond picked at his food and thought he might tell the cook what he planned. Then he figured that was the same as telling Hiram Flowers. Mac and the trail boss were thicker than thieves. Expecting Mac to keep a secret wasn't too smart.

"What's eating you?"

Desmond jumped a foot and spilled some of his beans on the ground. He hastily kicked dirt over them. They had enough trouble with bugs without advertising for more.

"Nothing special. Just thinking about the drive up to Denver. You ever been there before?"

"Nope," Mac said. "This is all new country for me. Can't say I like it as much as East Texas, but it has its appeal, I suppose. From what Mister Flowers says, once we get to Colorado, the land's a whole lot different. Tall trees, cooler, greener."

"That's good."

"Are you feeling all right, Desmond? You act like you're a million miles away."

"I'm just a tad tired. I rode night herd last night."

Mac looked at him strangely, then shook his head slowly and said, "No, you didn't. At least somebody who snored like a ripsaw cutting through tall timber curled up under your blanket all night long."

"Must have been the night before."

"No, that was—"

"I don't want to talk about it." Desmond shot to his feet, tossed his plate into the slop bucket, and marched away. He knew Mac stared at him, unconvinced. It didn't matter one little bit. He had made up his mind, and nothing would change it. Nothing.

Around midnight, just as the first of the night herders came in and the next wave of wranglers went to keep the herd bedded down safely, Desmond saddled his horse and packed what supplies he could in a pack. He rummaged through the chuckwagon for food. His fingers touched cool glass. The whiskey bottle taunted him.

"Medicinal," he said. "That's for medicinal use only." He held it in his hand, considered popping the cork and taking one long pull to get him on the way, and made his decision. He replaced the cork without so much as taking a sniff of the potent rotgut.

With the bag of food, he silently walked from camp and stowed the supplies on his horse. A pang of guilt hit him. He was stealing from the drive. A deep breath settled his thoughts. His ma owned the ranch and cattle. In a way, they were all his, so how could he steal from himself?

He stepped up into the saddle, wheeled around, and cut across country for the Abragon ranchero. Don Jaime wouldn't turn down an experienced cowboy, not when he had only ten men to handle his entire herd.

Desmond looked forward to the trip into Mexico with Estella riding alongside. He might even learn some Spanish.

Chapter 22

"You all packed up until the noon meal?" Hiram Flowers chewed on his lower lip and kicked at a rock as he spoke. He hated the uncertainty. He wanted Mac to get ready for the drive to Denver, but giving that order meant he had to commit himself—and the herd. A mistake now meant Mercedes Sullivan wouldn't get as much as possible for the beeves.

"What do you need from me, Mister Flowers?" Mac jumped up and sat on the chuckwagon tailgate, swinging his feet back and forth. To be as confident, as at ease, as the young man eluded Flowers. He wanted nothing more than to turn around, go back to Fort Worth and the Circle Arrow ranch, and—

And what?

"Near her," Mac said.

Flowers jumped as if he had been stuck with a pin. He had been thinking about getting home to be near Mercedes, to just *see* her again.

"What?"

Mac frowned, licked his chapped lips, and combed his fingers through his hair. "Mister Flowers? Mister Flowers!"

"Sorry," Flowers said as he gave a little shake of his head. "Got my mind on other things. The herd, getting on up to Denver."

And Mercedes . . . but Flowers wasn't going to say that.

"You've decided the Army won't take any more cattle?" Mac asked.

"You heard what Luther Wardell did with the three hundred he bought from us, eh?" Flowers nodded slowly. Mac kept his ear to the ground, especially since he kept on talking about that rancher's daughter he had met in town.

"He's trying to run the Abragons off their rancho," Mac said. "Now that the Army has all the cattle they can use, Don Jaime can't sell any of his cattle to the quartermaster. And neither can we."

"I about came to that decision on my own," Flowers said. "With the grasslands around here being so lush, the ranchers are raising big herds. Wardell, Don Jaime, several others. I think that fellow, the newcomer, Maxwell, has a decent herd, too."

"He's just started breeding. It'll be a year or two before he's ready to start selling," Mac said. "But you're right about too many head looking for a market." He paused. "Denver? When are we heading out?"

"You don't sound too happy about it. You will stay with the drive for another thousand miles? We can sell the rest of the herd for good money. The pay'll be worth it."

"It's a long way back to Texas."

"Don't sound so down in the mouth. We can take the train across to Abilene, then ride on down to the Circle Arrow from there in a week or two. There's no reason we have to backtrack the trail from here to Denver."

"Crossing the Pecos again, even without a herd, is not much to my liking, so I'm glad of that."

"What's Desmond think?" Flowers looked around. "Where is he, anyway? I saw him on night herd."

"He ate breakfast, or at least he grabbed a couple biscuits. I thought you had him watching the herd this morning."

Flowers suddenly had a bad feeling. "Show me where he spread his bedroll."

"You think something's wrong, Mister Flowers?" Mac asked as he slid down from the tailgate.

The trail boss took a deep breath and let it out slowly. His heart sped up, and he heard blood hammering in his ears.

"I don't look for things to go wrong, but that doesn't mean they don't find me now and then. Desmond was sweet on the same girl you are. I heard the two of you arguing about her. Estella? That was her name?"

"Estella," Mac confirmed. "We weren't arguing, exactly. He owed me some money from when we met her in town." Mac spat. "He owed me more than the money. I put in four hours working for the restaurant because Desmond walked out on me."

"With the girl."

Mac's sour expression answered his suspicions.

"Show me where he flops," Flowers said.

Mac walked around the chuckwagon hunting for a spot nestled between three mesquite trees and a large creosote bush. The ground showed where Desmond had scooped out for his hips and shoulders, but the blanket and the rest of his tack were missing.

Flowers stared at the empty, sandy patch, his mind racing. Mac completed a circuit of the area and came back, shaking his head.

"He's nowhere to be found. Did you send him out to ride herd?"

"I gave him the day off. He said he was feeling poorly, but it might just be that he was feeling frisky. Do you think he's off to pay court to Estella?"

Mac said nothing, which answered the question better than a lie. Flowers wrestled with the problem. He had hired on to get the herd to market. Watching after Mercedes's boy had become an additional chore, one he wasn't paid for, but if he let anything happen to Desmond she would never forgive him. Being in Mercedes's bad graces was worse than ignoring his duty as trail boss. He wanted nothing to happen to the boy, but choosing what to do tossed him on the horns of a dilemma broader than the span of a longhorn.

"Tell Messy he's in charge while I'm gone."

"You thinking on being gone long?"

"Can't say, but I intend to be back to get some of those biscuits you fix up so good." Flowers sighed. "The fact is, I might be longer. You go tell Messerschmidt for me."

He felt Mac's eyes boring into his back as he walked away. The cook knew what was going on and that his trail boss had just abandoned the herd in favor of finding the boss's kid. What trouble Desmond might be in mattered less to Flowers than getting him out of it. As always. Whether it was a whorehouse in Hell's Half Acre or stepping between him and an irate gambler, or now keeping him from getting mixed up in what might turn into a range war, it was always the same. Desmond Sullivan blundered into a mess, and Hiram Flowers got him out of it.

He got the boy out of it because of what he felt for the boy's ma.

"Damn me." He saddled a mount from the remuda, stepped up, and said, "Damn me," again for good measure. Tapping his heels, he got the horse galloping in the direction of Don Jaime's rancho.

He knew vaguely where the place was, and his instincts steered him right, as usual. When he reached the front gate, he slowed his breakneck pace and looked around. Something was wrong. His stomach knotted tight and his heart hammering away, he rode to the hacienda. Before he dismounted he took another look around. The place felt like a ghost town. The usual bustle around a place where people lived was gone.

Dropping to the ground, he walked to a wrought-iron gate in a thick adobe wall. As with most houses of Spanish design, this opened into a courtyard surrounded by the house itself. He stopped to admire the garden, then jerked around when he heard soft footsteps coming from the house.

Flowers was quick on the draw. He might be an old man, but he cleared leather and fired accurately with the best of them. Quick Willy Means had found that out the hard way, and all that had happened to him was being whomped on the head with a pistol—before he kidnapped Desmond. Flowers wished they had found the body. He was certain he had put at least one hunk of lead into the bounty hunter's worthless carcass, but he wanted to bury the son of a bitch.

"Who are you?"

Flowers took off his hat respectfully as he faced the servant, dressed Mexican style in a flowing skirt, snow-white blouse, and with a red sash tied around her ample waist. They were of an age and, if Flowers judged matters rightly, of similar positions. He worked for Mercedes Sullivan in an important job. This woman had the same air of command he did when he rode with the herd.

"I'm looking for a young man, Desmond Sullivan. Red hair, about so tall—" He started to indicate Desmond's height but the woman put up both hands, palms toward him, and waved them to stop him.

"I know of him. He is no good."

"We can agree on some things, then," Flowers said. "I want to get him back to his job working the Circle Arrow herd. Where is he?"

"Gone. He is gone with the rest of them."

"What do you mean?" He looked around again and the sense of abandonment hit him even harder. The only two people in the house were standing in the garden. Everyone else was . . . gone.

"Don Jaime has taken the herd to Mexico to sell. To Don Pedro." She spat the name out as if it burned her tongue like a red-hot chili pepper.

"What about Desmond?" The sinking feeling became more akin to drowning now. He hardly dared breathe.

"He rides with Don Jaime." She shook her head angrily. "No, he rides with *her*. I thought she had better sense. She likes him."

"She? Estella Abragon?"

"Who else?" She looked at him as if he had been out in the sun too long. Maybe he had.

"Don Jaime and his vaqueros are driving the herd into Mexico and Estella rode along? With Desmond, too?"

She glared at him, tapped her toe, and crossed her arms. Never had he seen a more emphatic dismissal.

"Did they leave at dawn?"

"They did. And I do not know where Don Pedro's rancho is. Mexico. That is what I do know." She pointed to the gate leading out to where he'd left his horse.

He put his hat on, touched the brim politely, muttered a "thank you," and hightailed it. Astride his horse again, he spun in a circle, trying to figure out what to do. As if by its own accord, the horse walked southward. Here, Flowers saw where Don Jaime's men had rounded up their horses for the drive and headed south. If the herd was of any real size, tracking it would be simple. *If* he went after Desmond. For two cents and a plugged nickel he'd let the boy go off on his own. What did he owe him, anyway? Desmond had been nothing but trouble.

He had been hired to get the Circle Arrow herd to market and wrangle the best price that he could. Selling about a third of the beeves for a hundred a head made him glow with pride. The reason Luther Wardell paid so much hardly mattered. The money covered all the Circle Arrow hands' salaries and then some. The sale of what remained, in Denver or elsewhere, was pure gravy.

Flowers rode steadily back to the Circle Arrow herd. The closer he got, the less sure he was what to do. By the time he reached the chuckwagon, he was too confused to know which end was up. Mac was working to clean the harness for the chuckwagon team and looked up when Flowers came closer.

"You find him?" Mac tossed aside the harness and saddle soap.

"He's on his way to Mexico. With Don Jaime and his herd."

Mac pursed his lips. Flowers saw the wheels spinning in the man's head as he ground everything into a fine dust before spitting it out.

"You're going after him, aren't you?" Mac said.

"No! He's old enough to make his own decisions."

"What's Miz Sullivan going to say? She wanted you to look out for him."

"I never agreed to that."

"But you didn't have to say it out loud," Mac said. "You and her, you've got a verbal contract. She stayed at the Circle Arrow, and Desmond was supposed to stay with the herd until it was sold. He was supposed to learn the business of running a ranch."

"You think I should go after him?"

Mac wiped his lips. His brain still churned. Watching the process would have been funny if Flowers hadn't had so much riding on Desmond and the herd.

"I do, Mister Flowers. How hard is it letting the herd stay here and graze?"

"There's no market here. Wardell sold our cattle to the Army. There aren't other markets big enough for seven hundred head. Almost that many." He did a quick inventory in his head. "Too many of them are steers for the local ranchers for breeding into their own herds."

"We could drive the herd down into Mexico. If Don Jaime has a market there, we might do all right, too," Mac said.

"I don't know anybody there. I don't know the markets, and I sure don't speak Spanish."

Mac laughed and said, "You don't hardly speak English."

Flowers glared at him for a second, then laughed, too.

"Got me on that." He relaxed a mite and thought as hard as Mac had been on the subject. Everything clicked into place, like dice falling in a chuck-a-luck cage.

"Messy can be the trail boss and get the herd started for Denver. I'll corral Desmond, bring him back, and catch up before a week's out."

"You trust the German with that much responsibility?"

"I've ridden with him and his buddy, Kleingeld, for a couple years. Nothing rattles him. And I don't intend being gone all that long. He's somewhere out riding herd. You can tell Messy what I decided. He gets my pay and his own while I'm gone. That'll please the hardheaded German."

Mac said nothing.

"You behave yourself, Mac. It's hard enough dealing with Desmond. I don't want you acting up, too."

Flowers led his horse to the corral, chose another that wasn't all tuckered out, mounted, and rode back. He nodded in Mac's direction.

Then he galloped off, knowing he had to put distance between himself and the herd or his resolve would weaken. Getting Desmond back mattered. That might not get him into Mercedes's good graces since he let her son light out for Mexico in the first place, but it helped. Let her fire him. In his heart he knew he was doing the right thing.

After a mile, he slowed to keep the horse from collapsing under him. If he kept up a decent pace, Don Jaime's herd would be within reach by nightfall, maybe sooner. From everything he'd heard, the rancher had only a few vaqueros. That would slow down the drive. Feeling good, Flowers began singing one of the songs the nighthawks crooned to keep the cattle settled down.

He jumped a foot when another voice joined in on the chorus. Hand on his revolver, he twisted around in the saddle.

"Mac!" he exclaimed when he saw the cook trotting toward him on horseback. "What are you doing here? Something wrong?"

"Nothing's wrong." Mac pulled even with him and made no move to stop or head back toward Fort Sumner.

"Messy refused to be trail boss?"

"He liked the idea. You might have to fight him to get your job back."

"So why are you here?"

"I decided to help you fetch back Desmond. I owe him."

"You're that good a friend?" Flowers laughed harshly. The two young men had a wary truce and nothing more.

"More like a grudging respect. Desmond is fighting to climb out of a bad hole and is doing a good enough job."

"What you're saying in polite words is that he's not as big of an asshole as he once was."

"That," Mac said. "And we worked good as partners before."

"We won't have Quick Willy Means to deal with anymore. Not like in Fort Worth." Flowers hesitated, then asked, "What're the men going to do for a cook if you're coming with me to Mexico?"

"Kleingeld claims he can do better. Let him try with his stuffed skunk cabbage and sausage. If I get back and the men like him better, I'll move on and everyone will be happy."

Flowers heard something more in what Dewey Mackenzie said. If he liked Mexico, he'd never go back to the Circle Arrow herd. Desmond might be traveling with the herd again, but the drive was going to lose a cook, a damned good one, to boot, sooner or later.

He'd deal with that problem when it happened. First, he had to hog-tie Desmond and drag him back. Then he'd worry about Mac.

Chapter 23

The day was as perfect as it could get. Luther Wardell shifted his feet, hiked them up on the porch railing, leaned back a bit farther, and sipped at the Kentucky bourbon he had special ordered six months ago for celebrations. Snookering Don Jaime counted as reason to sip at the whiskey and enjoy the fine late summer day, with the wispy clouds high in the bright blue sky, the gentle breeze, and land that he owned as far as he could see. Even if he climbed to the roof of his two-story house, he wouldn't be able to see the boundaries of his ranch.

After he bought Don Jaime's ranch for the price of a few mortgage payments, he wouldn't be able to ride around the perimeter of his land in a day. Two, maybe, but even galloping on a fast horse wouldn't take him off his own property. He was on his way to being a power in De Baca County. Some of Don Jaime's land stretched out to Lincoln County. That would be the next direction to expand.

He laughed.

"What's so funny, boss?" Joe Ransom asked as he came up to the porch.

He motioned for his foreman to join him.

"Ransom, my good man, I am going to expand my spread. Don't you like the play on words? I'm going to own all of southeastern New Mexico Territory within a couple years."

Joe Ransom dragged a chair over and put it at polite distance from his employer. He looked at the chair as if not understanding what good it was, then settled down into it.

"Something's eating you, Ransom. What is it? Don't ruin my good mood."

"I'd better go check the herd on the south forty." He started to stand, but Wardell motioned him to stay put.

"You *are* going to ruin my day. I can tell. What's wrong?"

"Don Jaime and the bank," Ransom said. "I just heard that the banker's giving him another month to make his back payments before putting the ranch up for sale."

"So? Another month? I'm a patient man. I can wait that long." Wardell fixed a cold stare on Ransom. The man was more gunman than foreman and had ice water in his veins. That he looked downright fidgety now caused Wardell to knock back his whiskey. It burned down to his belly. He didn't taste it, and that put him in a foul mood. He had spent a hundred dollars getting a couple of bottles from the distillery.

"Don Jaime rounded up all his cattle and is driving them to Mexico."

"He's abandoning his ranch? Good. That'll make . . ." Wardell's words trailed off. The reason for Don Jaime's trail drive wasn't cowardice or welshing on the bank loan. "He has a buyer for the entire herd? Willing to pay enough to cover his debts?"

"All of them, if my ciphering's right, boss. He sent a telegram to Don Pedro Escobar. I asked around. The two of them don't get along, but Don Jaime's got the cattle and Don Pedro's got the markets farther down in Mexico. He sells to the Federales and a half dozen Indian tribes, including the Yaquis." Ransom grinned wolfishly. "Rumor has it he also sells guns to the Indians. That might be where his real money comes from."

"Real money," Wardell said. He spat. "He's got plenty to buy cattle. Do you think Don Jaime might be smuggling guns into Mexico?"

"He wouldn't have the crust for that."

"That's the way I see him, too," Wardell said.

"I can catch up with his herd and gun him down."

"That won't get me his ranch anytime soon. If it gets tied up in court, I have to buy off judges and lawyers. You know what crooks they are."

"So he doesn't end up with a couple ounces of lead in his belly?" Ransom sounded disgruntled at this. His fingers twitched, as if they circled the butt of his six-gun and pulled back on the trigger.

"There're all sorts of dangers to face on a trail drive. Stampedes can destroy most of your cattle. What if his horses were stolen and his vaqueros had to walk?"

"He has to pay off the loan in a month. The banker won't give him more time."

"Why'd Amos Dunphy give him one second longer to pay up? Dunphy would foreclose on his own grandmother if there was an extra nickel in it for him." Wardell thought hard. Then he shook his head in disbelief. "I can't believe he gave Don Jaime the extra time because he's sweet on Estella."

"The fat banker man and a *chica bonita* like that?" Ransom laughed. It was an ugly sound that made Wardell wonder if the gunman wasn't sweet on her, too

"It makes sense. He thinks giving Don Jaime a break might ingratiate him to his daughter. He either doesn't see too clearly how she'd react to an arranged marriage with a fat, pasty-white banker or there's something more at stake."

"What does it matter? He gave Don Jaime the time."

"Will he give him one second longer if he doesn't get his money? Maybe with a bonus tacked onto it."

"I can see that. Dunphy gets a bribe, paid under the table so his shareholders never find out. That's what I'd do, then find a way to foreclose on his ranch." Ransom sounded proud of such a scheme. Wardell knew that much was true, but Estella's hand, with the ranch as dowry, still intrigued Ransom.

"How many men can you get into the saddle?"

"To overtake Don Jaime? A half dozen. If I take any more, tending the cattle out on the range will suffer. We've got Mescaleros raiding almost nightly. Without enough guards, they'd run off the entire herd within a week."

"Damned Indians," Wardell groused. "Get the men ready to leave as fast as possible. I'll stay here to deal with the Apaches."

"And the banker?" suggested Ransom.

"Dunphy must have a weak spot. I'll find it and dig my thumbs in to see how deep the bruise goes." Wardell recovered some of the good nature he had experienced before Ransom delivered such bad news. There wasn't any call to get upset. Things would work out for him soon enough. All he needed was patience.

Patience and a way of applying pressure to Don Jaime and Amos Dunphy and anyone else who got in his way.

Chapter 24

Mac pulled his battered hat down until the brim was just over his eyebrows. This shielded his eyes enough to slowly survey the land ahead even as it let the hot sun bake down on the top of his head through the hole in the hat's crown.

Small ranges of low mountains perked up all around, but the main path any cattle would take lay wide and green with juicy grass. Try as he might, he couldn't find Don Jaime's herd. This worried him. The rancher might have taken some other route from Fort Sumner. Going straight into the Sacramento Mountains had to be the worst choice. They were high and passes would need to be found. Mac had never driven a herd through mountains, but it didn't look easy.

He turned more to the south. The Circle Arrow herd had come from the southeast. Don Jaime had no reason to cross the Pecos. Texas was filled with longhorns, and the price of any given steer was too low to get him the money he needed.

"There," Hiram Flowers said, pointing due south. "He's made good time to get that far."

"Are you sure?" Mac finally spotted the dust on the far horizon. "It's only a dust devil."

"Don Jaime's herd," Flowers insisted. "He's in a hurry."

"He'll run those beeves until they're nothing but skeletons." Mac pushed his hat back up in a more comfortable position. He eyed the dust as it died down. The brown haze lay in the right direction.

"Let's ride. We can overtake them by sundown."

"We should have brought a second horse for each of us. Swapping out when one got tired would have let us double the distance we can ride."

"We'll get there, Mac. What worries me most is if something's happened to Desmond. Sometimes, he doesn't have the sense God gave a goose."

"You mean you worry that Don Jaime catches him fooling around with Estella?" In a perverse way, Mac hoped Don Jaime did catch them and booted Desmond off the drive. He smiled, just a little, at the notion of Estella turning from Desmond to someone else. *He* was that someone else. Ever since he had seen her in the restaurant, she had dominated his thoughts and dreams.

Desmond had been able to corner her when he hadn't. Desmond gave her a way off the ranch that her pa was driving into the ground. Mac wasn't sure what he offered her, but it had to be better than the ne'er do well. Desmond had hardly worked a day in his life before the trail drive.

Mac had worked every day since he was eight or nine. His pa had made sure of that. When he moved on after his parents died and his brother Jacob upped and left without so much as a good-bye, life had turned difficult. All the time he'd spent in New Orleans had shown he coped well and met any challenge, even the snake eyes he rolled with Pierre Leclerc.

A momentary pang caused him to catch his breath as he thought of Evie. She had been so lovely. For all he knew, she enjoyed her life with Leclerc, though he doubted it if she got wind that the shipping tycoon had murdered her pa. He shuddered, remembering how he had found Micah Holdstock's body tied up on the oak tree, his body slashed and his throat slit with Mac's knife.

He still used that knife for cooking on the drive.

"What's wrong? You forget something? Your knife's sheathed at the small of your back, if that's what you're feeling around for." Flowers looked curiously at him.

"I worry about forgetting things. I'm ready to ride."

"Gallop a mile, walk half, trot for a half, then gallop until the horses tire. If we change their gait they won't get as worn out." Hiram Flowers patted his horse's neck. The animal turned a big brown eye around to glare at its rider, as if it understood what the trail boss said and disagreed.

"You've done this before," Mac said. "Was it chasing after Desmond then, too?"

"You've got a mouth on you, boy. You just shut it and ride. Otherwise, you'll end up with a mouth full of bugs and dust." Flowers lowered his head and brought his horse to a gallop.

Mac followed him. His horse wasn't anywhere near as strong as the trail boss's but kept up well enough, lagging only a few dozen yards by the time Flowers drew back to a walk.

Mac closed the distance and said, "You see what I do?"

Flowers jerked around, eyes narrowed.

"What are you talking about?"

Mac felt a momentary pride that he had paid attention to his surroundings and Flowers hadn't. The satisfaction died when he realized how second nature that had become to him with bounty hunters on his trail and a murder trial waiting for him in New Orleans.

"Not a mile to the west. At least five riders. They're making tracks for Don Jaime's herd, too. They might be rustlers."

"That's mighty quick of them, if they are. From what I can tell, Don Jaime got the bug up his ass to drive his cattle to Mexico in the last day or two. Maybe only hours before he set out."

"This isn't the usual trail that a cattle drive takes, is it?"

"The Goodnight-Loving Trail is miles and miles to the east and doesn't go anywhere near Mexico. Men don't ride this section of the territory for fun, not with the Indians always riled up about something."

Mac hazarded a guess. "Apache scouts?"

"Apache war party is more like it. You didn't get any better look at them, did you?"

Mac started to snap back an answer. He had seen the riders; Flowers hadn't. How much more was he supposed to do? Count the number of gold teeth in their heads? Find out their horses' names?

He held back his sass.

"From the way they're headed, we can cross in front and find out what they're up to. Or we can dog their back trail and sneak up when they camp."

"And spy on them?" Flowers spat out the words. "That's downright uncivil."

"If they're honest men traveling for honest reasons, that's not overly polite. You're the one who said there's no such critter as an honest man out in this part of the territory. Other than us. And Don Jaime and his vaqueros."

"We take it on faith they're up to no good. Asking their business is likely to get us filled full of holes, no matter what their intentions."

Mac put what he knew into his head and let it all tumble around to see what finally came out. The determination of the gang, the way they rode fast and hard, heading straight for Don Jaime's herd, decided him. They were up to no good.

"Don Jaime got all the men he could from his ranch. These gents aren't intending to join up and help him get his cattle south of the border. If I was a betting man, I'd lay odds on them being sent by Luther Wardell."

"Why's that, Mac?" Flowers worked on his own ideas, but this one distracted him.

"If Don Jaime gets the money to save his ranch, Wardell wasted the money he spent buying our beeves and almost giving them to the Army. The Circle Arrow and the Army will be the only winners. And Don Jaime, if he collects enough for his cattle. Wardell loses all around."

"That makes sense," Flowers said. "The question comes to mind, what do we do? If we mix it up with them for no good reason, that's not going to get Desmond back."

"If the gang tries to rustle the herd or just stampede it, Desmond is in serious danger. He's barely got the experience to wipe his own nose."

"He can do more than that. He saved your damned chuckwagon crossing the Pecos. Don't you forget that."

Mac recognized a desperate defense when he heard one. The trail boss knew that Desmond had been caught in the stampede during the thunderstorm and would have died if he hadn't saved him. After that, Mac had taught him close to everything he knew about being a cowboy. Mac remembered how Desmond had come close to shooting off his own foot until taught how to draw and fire. He needed more practice with his revolver, but the lessons Mac had given him were enough to keep him alive. Unless the hothead did something he thought was heroic to impress Estella.

"It won't hurt to watch them," Mac said, choosing his words carefully. "If it looks like they're going to try their hand at some rustling, we can always let Don Jaime know. After all, it's his herd to protect."

"That's sensible enough," Flowers said. He spat, turned his horse, and slowed to a walk.

Mac kept pace beside him, letting his horse rest up. They might have to hightail it. He wanted as fresh a horse under him as possible if it came down to shooting.

They made their way through the desert, finding ways to stay out of sight until Flowers couldn't stand it any longer. He dropped to the ground, tossed his reins to Mac, and started up a steep hillside for a look.

"Don't let them see you," Mac called. He got a dirty look in return. Flowers was savvy enough not to silhouette himself against the sky, even if the sun had moved around and would be in his eyes.

He reached the crest, hunkered down, and inched forward. He flopped on his belly so fast that Mac jumped. In less than a minute Flowers worked his way back downhill, stood, and ran the rest of the way. Panting harshly, he grabbed the reins from Mac's hands and pointed to the rifle in the saddle sheath.

He gasped out, "Rifle. Get your damned rifle. They're on the other side of the hill fixing to start a stampede."

"You heard them?"

Flowers's head bobbed up and down. He mounted, drew his own rifle, and levered a round into the chamber. Not waiting to see if Mac followed, he lit out around the base of the hill.

"Wait for me," Mac cried. He felt a little queasy going into a fight and not knowing what he faced. How many rustlers were there? Or had he been right that these men worked for Wardell and intended nothing but mischief to keep Don Jaime from selling the cattle to save his ranch?

He found out quick. Trailing Flowers by a dozen yards, he pounded around the hill. Nestled between two smaller hillocks, eight men worked to fasten bandanas over their faces and checked their revolvers. They looked up when Flowers and Mac raced toward them, but they didn't react. Mac saw them call out to one man, their leader.

"That's Ransom, Wardell's foreman," he shouted to Flowers. He had seen the man in Fort Sumner and learned his name.

The trail boss never heard. His horse's hooves pounded too hard against the dry ground. Then he opened fire. His rifle spat foot-long tongues of orange flame and filled the air with white gun smoke.

Mac raced right behind him. The notion of shooting down the men churned at his gut. This wasn't self-defense, not strictly. To ease his conscience, he saw that all his rounds missed their intended targets, but the volley they fired spooked the mounts under Wardell's henchmen. Confusion, rearing horses, animals bolting threw several of the riders to the ground. As Mac charged past one, he heard a sick crunch as his horse's front hoof collided with the man's arm. The bone not only broke but poked out through his duster. He fell away, screaming in pain and adding to the commotion.

"It's just two of them. Don't let them scare you!" Ransom fought for control of his horse. He waved his gun around, but every time he leveled it, the horse sunfished and threatened to throw him off. "Kill them! Shoot the bastards!"

Mac tried to do just that to Ransom, but he had raced clean through where they'd gathered. He leaned to the side, avoided a couple bullets sent his way, turned his horse, and came back for a second attack. He changed his tactics when he saw Flowers on the ground, his horse next to him. The horse was dead. Hiram Flowers had drawn his revolver and fired as accurately as he could as he knelt behind the meager shelter of the horse's body.

To protect the trail boss, Mac rode between him and three men closing in on him. Two rounds cracked from his rifle, but then it was empty. He whipped out his S&W. The trusty gun fired four rounds with accuracy unlike anything he had experienced before. Or it might have been Lady Luck smiling on him. He winged one of Wardell's gunmen, shot another's horse from under him, and caused the third to veer away.

"Get up behind me," Mac called. He had to use both hands on the reins to stop the horse close enough to Flowers. Otherwise, it would have kept running until it died under him.

"Two of us will tire it out."

"*Get on!*" Mac was in no mood to argue. His tone lit a fire under the trail boss. Flowers jumped up, caught at the saddle, and awkwardly pulled himself forward.

Mac saved his last two rounds for when he might need them. He bent low and rode straight into a tight knot of would-be stampeders. Two scattered. Another was thrown when his horse reared.

"What are you doing?" He looked behind. Flowers had jumped away. He saw the reason. The riderless horse had stepped on a rein and jerked its head around. As it tried to figure out how to get away, Flowers snatched the rein, pulled it free, and vaulted into the saddle.

They were both mounted again.

Mac used his final two rounds to send Wardell's men running. It took all his willpower not to keep firing on empty chambers. The click-click-click might have drawn them back to fight some more if they knew he had run out of rounds.

Flowers hooted and hollered and dropped the man who had been tossed from his horse as he tried to scramble over a hill. Flowers grabbed and caught the bridle of the now stray horse.

"We showed them," Mac said. Reaching into his coat pocket, he pulled out six cartridges and reloaded his revolver. It took longer to find a box of shells and get his rifle reloaded. "Let them come back. I'm ready for bear."

"How many are dead?" Flowers swayed as if a high wind buffeted him. He turned in a full circle, then threw up his hands. "How many?"

"They're running, Mister Flowers. They won't stop until they get back to Fort Sumner." Mac had to grin. "Chances are good they won't go back and tell Wardell what happened. They'd prefer him to think they're dead, rather than cowards who couldn't tangle with two cowboys and win."

"Their leader. Ransom. He's a mean one. He won't go back. He'll get mad."

"He'll be alone. I saw the expressions on those owlhoots' faces. They won't come back."

"I hope you're right, Mac. I hope you're right." Flowers tipped his head to one side, listened hard, then pointed. "Don Jaime's herd is over that way. I hear them stirring."

"They stayed put and didn't stampede. His vaqueros can settle them down."

"That's none of our business. Getting Desmond back to the Circle Arrow is."

Mac heaved a sigh. The trail boss had a one-track mind. This time that proved to be a good idea. Ransom and the rest of Wardell's gunmen had run away, but if they took long enough, they'd forget why they ran, build up some courage—maybe with the help of a bottle of whiskey—and decide they feared Ransom and Wardell more than two cowboys.

He settled in the saddle, hunted for any dropped weapons, and found two revolvers. It took him a few seconds to dismount and grab them. The more firepower he carried, the better their chance of fulfilling Flowers's pipe dream of prying Desmond loose from the Mexican's trail drive.

Desmond had plenty to prove. He'd take every chance he could to show off for Estella Abragon. Mac caught up and cantered beside the trail boss until they sighted the trailing edge of the herd. Two vaqueros turned in their direction. Both uncurled ten-foot-long whips and cracked them behind the steers. This moved the reluctant beeves—and it gave ample warning to the pair of intruders not to cross them.

Mac politely waved. Flowers rode, eyes straight ahead as if he pierced the cloud of dust and saw Desmond. A few minutes' ride brought them around the side of the herd where Don Jaime rode. His fancy embroidered sombrero had turned dust brown. The gold threads poked through in places but both the quality and craftsmanship were veiled by trail dust already.

"What do you want?"

"A good day to you, too, Don Jaime," Flowers said. "We're here to take Desmond back where he belongs."

Mac rode between the two men. Flowers lacked even a hint

of diplomacy in his makeup. He focused on one thing only, and nothing moved him until he finished it. In a trail boss that kept the herd together and the crew safe. For retrieving the boss's son as he worked another herd, it lacked a great deal of diplomacy.

"Desmond Sullivan's needed back in Fort Sumner," Mac said. "We'd like your permission to talk it over with him."

Mac saw the ranch owner thaw a little at that. "He has hired on to work for me until we reach market in Mexico."

"We understand that, Don Jaime. We only want to talk."

A cloud of dust rose when Don Jaime took off his sombrero and waved it above his head. He loosed a whistle that hurt Mac's ears before the dust from that broad-brimmed hat choked him. Riding through a New Mexico dust devil had nothing on the tiny storm stirred up by simply whacking the hat a few times.

"There he is." Flowers started to ride to Desmond until Mac reached out to hold him back. Flowers angrily jerked free. "Don't you ever try to stop me, boy. Never."

"He's coming to us, Mister Flowers. Rock the boat now, and we return empty handed."

Mac was aware that Don Jaime took in every word they said. What his role was in letting Desmond ride with the herd remained to be seen. Having the young man on the same drive as his daughter had to be a burr under his fancy saddle.

"What are you two doing here?" Desmond drew rein and glared at them. "I'm not being kidnapped."

"Not again," Flowers said, his tone surly. "You've already done that so you keep making new mistakes. Go fetch your gear. We're going back to the Circle Arrow herd right away."

"I gave Don Jaime my word. I promised I'd work as a cowboy—a vaquero—until he reaches a market below the border."

"Your ma won't like you running off like this." Flowers turned even more belligerent. Mac saw this was the wrong thing to say, the wrong tack to take.

"Why don't we get a cup of coffee and talk this over?" Mac suggested.

"The chuckwagon's a mile that way," Desmond said, pointing due south, the direction of the herd. "You mind, Don Jaime?"

The rancher dismissed them with a wave, shouted in Spanish, and rode to chew out one of his vaqueros for some minor offense. Mac felt sorry for the man because he hadn't done anything but provide Don Jaime a convenient reason to leave his unwanted visitors to work out their problems alone.

Mac, Flowers, and Desmond rode in silence. The herd moved like a sluggish river beside them. The cattle were well fed from the lush grasslands around Fort Sumner, but Mac saw how fragile they looked in comparison to the sturdy longhorns. Without cutting into one of the cows, he figured their meat lacked the tenderness and flavor of the Texas cattle. Life in New Mexico Territory was hard enough that it toughened the animals.

"Here," Desmond said. "Here's the chuckwagon. Dinner will be ready in another hour."

"We won't be around that long." Flowers dismounted and lashed his reins to the wagon's rear wheel. He took a deep breath. The odor of cooking food obviously pleased him.

It certainly did Mac. He had learned to cook as much by smell as by taste. If food smelled bad, no amount of salt and pepper turned it palatable. The man with an apron wrapped fully around his waist and then half again worked on a mess of pinto beans. He stirred them, then worked to fry tortillas.

"That's Felipe. He's been with Don Jaime going on twenty years." Desmond reached out to pluck a morsel from a Dutch oven. He jerked back when Felipe rapped his knuckles with a wooden spoon and loosed a string of Spanish that none of the three men understood. But the meaning was clear.

"You eat with the rest of the vaqueros."

Felipe went about his work with quick moves and efficiently produced enough food for a small army. Mac approved of the man's skill and, if the taste matched the smell, his cooking was even better.

"We should hit the trail right now," Flowers said. "Trouble's brewing that isn't your concern."

"What do you mean?" Desmond perked up. His hand pushed back his duster so his revolver rested where a quick draw was possible.

Mac wondered if Flowers intended to force Desmond to stay with Don Jaime. Everything he said backed Desmond into a corner where he either fought or ran. No matter which he chose, he wasn't heading back to Fort Sumner and the Circle Arrow herd.

"We shot it out with some owlhoots. They had the look of working for Luther Wardell."

"That snake," blurted Desmond. "He's out to get Don Jaime's ranch. If this herd's not sold for a decent price, the bank forecloses and Wardell buys it for a song and dance."

"That's his worry, not yours."

"Mister Flowers, let me talk to him." Mac had to repeat his request before it soaked into Flowers's thick skull. He waved him off to one side.

Mac took Desmond by the arm and kept him from jerking free. When they were out of earshot of both Flowers and Felipe, Mac spun on him and shoved his face within inches.

"You want to get yourself killed? There's a range war brewing. You're going to be smack in the middle of it."

"I'll side with Don Jaime. Estella says—"

"There's the problem," Mac said. "Estella. She's got your brain all scrambled up. This isn't your fight. It's hers. Hers and Don Jaime's. They'd as soon shoot you as any of Wardell's men. And Ransom—Wardell's foreman—has the look of a gunslick. He's a hired killer. He won't think of you twice except to decide how few rounds it'll take to kill you so he can save the bullets for Don Jaime."

"For Don Jaime and Estella. I'm not leaving her to a man like that."

Mac backed off. Desmond hadn't budged. In his way he was as mule-headed as Hiram Flowers.

"We're not friends, not exactly, but we've saved each other's life. We've come to a truce, if you can call it that. I'm telling you, not so much as a friend but as an outsider with no stake in this game, go with Flowers. Get back to your ma's herd and drive them up to Denver. Sell them, go back to Fort Worth, and put in the hard work raising next year's longhorns."

"You just want me to go so you can cut in on Estella," Desmond accused. "I know how you look at her. If she's going to end up with anyone, it'll be me."

Desmond looked past Mac, who turned and saw the woman helping Felipe prepare the food.

"She's almost as good a cook as Felipe." Desmond sounded proud of that.

"As good as your ma? Is that what you see in her?" Mac ducked as Desmond swung. Even so, the fist grazed his cheek and caused him to reel back, off balance. His heel caught on something and he sat down hard.

Desmond stood over him, hand on his revolver, fire in his eyes.

"I taught you how to use that," Mac said. "I hope I also taught you when not to use it."

"Go to hell." Desmond stepped back and took his hand off his pistol. He stormed off to go talk with Estella. She looked at Mac wide-eyed and with some fear, as if she knew about Desmond's unchecked anger. They walked away from camp, arguing.

Flowers came over and crouched down beside Mac.

"I'm glad I let you handle him. I'd've made him so mad he couldn't be pried from this herd using a crowbar."

"What are we going to do?" Mac let Flowers help him to his feet. He brushed off the dirt from his jeans.

"You can go on back to Fort Sumner and save the men from Kleingeld's cooking. Me, I've got no choice. I go along into Mexico to be sure he stays out of trouble. If anything happened to him, his ma would skin me alive."

Mac watched Desmond and Estella standing inches apart. He wasn't sure but the tension between them turned the distance into miles.

"I'll go along to keep you company. Might be I can help Felipe whip up chow for the crew."

"I'll lend a hand herding the cattle. We won't get paid, but I'll see that Mercedes puts a little extra into your pay when we get back."

Mac considered the bonus, then thought about staying in Mexico. The bounty hunters had gotten too close, and Ransom was the sort to carry a grudge all the way to the grave. Money was good. Freedom from being hunted like an animal was better. He'd have to see.

South of the border.

Chapter 25

Quick Willy Means stared down at the man who had been his partner for the better part of a year. Charles Huffman moaned and thrashed, his arms pulled in tight to his belly to stop the bleeding. It didn't work. Red leaked out around his hands and dripped to the thirsty ground to make a gory mix of mud and sticky sand.

Means hadn't helped his partner's wounds any by dragging him away from the gunfight, rolling him down a hillside, and then draping him over his saddle to lead them out. There had been nothing he could do for Frank Huffman—he was deader than a doornail from Hiram Flowers's deadly aim.

"Do somethin', Willy. I'm hurtin' something fierce. My guts are on fire and there's a ringin' in my ears so loud I can hardly hear."

Means stared at him. There wasn't anything he could do. There wasn't anything a doctor could do. Three hunks of lead had lodged in the man's stomach. Another had caught him high in the shoulder. Even if the other three hadn't spelled certain death, the one in the shoulder would have eventually killed the man since it was still lodged deep against the bone.

"Frank's dead. He died in the gunfight. It's a wonderment to me that you're still kicking."

"Kickin'? Hurts to move anything. Can't hardly feel my feet. Are my boots on? I don't want to die with them on. I promised my ma that I wouldn't die with them on."

"You lied." Means came to a decision after listening to the caterwauling and whines of pain. He slid his gun from its holster, aimed and fired. The bullet struck Huffman in the middle of the forehead. He died before he knew what happened.

Means slowly replaced his revolver. It had been a waste of ammunition to put Huffman out of his misery since Huffman was dying anyway, but he would have done the same thing for a horse that had broken its leg.

"Getting shot was a mistake." Means flexed his own arm and knew he had come close to sharing the Huffmans' fate. Four bullets had torn through his coat and shirt sleeve. Only one had drawn blood. This left his arm achy and stiff, but not enough to affect his draw or his aim.

He closed his eyes and took in the world around him. The drone of flies coming for Charles drowned out other, more subtle sounds. But he noted the sun against his face, the puff of wind through his hair, the feel of the earth beneath his boots. He experienced it all.

Then he mentally pictured the men who had done this to him. Dewey Mackenzie had a bounty on his head. Bringing him in—bringing him down—would be a pleasure. Whatever money Leclerc offered for Mackenzie's scalp would put a decent bonus in his pocket. But Hiram Flowers wasn't a wanted man, not so far as Means knew.

That took away any profit from cutting him down, but not the sheer animal pleasure of seeing him die. Means imagined facing the grizzled old cowboy, seeing his face wrinkled and tanned by the hot Texas sun begin to furrow even more as he realized he was going to die. A quick draw, an accurate shot, Hiram Flowers gasping as death ripped through his chest. That was how it would be, and Means would watch him crumple to the ground, kick feebly, and then die in the hot sun. The old man had pistol-whipped him. That had left a deep scar on Means's soul.

Flowers and Mackenzie gunning down all three of the Huffman brothers called for punishment beyond a quick death. A dozen tortures came to mind, many of them stolen from the Apaches. But when all was said and done, Quick Willy was a businessman. Taking the time to properly torture Flowers would keep him from tracking down outlaws wanted by the law.

"You'll die fast, old man." He opened his eyes and stared at Charles Huffman. The man's face was black with flies and crawling insects.

He considered burying him to keep the coyotes from feasting on his dead flesh. Means decided not to waste the time. Charles Huffman hadn't been that bright, and he had never liked taking orders from anybody but Frank.

Means spun around and walked to his horse. Both Huffmans had lost their horses in the gunfight. A spare horse would have meant quicker, easier riding. So, of course they had let their mounts run off to make life that much more disagreeable for him. When he killed Mackenzie and Flowers, taking their horses wouldn't be that much of an advantage. He had seen the scrawny nags the Circle Arrow crew rode.

His horse pawed nervously at the ground. The gunshot had scared it, but not as much as the smell of blood. Means stepped up, wheeled the horse, and started for Fort Sumner. When Flowers and Mackenzie had saved the young punk, the only place they'd ride would be back to the Circle Arrow herd grazing outside the town.

Ignoring the aches and pains in his body proved difficult. He needed a shot of whiskey. Hell, he needed a bottle to ease the anguish wracking him from head to toe. As he rode past the fort, he garnered a few curious looks from sentries patrolling the perimeter. Like most frontier forts, there wasn't a palisade, just a low adobe wall to keep the livestock from running away. He wondered what kept the soldiers from deserting. This was a lonely, terrible place.

He almost fell from the saddle in front of the first saloon he rode up to. Means straightened, worked the kinks from his shoulder, and rubbed his arm before entering. The cantina was in a small adobe house with a bar hardly eight feet long. On a wooden shelf behind the barkeep proudly stood four bottles. They were the only things in the cantina not covered with a thin coating of dust.

"You don't have much selection," Means said.

"Nope. We got rye, we got bourbon, we got brandy, and there's a bottle of—" The barkeep peered at the fourth bottle, then leaned closer to it as he tried to read the label. "We got whatever that is."

"You don't sell a lot of it, do you? Give me a shot."

"From this one? Mister, that's living high, wide, and dangerous." The bartender sloshed the muddy fluid around in the bottle. "It might have been tequila."

"It's almost black," Means said.

"The worm fell apart?" The barkeep hesitated and asked, "You still want it?"

"Gimme a shot and information." Means let a silver dollar spin on the bar, then come to rest, its ringing pure music to the bartender's ears.

"Anybody who'd drink this can hear whatever I got to say." He poured a shot into a glass. With some distaste he pushed it across the bar to Means.

"The cowboys from the herd grazing outside town. What do

you know about them?" He toyed with his glass as the barkeep spewed forth everything he already knew. He lifted the glass, sniffed, and then knocked back the vile liquor. It tasted like nothing he had ever sampled before. There wasn't much kick. Then there was. He felt as if he went bare knuckles with the liquor, ducked a feint, and then got hit by a sucker punch.

"What's it taste like?" The bartender leaned closer to hear, in case it had robbed Means of his voice.

"You want to know, you try it."

"No, sir, not me. You're a better man than I am."

"That's as plain as that big nose on your face," Means said. "Do the trail boss and cook come in here?"

"Naw, they ain't much in the way of drinkers, or so the Circle Arrow cowboys say. But there's a new trail boss, and I seen a German fellow who don't speak much English over at the mercantile. Now that I think on it, the new trail boss is German, too, but he speaks good English, unlike the cook."

"What happened to the old ones?"

Means listened to a highly improbable tale unfold, then the barkeep mentioned Desmond Sullivan and how he had gone south with Don Jaime's herd because of Estella. This explained both Mackenzie and Flowers leaving their jobs and close to seven hundred head of cattle to be sold. Desmond Sullivan. He didn't know what draw the arrogant little pup had over the other two, but it explained them leaving. They were off to rescue him. Again.

"Keep that bottle ready for me. I'll be back to celebrate."

"Ain't been nobody daring enough to even smell it in a year. It'll be here for you. First one's on the house."

"I'll hold you to that," Means said, hitching up his gun belt. He had some riding to do to overtake the herd driving south toward Mexico. He hoped Don Jaime wouldn't miss that extra gringo helping with his herd. And he wondered how long his daughter would bawl her eyes out when her gringo lover was shot down along with Mackenzie and Flowers.

Means tried to make sense of the tracks in the sandy ground. The wind had scrambled much of the evidence, but picking out the bloody patches reminded him of his own fight with Flowers and Mackenzie. Someone had died here, judging by the amount of blood soaked into the ground. Rocks had been painted a dull red and more than a few bright scratches showed where bullets had ricocheted off into the distance.

"So a couple riders came galloping in from that direction." He imagined seeing the riders. A sneer crossed his lips. "Flowers. Mackenzie." He walked around the spot. "They rode down on men waiting here and shot them up. Why were the men here?"

He scratched his stubbled chin trying to work through what happened. All he could tell was that two or three men were ambushed and escaped. Two or three others had been killed or severely wounded to spill that much blood. He ran his finger over a rock. The blood had died fast in the hot sun, making it difficult to determine when the fight had happened.

"Within a couple of days," he mused. "And they're after Don Jaime's herd. Rustlers?" That didn't ring true. Or maybe it did. The rumors he had heard in Fort Sumner alerted him to a fight between Don Jaime and Luther Wardell. "These were Wardell's men," he decided.

He mounted and circled the area, finding the direction taken by the two riders who had charged into camp. Letting his horse have its head, he meandered southward. The tracks disappeared over sunbaked ground, but he pressed on. Just before sundown Means felt a little prickly. The hair rose on the back of his neck, a sure sign he was being watched.

Spied on or riding into trouble. Not slowing, not looking

around, he slid first one gun from its holster and then the other, checking to be sure he carried full wheels in each. The rifle under his right knee begged to be checked, too. The rifle was an old Henry, but it served its purpose in a fight. He was a crack shot with it, and that mattered more than having a Yellow Boy or some other fancy long gun.

In the distance he heard cattle lowing. He kept riding, but at an angle to his original path. The setting sun caught metal and gave off glints that allowed him to locate the source of his uneasiness. Not a half mile off he made out the dim shadows of three riders intent on working their way toward the herd. If they'd been vaqueros or otherwise working for Don Jaime, there'd be no reason for skulking. He caught his breath. It hardly seemed possible that his luck had dealt him a hand with three aces—Mackenzie, Flowers, and the snot-nosed kid.

He shook off that notion. From what he'd been told in Fort Sumner, Desmond Sullivan rode with Don Jaime as one of the cowboys. If Mac and Flowers had gone to fetch him back to the Circle Arrow herd, the three of them would be at odds. These riders huddled together, taking turns leading the single-file advance that took them toward the beeves.

Standing off and watching what Wardell's men did next made sense. Tackling Hiram Flowers, Mackenzie, and Sullivan on his own did not. Help might be at hand. Help or pawns to be sacrificed as he took his revenge on the Circle Arrow trio for what they'd done to his partners. His mind raced until everything came together.

He rode slowly toward the men, making sure they heard him coming, then saw that he wasn't a threat. Keeping his hands outstretched to show he wasn't aiming a gun at them, he stopped a few yards off.

"Evening," he said. "I'm looking for the trail down into Mexico. You gents heading that way, too?"

"Who're you?" One of the men stepped out, hand resting on his pistol. Means sized him up fast. Not only was he the leader, he thought he was a fast hand and smarter than anyone else.

"My name's . . . Shiloh. Antietam Shiloh."

"You're a damned liar!"

"Why? You come across somebody else claiming that name?" Means almost laughed. He had given the first names that had come to mind. His uncle and his pa had died at Shiloh and Antietam, fighting for the wrong side. If the need arose in the future, he'd have to come up with a name that wasn't so outrageously fake. But the deed had been done, and he had to live with it. For the moment.

"Those are battles, not names."

"My pa had a fondness for those places long before they were battle sites. What kind of man makes fun of another's name?" Means waited to see the reaction.

"My name's Ransom."

Means laughed. "That a name or is that what you pay a kidnapper?" He saw he had taken the right path. The two men with Ransom laughed, causing their boss to turn and shush them.

"It's your worst nightmare," Ransom said.

"You mean it's my worst nightmare, Mister Shiloh." Means paused a few seconds, then said, "I was looking for trail companions. I'll keep looking." Before he turned his horse, Ransom snapped at him. "You hold on, mister." He swallowed his pride. "Mister Shiloh."

"Yes, Mister Ransom?" This reply put oil on troubled water.

"You got the look of being able to use those revolvers." Ransom moved closer to get a good look. "Fact is, you got the look of a man on the run from the law."

"Yes, no."

Ransom sputtered.

"Yes, I know how to use my sidearms. No, I'm not on the

run from the law, local or federal. I just want to go to Mexico and see if I can't find a job. I've heard tell men with my skills are in demand to protect the towns and ranches from the Indians."

"The cavalry does that north of the border," Ransom said. "That's why New Mexico Territory is filthy with Army posts, all a day's ride apart."

"I've found that out. I get antsy if life's too quiet." Means considered adding more. Better to let Ransom lead the way.

"Do you have any problem taking a job right now? To get back cattle that've been rustled from my boss?"

Means had wondered what lie Ransom would tell. As fibs went, this wasn't too bad. He wouldn't have to press Ransom for more details.

"You ride out of Fort Sumner? There are plenty of ranches up there with fat cattle just itching to be rustled. That's the way I saw it, at any rate."

"You want to hire on for Luther Wardell's spread, five dollars a day until we get the stolen cattle back to their pastures?"

"That's a mighty rich payoff. All the cattle in the herd along the trail yours? Mister Wardell's?"

"How'd you know—?" Ransom laughed harshly. "You were on the same trail as the herd."

"Hard to miss that many cow chips. Fresh ones, to boot."

"Not all the cows are Mister Wardell's. We'll have to cut out the ones that are and to hell with the rest. They might be from other ranches around Fort Sumner. That's not our concern. For all I care, what's not our property can be sold in Mexico."

Means nodded slowly. "Sensible way to approach it. You don't want to shoot it out with the rustlers? Just sneak in, get your beeves back, then go home?"

"Something like that," Ransom said.

Quick Willy Means grinned, dismounted, and went to Ransom, his hand outstretched.

"We got a deal. Let's go get some strays all rounded up, and damn the rustlers."

Ransom shook. From the small tremor, Means knew he'd have no trouble throwing down on Ransom and leaving the man dead in the dirt, if the need arose. Up close, he studied the man's face and knew he had a hundred wanted posters that might carry the man's visage.

A bounty hunter's job never ended.

Chapter 26

"Go. I do not want you." Don Jaime Abragon crossed his arms and rocked back as if distancing himself from Dewey Mackenzie and Hiram Flowers would get rid of them.

Mac almost laughed. If anything, this made him even more intent on staying. The man would do anything to protect Desmond, even take on the rancher as he made his way into Mexico.

Mac cut off the trail boss's response, knowing whatever Flowers said it would only make Don Jaime madder. He wanted to smooth ruffled feathers, not pluck them out.

"Don Jaime, please. Our interest is Desmond and nothing more. We have the same goal, I suspect." He glanced to where Desmond sat close to Estella Abragon. She made no effort to push him away. "His ma would have a fit knowing he ducked across the border when he was supposed to be going in the opposite direction."

"He is young." The rancher's lip curled. "So is she."

"Too young to understand what they're doing," Mac hurried on, realizing he was hardly older than Desmond. His own travails with women had almost gotten him hanged. "We agree on so much more. You want to get your herd to market. That's none of our business. Desmond's well-being is."

"You think to hog-tie him and take him with you?" Don Jaime laughed harshly.

"It'd work," Flowers said.

"It would work. And then my daughter would go after him. That distracts me. I would have to go after her, and then who drives my cattle to Don Pedro?"

Mac realized Don Jaime was right.

"You'd lose your ranch to Luther Wardell," Mac said. He took a deep breath and looked at Desmond and Estella making cow eyes at each other. "You'd lose your daughter, too. She'd never forgive you."

"You see a great deal," Don Jaime said. He uncrossed his arms and gestured with his hands, waving them in the air. "I do not know what to do. Do you know?"

"We can drag him off so she'd never know where he went," Flowers said. "We can hide our trail."

"She's not stupid, Mister Flowers," Mac cut in. "There's only one place he would go—back to Fort Sumner and the herd."

"It's his herd!"

"Whether she believes that or not doesn't matter. She'll go there and Don Jaime has the very problem he wants to avoid. The problem *we* want to avoid," Mac emphasized. "There is a way around this."

Both Don Jaime and Flowers stared at him as if he had grown a hand out of the top of his head.

"What is this magic? You know a *brujo* to cast a spell on her?"

"She'll stay with the herd as long as he's riding with you as a vaquero. So Mister Flowers and I go along until you sell your cattle in Mexico. We'll work. You don't have to pay us."

"So?" Don Jaime frowned, trying to figure Mac's angle.

"At that age, passions run high and burn out fast. By the

time we get to Mexico, they'll be tired of each other. There'll be an argument. They will see someone else who excites them more. I understand there are many pretty señoritas where we're going." He had no idea where that was, but assuming there were women there helped his argument.

"He is not so stupid. He would never turn from my Estella." Don Jaime smiled broadly after a moment. "But she will see many of the young bucks from wealthy families. They are in favor in the Spanish court, with the king. They appreciate my land grant."

Flowers started to say something about forcing Estella to marry the son of a wealthy landowner. Mac elbowed him and got a dark look. Flowers subsided.

"We look after Desmond, and you do the same for your daughter." Mac saw Don Jaime come around to his way of thinking. He wondered if Don Jaime cottoned to the idea of Desmond fading away, only to be replaced by another gringo. Mac had never seen a lovelier woman than Estella and knew he offered her more than Desmond ever could, in spite of the youngster being heir to the Circle Arrow.

"Do not get in my way." Don Jaime pointed. "And keep him away from her. As much as possible." With that he stalked off, barking orders to his foreman. Men hurried around as he gave orders to bed down the herd for the night.

"I don't know if we came out on top or not, Mac." Flowers scratched his head. "We got to work for him all the way to market? For nothing?"

"Not for nothing. Miz Sullivan's still paying us, only not to be trail boss or cook. She'll be paying us to watch over her son."

"You're playing some other game, aren't you, Mac? I can tell. You and Desmond weren't such good friends that you'd do all this for his sake."

"You accused me of wanting to disappear into Mexico before. Let's take it one day at a time."

"We already helped Don Jaime more than he knows, scaring off Wardell's men the way we did."

"There'll be other problems. Rustlers. Indians. Once we get into Mexico, I have no idea what we'll face. Have you been in Mexico?"

"Not for years. There's nobody left who remembers me, not that this is where I was in Mexico. I crossed the Rio Grande down south of Eagle Pass."

"And?" Mac nudged him to tell more. There had to be a good story, one that'd keep the cowboys laughing around the campfire.

"And nothing. You're too young to hear. It'd burn your delicate ears."

"Show me when we get to Mexico," Mac said, laughing.

"We better get mounted and see if Don Jaime wants us to take a turn at night herd." Flowers stretched. "Been a while since I rode like that."

"You're always up, checking on the cowboys who are on night herd," Mac said. "I've done it a few times, but mostly preparing food is the one thing that keeps me busier than a cat in a mouse factory."

Mac stepped up and brought his horse alongside Flowers. They rode slowly until they were away from the main camp and not likely to have anyone overhear what they said.

"Keep an eye out for rustlers," Flowers said. "We've seen more than enough evidence that this herd is a prime target." He sniffed. "Prime. Not the beef. The Circle Arrow longhorns are better. Prime Texas beef."

Mac slowly drifted away from his trail boss, letting Flowers carry on because the sound of the man's voice soothed the cattle. On the far side of the herd a vaquero sang in a deep, melodic voice some song Mac did not recognize. He didn't know if it gentled the cattle, but it made him begin to nod off. Now and then he jerked awake. He had been through too much that day not to be exhausted. His horse walked without stumbling; he wasn't sure he could do the same.

As he circled the herd and shooed a few cattle back to the main herd, a clicking sound brought him fully awake. A smooth move pulled his revolver from its holster. Turning from the cattle, he rode due south in the direction the herd would travel the next morning. A sliver of moon poked up in the sky, but the brilliant stars provided most of the light. Eerie shadows danced as he rode, only to stop dead a quarter mile from the herd. The clicking sound was louder here.

Mac lifted his pistol in that direction. A small shadow became a larger one as a rider appeared. The rider stopped. Mac kept his pistol aimed in the rider's direction. The rider lit a quirley and puffed on it. The sudden flare of the lucifer gave Mac an instant to see the man's face. He had a serape slung over his shoulder and wore a broad-brimmed sombrero. He took his time with the smoke, then tossed the stub away. It trailed embers all the way to the ground where it vanished. With a shrug, the rider pulled the serape around, turned his horse, and walked off. Again came the clicking sound of steel horseshoes against rock. He listened until only the soft wind disturbed the desert silence.

Going after the rider gained him nothing. Mac returned to the herd, completed his circuit and two hours on duty. In camp, he found himself a place to spread his bedroll, forcing himself to stay away from the chuckwagon. He felt out of place having the stars overhead as he stretched out, rather than looking up at the chuckwagon's bottom. In a short time he had developed habits that proved hard to break.

He slept fitfully, waking before dawn. To be sure he was ready to ride, he gathered his gear, tended his horse, and called out when he saw Don Jaime.

"I wanted to tell you what I saw last night."

"Do I care?" The ranch owner's foul mood almost made Mac hold his tongue.

"You should." He described the rider and how the man had watched the herd, as if judging the number of vaqueros in preparation for an attempt to rustle as many head as possible.

"We are close to the border. He rode from the south?"

"Yes, sir, he did. I didn't see anyone with him, but his confidence tells me he's not alone."

"You did well to tell me. The Rurales are in cahoots with many bandidos. We must avoid them as well as any lone rider thinking to lure us into an ambush."

"You're the boss."

Don Jaime's eyes narrowed as he studied Mac, hunting for any trace of sarcasm. There wasn't any, but he still thought less of what Mac told him than if one of his own vaqueros had.

"Get breakfast. We hit the trail in an hour." Don Jaime went about his business, rousting his men and bellowing for chores to be done.

Mac made his way to the chuckwagon and watched Felipe work. The cook prepared food differently, in an order that made Mac want to help. Somehow, in spite of what had to be a poor use of time and food, the cook had everything ready for the men. Mac missed his own biscuits, but the freshly fried tortillas made up for the lack of them. He used bits of the last tortilla, as he would a biscuit, to sop up whatever remained on his plate.

Felipe took his tin plate without a word. His reluctance to acknowledge Mac carried over to the rest of the vaqueros. As he mounted, Mac saw one exception. Estella Abragon had no trouble chatting brightly with Desmond. The two of them rode side by side until Don Jaime trotted up and sent Desmond out to the front of the herd. Mac had to smile. Assigning Desmond the responsibility of keeping to the trail showed Don Jaime had grown some respect for the cowboy.

Or was there something else going on?

He caught up with Flowers to share his concern.

"He sent Desmond ahead, and there might be trouble brewing."

"I know," Flowers said. "Last night I went scouting after I finished night herd and saw a campfire a few miles ahead of us. From the size of the fire, there were a dozen men there."

"Rustlers," Mac said. "That's what I think."

"And Desmond will be the one who springs the trap. Don Jaime is using him as bait."

"There," Mac said, "is a path leading off the main trail. We take it and come up from the side at about the place where Desmond calls a halt for Felipe to set up the chuckwagon."

"The chuckwagon," Flowers said. "I knew I'd missed something. The chuckwagon is behind the herd, not in front of it." He looked around hastily. He saw the path Mac had mentioned. He pulled out his rifle and checked it.

"Let's ride," Mac said. He had already made certain his weapons were ready for a fight.

They set off at a gallop. Slowing to a canter let their horses regain their wind, then they galloped for another two miles before reaching a small canyon opening out into a wider plain. Desert plants dotted the sandy ground. Waiting behind half a dozen mesquite trees were bandidos, bandanas pulled up over their faces and their pistols drawn.

"That's half of them. The rest are over yonder." Flowers pointed.

Mac couldn't see them but believed the older man. Flowers had been on enough trail drives to have an instinct for such things. Mac felt a tension that showed he was developing a similar nature.

"There's Desmond," Mac said quietly as he spotted the young man ambling along a couple of hundred yards to the right. "They'll let him ride in and then what? Reckon the herd will come on because he didn't warn the vaqueros?" Mac stood in the stirrups and shaded his eyes. "There's a second rider, one joining Desmond." His stomach tightened into a knot.

Both he and Flowers exclaimed at the same time, "Estella!"

Their outcry ruined any hope they had of a surprise ambush

on the rustlers. The one closest spun, shouted a warning in Spanish, and opened fire. He used a six-gun and was out of range, but others had rifles and turned them on Mac and Flowers.

"Desmond, run! Get Estella out of here!" Mac shouted, then had to duck as the air around him filled with lead. He swung his rifle up and fired, but his horse started crow hopping and ruined his aim.

Flowers had better luck. His first shot winged the bandido nearest them. Then he, too, was forced to break off and try to reach safety.

Desmond and Estella had wheeled their horses and were galloping away from the canyon. Mac saw Estella's horse go down suddenly. It had stepped in a prairie dog hole or somehow else failed her. She hit the ground and rolled. Desmond didn't seem to have noticed what had happened.

"Keep down!" His shouted warning was drowned out by a rising thunder of gunfire. He bent forward, head pressed low by his horse's neck as he raced toward Estella. The hail of bullets diminished thanks to Flowers and his accurate return fire. He had pulled up and was spraying lead among the bandidos.

By the time Mac got to Estella, she was sitting up, dazed. He reached down to help her up behind him. His horse balked, then screamed, reared, and keeled over. One of the rustlers had finally found the range and shot the horse out from under him. Mac had to kick his feet free of the stirrups and dive from the saddle to keep the horse from falling on him. He crashed to the ground, shook off the fall, and rolled onto his belly. Somehow he had held on to his rifle.

A flash of sunlight off a rifle's front sight presented a decent target. Mac got his first killing shot in, saw the bandido throw up his arms and topple from his horse. This did nothing to slow the rate of firing.

"Desmond!" the young woman cried out, and reached up.

Mac saw Desmond galloping toward them. He hit the ground

running and dropped beside Estella, holding her. She clung to him and buried her face in his shoulder.

For a brief second, the shooting stopped. In that pause, Mac saw he had no chance with Estella, not with Desmond around.

"Get down, both of you." Mac broke the lull in the fight in an attempt to get both Desmond and Estella to safety.

He jerked as two bullets hit him at the same instant. One ripped away part of his duster and left a crease in his left side. The other slug jerked him around as it tore at his scalp. His left temple felt as if it would explode. He fell face down and lay stunned. Through the ground he felt vibration.

At first he thought it was Flowers's galloping horse. He pushed himself up and saw Flowers a dozen yards away astride his mount. Not moving. Flowers kept his horse steady with his knees as he fired methodically. The vibration didn't come from his horse's hooves. Twisting his head around despite the thunderous pain inside his skull, he saw the real cause of the earthquake.

Don Jaime's herd was stampeding directly toward him. He forced himself to his feet, wobbled, and found it impossible to keep upright. Mac crashed back to the ground in the path of the frightened cattle.

Chapter 27

How many times could one man get trapped in the path of a stampede and survive? Mac didn't know, but he had a hunch the odds had just caught up to him.

He hoped he would die quick. Being maimed and hanging on to a thread of life for days or weeks wasn't for him. Mac worried even more about being so crippled for life he couldn't get around. Fumbling, he tried to lift his rifle and shoot himself rather than be stomped on by the cattle. His fingers had turned into sausages, big and greasy and not working.

Then he felt light and floating.

"Walk, damn you," a voice said urgently in his ear. "Help me."

"What?" He turned his head and almost lost his balance again. "Desmond?"

"Walk. Run, if you can. Get over there with Estella. It's not far."

"Not far." The words echoed in Mac's head. His dizziness passed, just a little, and he saw Estella Abragon hunkered down behind a mesquite perched on the edge of a deep arroyo. Everything clicked in his head. If he could get there, the steep bank would protect him. The cattle would blunder into the thorny bush and veer away, no matter how frightened they were.

His feet worked a little better as Desmond's arm around his shoulders supported him. Then he ran—stumbled. He fell forward and hit the bottom of the arroyo with enough force to send pain jabbing into his head. And side. And everywhere in his body. Hands pulled him upright, so he pressed his back against the tall, crumbling, sunbaked arroyo wall. In the distance he heard gunfire and pounding hooves and shouts.

Closing his eyes helped him regain his senses. Then he forced himself to look around. Desmond held Estella, cradling her, and turned so any steer coming over the edge of the arroyo would hit him first.

"The herd's not stampeding anymore," Mac croaked out. He pressed his fingers into the side of his head. They came away sticky with blood. He straightened and examined his side. His duster was shredded and stained with blood seeping from the shallow wound in his side. Moving around, he gingerly examined the wound. He wasn't so bad off, after all.

"They turned the herd," Desmond said.

Mac looked at him. Estella hung on him, her arms circling him as if she were drowning and he was her lifeline.

"Thanks," Mac said. "You pulled my fat from the fire."

"You saved me," Desmond said. Then he wasn't talking. Estella kissed him.

Mac turned away. This wasn't any of his business. Then he saw Flowers riding down the arroyo. He waved, but Flowers had already spotted him—them.

"Well, isn't this a fine reunion," the trail boss said. "Everybody still have all their parts attached to their bodies?"

"Mostly," Mac said. He grabbed an exposed root and pulled himself to his feet. "What's happened to the bandidos?"

"The ones that weren't stomped to death mounted up and galloped away. Don Jaime says we're already over the border and in Mexico, so there's no reason for the cavalry to go after them."

"What about the Rurales?" Mac took a few hesitant steps. The dizziness passed, and he was sure he was going to be all right. But he needed a horse if he intended to get very far. Hoofing it in this desert, he wouldn't get half a mile before he keeled over.

"They don't risk their necks unless they're paid," Flowers said. "Might be some of the rustlers were Rurales. I thought I saw a couple of them wearing uniforms. Might be they took them, might be they threw in with the rustlers."

"How far do we have to go?"

"Not more than three days," Estella said. "I went to Don Pedro's rancho a few times when I was younger. He owns land stretching for many miles along the border and then down into Mexico."

"He sounds like a prosperous rancher," Flowers said.

"He is. He is also a terrible man. But *muy rico*."

"Let's get back to work," Flowers said. "You need a ride?" He reached down to help Mac up behind him. The trail boss chuckled. "I'd rather have her riding behind me, but Desmond beat me to it."

"He'd fight you off," Mac said. Estella had already settled behind Desmond on his horse as they made their way up the brittle slope. He kept it to himself how Desmond had saved his life. In spite of the way he had started out, Desmond was turning into a decent man. There hadn't been any call for him to come to Mac's aid. He could have stayed with Estella and protected her. He'd saved her, and he'd saved Mac.

Seeing the two on horseback made Mac wonder what Flowers would do when Desmond refused to return to the Circle Arrow. He fell into the rhythm of Flowers's horse, almost going to sleep by the time they caught up with Don Jaime and the herd.

* * *

"He won't let me use any of his horses," Mac said to Felipe. The cook shrugged. "I can't ride herd, so I'm stuck here with you."

Felipe glared at him as he peeled potatoes. He glared even more when Mac sat next to the sack of potatoes, hefted a spud, and pulled out his cooking knife. The blade flashed four times and the potato skin surrendered. The naked potato went into the pot and another joined it a few seconds later.

"I do not need help."

"Then teach me." Mac's simple statement made Don Jaime's cook jerk around and stare at him.

"What do you mean?"

"I'm a cook, a danged good one, but what I fix for the Circle Arrow crew isn't anything like you do. Those pinto beans are about the best tasting beans I ever had."

"Green chile," Felipe said. "That is how I do it. And some other spices."

"Show me, and I'll do whatever work you don't want to."

"You are a strange gringo."

"I'm a cook. I like it, I want to do it better."

"Then you will learn from a master." Felipe grinned broadly.

Mac settled down and watched, with Felipe speaking only a little. When Felipe asked questions about why Mac prepared parts of the meal the way he did, Mac knew he was accepted. Working as a wrangler, a cook's assistant, didn't bother him too much. He earned a few dollars, or more likely his choice of horse from Don Jaime's remuda when they arrived. Estella had said it would be a couple more days.

That suited him just fine. He wanted to ask what life was like in Mexico so he could make a better decision whether to drift on further into the center of the country or return with Flowers. Estella would follow her father back to Fort Sumner once the money was securely in hand, but Mac began to doubt if Desmond would budge an inch without the woman. Flowers had lost himself any chance of winning Mercedes Sullivan's approval by taking her son on the drive and teaching him ranching.

Whether Don Jaime allowed the Texan to stay and work on his ranch was another matter. Mac foresaw gunplay if the land grant holder tried to separate Desmond from his daughter.

Thinking on it as he prepared food for Don Jaime's vaqueros, Mac decided he would back Desmond's play, whatever it was. If he even returned to Fort Sumner.

"You're looking mighty thoughty," Flowers said, settling down and holding out his tin plate for Mac to slop a little of this and more of that on it.

"What are you going to do about Desmond?" There was no call to explain what he meant. Flowers had to have the same ideas.

"I've been talking to Don Jaime. He's not too keen on having a gringo as a son-in-law. He's planning on arranging a marriage between Estella and some Mexican rancher's boy."

"Does he have anyone in mind?"

"He's going to shop around and see what the best match is." Flowers began shoveling the food into his mouth, chewing once and swallowing almost whole. The way he wolfed it down made it seem he was in a hurry.

Mac asked about that.

"Estella said we were a couple days away from Don Pedro's ranch. Truth is, we're not only south of the border, we're on the ranch and the two of them, Don Pedro and Don Jaime, are fixing to meet around sundown to discuss the sale."

"So soon?" Mac held back a moment's panic. Being rushed into a decision put him on edge after he had anticipated another couple of days to mull over his choices.

"Don Jaime refused to go to Don Pedro's hacienda. There's plenty of bad blood between them. From what I overheard of the vaqueros gossiping, and my Spanish is not too good, Don Pedro didn't want Don Jaime inside his house, either. There was talk he'd only meet him out by the pigsty. Whatever's gone wrong between the two of them, it's bad wrong."

"Will Don Pedro try to cheat Don Jaime on payment?" Mac's hand drifted to the S&W at his side. He hadn't signed on to be a hired gunman, but protecting Desmond and seeing him returned to his own herd might require some exchange of lead.

"Don't know. I do know Desmond is riding out with Don Jaime because Estella is going along, too." Flowers scraped the rest of his food straight from the plate into his mouth. A gulp got it down, followed by the full cup of coffee made from boiled mesquite beans. "You up for a twilight ride?"

"Thought you'd never ask." Mac finished his chores to Felipe's satisfaction and went with Flowers to the rope corral.

"Go on, take a horse. You can always say you're riding night herd."

"In a way, I reckon I am," Mac said. He wasn't going to work long enough to justify being given a horse. The few pesos Don Jaime might pay him for helping Felipe would hardly buy a shot of tequila.

They rode through the gathering gloom, the desert coming alive with hunters and hunted. Mac knew the feeling. In spite of riding with Flowers to make sure that Desmond didn't get into too much trouble, he watched over his shoulder constantly in case somebody was creeping up on him. It was ridiculous to react like this, he knew. He had rid himself of bounty hunters and others wanting to ventilate him.

"There they are," Flowers said.

Peering through the shadowy desert, Mac saw what Flowers already had. Two groups stood a few feet apart, looking for all the world like they were going to throw down on each other. Behind Don Jaime stood Desmond, two vaqueros, and at the rear, Estella.

Despite everything that had happened, despite knowing better, Mac felt a pang of desire for her. So lovely. But so devoted to Desmond. Mac forced himself not to linger on her grim form silhouetted in the night against the starlit sky.

Facing Don Jaime was a shorter man, stockier and even more voluble as he waved his arms around. Compared to the Fort Sumner rancher, he had an army with him. Mac lost count at eight vaqueros.

The voices carried in the still night, but Mac didn't understand enough Spanish to know what insults were being swapped. Whatever Don Pedro said, it wasn't complimentary. Don Jaime's answer was no less biting.

"What's happening?" Flowers came up in the stirrups, hand going to his gun. "They're moving toward each other."

"Papers," Mac said. "Don Jaime has papers. That must be the bill of sale for his herd. Don Pedro is handing over money."

The business transaction continued with more insults bouncing back and forth. Mac held his breath when Don Pedro thrust out his hand. And waited. Don Jaime finally shook, completing the deal. Don Jaime handed the money to Estella, who clutched it to her breast. She spoke quietly with Desmond. Then they backed away a few paces, turned, mounted, and rode off.

"What do we do?" Mac felt at loose ends. He had a horse that would take him into central Mexico. Leaving behind the suspicion he felt every time he saw a stranger coming toward him meant a simpler life. If he stayed in the U.S., every man might turn out to be a bounty hunter after him. In Mexico, no one knew him or cared about his past.

"Follow Desmond back. The sooner we're out of this country, the better I'll feel. We tangled with rustlers. Some got away. Sure as hell and damnation, they'll recruit some of the Rurales to come for us. Then we're fighting the whole damned Mexican Army."

"Don Pedro sounds like the kind of man who'd set them on Don Jaime to steal back his money. If he split it with the soldiers he'd come out way ahead."

"More than that, Mac. He hates Don Jaime enough to let the soldiers have all the money. He's got a big herd of prime cattle at a bargain. Killing Don Jaime is a bonus for him since his hands would be clean of the deed."

This decided Mac about where to ride and what to do. At least for a while. Don Pedro controlled the entire stretch of border. Killing everyone who rode with Don Jaime seemed to be something that the Mexican cattle baron would revel in.

Without a word, Mac swung his horse around and trotted after Don Jaime and the others. He quickly discovered how fast they rode, wanting to get away from Don Pedro. Within a half hour they had returned to the herd. Don Jaime was already bellowing orders about packing up and heading north.

The vaqueros complained about riding in the dark, but Don Jaime cursed them and used a short whip on one to roust him from his bedroll and get him on the trail. Mac dropped to the ground to help Felipe pack up the chuckwagon. The cook had left out the fixings for breakfast.

"We return home," Felipe said. "It is good Don Jaime has the money."

"I've got experience driving at night," Mac said. "You want me to take the reins?"

"My chuckwagon, my duty," Felipe said. He slapped Mac on the shoulder. "You are a good cook." With that compliment, he climbed onto the driver's box and got the six-mule team pulling hard. Seeing how balky a pair of them were, Mac silently thanked Felipe for insisting on driving.

He mounted and rode to where Flowers spoke in low tones with Desmond. Mac left them alone and went to Estella. He remembered her pa had given her the sale money. She had stuffed it down the front of her riding blouse. A dozen unworthy thoughts raced across Mac's mind.

"Did your pa get the price he asked?"

She nodded. With a quick toss of her head, she moved the

broad-brimmed dark hat back and let it drop behind, held around her neck by a stampede string. She was just about the loveliest woman Mac had seen.

"He worries there will be treachery from Don Pedro."

"So much so that he's not going to stay and find you a husband?"

Mac almost laughed at her reaction. She whirled around, her dark eyes flashing anger.

"I have told him I will have no part in such a thing. I . . . I have other plans." She looked toward Desmond.

"You and your pa are going to lock horns over him." Mac thought a moment, then said, "He's a better man since he met you."

"You are his friend?"

Mac shook his head. Exactly what Desmond was to him remained a mystery. They had saved each other's lives more than once, but he felt no bond with the young ranch heir. Desmond rode his own trail. Mac had to, also, and it wasn't in the same direction.

The tight knot of vaqueros rode past them, joking and laughing. After the night's sale, they were getting paid. Don Jaime's ranch was safe from being sold at auction by the bank. All was well.

But the longer Mac rode alongside Estella, the uneasier he felt. Desmond cantered over, and he and the woman rode together a few yards from Mac. The night had turned even darker, making it difficult to see, even in the bright starlight. The moon rose in a few hours, but it was a sliver and gave no real brightening to ride by.

He jumped when Flowers said in a low voice, "You feel it, too, don't you, Mac?"

He didn't know what he felt, but a vague dread clutched at him. Then all hell broke loose.

Again.

Chapter 28

Bullets tore past Mac, forcing him to fight to keep his horse from bolting. Flowers wasn't as lucky. His horse lit out like its tail was on fire. Mac knew the trail boss rode like his butt was glued to the saddle and would soon bring the frightened horse under control, so he whirled around to see what happened with Desmond and Estella.

Estella's horse stood stolidly, unaffected by the deadly lead filling the air around her. From the way Desmond's horse bucked and reared, it might have been grazed by a stray bullet meant for its rider.

"This way, this way!" Mac waved to the others. He spotted an arroyo leading away into a cluster of rocky hills that would provide good cover—if they reached it.

He foolishly sat upright in the saddle to get a better look at who was attacking them. The flash of gunfire off brass and medals told the story. As Flowers had worried, the Rurales had come for them with guns blazing. Whether dispatched by Don Pedro or they recognized easy pickings when they saw it, the Rurales put everyone riding with Don Jaime in danger.

Estella galloped toward Mac. Desmond had more difficulty because his horse wanted to run away from the gunfire. If it did, both rider and horse would be out in the open, good targets even in the dark. From what Mac saw, they were only a few minutes from being caught in the jaws of a cross fire set up by the Mexican soldiers. Don Jaime and his men had ridden through, but the Rurales waited for the stragglers. Maybe they knew Estella carried the money from the cattle sale.

Or maybe they simply saw an easy way to split Don Jaime's forces in half. Whatever the reason, they fought like wildcats, with Don Jaime on the far side of the group. If there had been a way to communicate with the ranch owner and his vaqueros, Mac saw that the Rurales would be the ones in a trap, fighting on two fronts. As it was, he and the others were forced to take refuge or die.

Desmond had finally gotten his horse under control. He rode around so he positioned himself between the soldiers and Estella. "Where's Flowers? Wasn't he with you?"

"His horse took off in the other direction," Mac said. "If we're lucky, he can get through the Rurales and tell Don Jaime to counterattack."

"Shoot the no-account bastards in the back," Desmond said. He glanced at Estella, as if he worried that such language offended her. She paid no heed. Her expression said that she had come to that conclusion without Desmond's profane urging.

Mac dragged his rifle from the saddle sheath. He spat. Checking his gear before riding from camp would have served him better now. This rifle needed patches of rust wire-brushed off the barrel. As he cocked it, he heard grinding. It hadn't been oiled in too long. If luck rode with him, the gun wouldn't blow up when he fired it.

The answer came faster than he liked. A soldier galloped toward them. Not even thinking, Mac lifted the rifle to his shoulder, aimed, and fired. The recoil almost knocked him from horseback. He recovered in time to see the Rurale throw up his hands and topple backward from his horse. The shot had been more luck than skill. His luck had run out after he pulled the trigger. Part of the bore had been peeled back as the bullet left the barrel. He tossed the useless rifle away and pulled his trusty revolver. He fired several times, driving back another soldier.

Desmond, Estella, and Mac drew into a crude circle at the mouth of the arroyo, their horses' hindquarters rubbing together. This let them fire outward and, temporarily, drive back their attackers. Mac saw immediately there wasn't any way to survive if they stayed here.

"Ride for the hills. I'll slow them down."

"Go," Desmond urged Estella. "We'll keep them from hurting you."

Mac was in no position to argue. He had fallen into the job of protecting Desmond ever since he and Flowers had pulled the young man from the Fort Worth brothel. Things had changed since then. They had to rely on each other, and Desmond willingly pulled his weight now.

Estella leaned over and gave Desmond a quick kiss. She missed his lips and pressed briefly against his cheek. Then she drew her right arm across her belly to cradle the money from selling the herd and lit out at full speed. Her horse tried to slow, showing good sense in the darkness. Heels raking, she dug her Spanish rowels into horseflesh. This convinced the reluctant nag to ignore the chance of stepping into a hole and to race like the wind.

Desmond looked at Mac, who grinned and said, "Let's see who gets to her first."

Desmond started to protest. He spoke to empty air. Mac charged out of the arroyo and cut off at an angle to give Estella more time to reach the foothills. Desmond quickly overtook him, his horse stronger and not ridden into the ground by a careless vaquero during the drive. They began to zigzag, drawing fire and forcing the Rurales to waste their ammo. Mac barely had time to tense as his horse gathered its hind legs and made a mighty jump over a huge patch of prickly pear cactus. He landed hard but held on. Desmond skirted the spiny clump.

A few more shots emptied his six-gun. Mac crammed it back into his holster and concentrated on outpacing the squad of soldiers now giving chase. He slid down an embankment, then crossed to a steeper climb into the rocky foothills. From here all he could do was follow a game trail meandering through increasingly large boulders. Even if he had a loaded gun, firing over his shoulder would have been futile. The rocks gave him cover. He popped out from between two towering rocks that formed a channel so tight he thought the horse might get stuck.

"Up here. Hurry!" Estella waved to him from a hundred feet farther along the trail. The elevation changed quickly, affording her a view of the desert behind them.

Mac was panting with exhaustion by the time he drew alongside the young woman.

"Where's Desmond?"

"He comes along a different trail." She pointed, but Mac failed to see. He closed his eyes and listened. A rider approached, making good time.

"Are you sure it's Desmond?" He broke open the S&W and kicked free the spent cartridges. Wanting to hurry but knowing that rushing made him clumsy, he reloaded with mechanical precision. The gun snapped back shut, ready for action, when a dark shape came from between two rocks to his left. He started to fire, then checked himself.

"Desmond!" Estella rode to him and they awkwardly hugged.

"We've got bandidos on our trail," Mac said. "You want to deal with them first?"

"There is no need," Estella said. "I saw Papa and a few vaqueros riding to fight them."

Mac strained to hear gunfire and was greeted with only the silence of the desert.

"They are chasing them away," Estella went on. "We are safe."

Mac wanted to see for himself. He dismounted, climbed to the top of a boulder, and studied the ground they had just ridden across. It was as desolate and devoid of life as any desert he had ever seen. Don Jaime might be chasing off the Rurales. It didn't matter. The soldiers were gone and no longer a threat. He turned in a slow circle, hunting for Hiram Flowers. If things had gone right, Flowers had eluded the Rurales and fetched Don Jaime and his men.

"I don't see him," he said. "Mister Flowers."

"He can take care of himself," Desmond said. Swinging his leg over the saddle horn, he slid to the ground and took a couple stumbling steps.

"*Mi novio*, you are hurt!"

Estella rushed to Desmond's aid. When he dismounted, his legs caved under him. He fell to his knees, still hanging on to the reins. He used his stirrup to pull back to his feet. The places he had been shot earlier pained him anew. His side ached like a son of a bitch and dizziness sent the world spinning around him. Carefully walking, letting his horse support him, he found a comfortable-looking rock and sank to it. His knees hurt from scraping along the rocks leading to this refuge.

He slowly regained his strength. Protecting Desmond looked less likely in his condition than Desmond protecting him—if Desmond ever noticed. He and Estella were too busy kissing and carrying on.

Mac sucked in a deep breath and let it out slowly. His heart raced faster as he did so. He sucked in another breath, taking it in so he caught every hint of scent on the faint breeze blowing from higher elevations. Trying not to look too obvious, he slid his revolver from its holster and laid it across his lap. Gritting his teeth at the noise, he broke it open and checked to be sure he carried a full load. When he was sure, when his strength was enough, he drew back the hammer, half stood, and looked into the rocks above them. His finger curled on the trigger the instant he spotted a hat rising up from behind the crest of a boulder.

The report startled both Desmond and Estella, but it took his target by even more surprise. The man rose, pushed his hat back from his head, touched the hole in his forehead where oozing blood turned inky black in the starlight, and slumped forward. Mac had drilled him through the brain with one shot.

"Who's that?" Desmond asked.

"Don't know, don't care," Mac said. He tugged at his horse's reins to get it back down the trail he had just ridden. Pushing between the tall rocks gave protection on either side. It also funneled a volley of shots coming from the rocks near the man he had killed.

"Those are not Rurales," Estella cried. "They are gringos. They do not wear uniforms."

"Chances are good they're Wardell's men," Mac told her. He silently cursed. They should have killed them, all of them, rather than believing they would hightail it for Fort Sumner. "Keep moving. Your pa has run off the Mexican soldiers. We have to go back that way." He ducked involuntarily as another round spanged off a rock beside his head. Hot chips of splintered rock stung his cheek.

"How'd you know they were up there?" Desmond pushed forward to stand between the gunmen and Estella.

"I caught the smell of tobacco. I don't partake, and I've never seen you build a smoke."

"You saved us," Estella said.

"We're not out of this yet. Check farther downhill and see if they're circling us."

"Wait, no!" Desmond tried to stop her but Mac grabbed his arm and spun him around.

"It gets her out of the line of fire. They're not down there. They're above us. All of them."

"How can you tell?" Desmond looked worried. He scowled when Estella vanished around a bend in the trail.

"Instinct," Mac said. Actually, he had no idea, but his show of confidence settled Desmond's nerves and focused him on the narrow gap between the rocks and the sandy pit just beyond where they had first taken refuge.

Mac looked around. Their attackers had chosen a poor spot for an ambush, unless they had intended to gun the trio down. Mac wished about now he was with Felipe riding along on the chuckwagon, heading for Fort Sumner. Might as well wish he was on the moon, he reflected wryly. Escaping wasn't going to be easy, especially with Desmond and Estella to look after.

"We can't make a stand here," Desmond said. "There's no way to move around. We either attack them straight ahead or get on down the trail."

Mac reached into his coat pocket and fingered the spare ammo there. Desmond was right. He had a dozen rounds plus the six chambered in the S&W. Then he remembered his shot that reduced the attackers' number by one. Five rounds in his six-gun. Even if Desmond had more, the men coming after their scalps could wait them out.

"I can't see what's happening," Desmond said. "It's too dark."

Mac avoided staring at the deep shadows and looked instead at the spots where the stars shone the brightest. On a cloudless night the illumination was enough to see clearly. In this tumble of rocks, he caught glimpses of movement but listening hard gave him more information on what the gunmen were doing. When he took another deep whiff, he raised his pistol and fired three times. He heard a grunt, then a curse. He hadn't killed the man trying to sneak up on them but he'd certainly winged him.

"Who are you?" Mac called. "We don't have any feud with you." He held up his hand to keep Desmond quiet. Whatever answer he got was likely to be a lie. All he wanted was a hint as to how many men they faced and where they had positioned themselves in the rocks.

"We're only bandidos," the answer came back. "We want the money you got from the cattle sale!"

Mac pressed Desmond back. They quietly retreated. He had located the one who answered. That had to be the leader.

They inched away and finally came to the base of the small hill. Estella waited anxiously a hundred yards away.

"Go to her, get away," Mac said softly. "I'll keep them back until you find Flowers or her pa."

"I'm not leaving you to face them alone," Desmond insisted.

"They want her, or the money she's got. The only way they'd know about it is if Wardell sent them to steal it."

"They might be Mexicans," Desmond said. Then, "Oh. They aren't. They don't have accents."

"I think I recognize the leader. His name's Ransom."

"Wardell's foreman!"

"You go on now," Mac said. "Make a lot of noise as you go so they'll think I'm with you. I'm going to lay an ambush for the ambushers."

He handed the reins of his horse to Desmond.

"I won't need it, and you have to decoy them. If they see or hear only one horse leaving, they'll know what I'm up to. Now *go*."

Mac knew Desmond obeyed when he heard the thudding of hooves going toward Estella. He bent double and ran to a spindly greasewood bush and crouched behind it. Hands sweaty, heart hammering, he waited. It took only a minute for a trio of men on foot to come from the narrow trail and spread out.

Ransom would be in the middle. His henchmen would flank him. Mac steadied his revolver, squeezed off a shot, and cried out in triumph when the middle man collapsed as if his knees had turned to water. Mac swung to the left and triggered a second shot, then hurriedly flung lead to the right. He winged one man and scared the other. Not letting himself think too much about what he was doing, he got his feet under him, ignored the pain twisting him around from his prior wounds, and ran forward shouting.

The man he had winged switched hands and tried to fire. Mac dispatched him with two more shots. He stumbled and went to a knee. This saved him from catching a wild shot from the third man. Using both hands to steady his aim, he fired.

The third man straightened, then toppled like a tall tree sawed off at the roots.

"Mackenzie!"

His head snapped up at the sound of his name. His heart jumped into his throat.

"You know me, Dewey Mackenzie. I could take you in to the law. I could drag your worthless carcass all the way back to New Orleans. But I won't. You know why? You killed three of my men. The Huffman brothers. All dead."

Quick Willy Means came from the rocks, widened his stance, and pushed his coattails back on both sides. He wore two revolvers and looked able to draw and fire both of them.

"The only thing missing is Hiram Flowers," Means went on. "I got a beef with him, but you were the one I was sent after. I can deal with him later since that's personal, not business."

Mac raised his gun and fired. The hammer fell on a spent chamber.

"I was counting, Mackenzie. Six rounds fired. How'd you survive this long being so careless?" Means started walking toward him. "Go on. Try to reload. I can plug you from here, but I want to see you squirm for all you've done."

Mac had nothing to say. Anything that came from his lips would be futile. Means intended to cut him down. Why goad him? Why give him even an instant's satisfaction? Mac wasn't the type to grovel or beg for mercy. Getting compassion or leniency from the bounty hunter was a waste of the last few seconds he had on earth.

He cracked open his S&W and ejected the spent brass. Means came down the slope even faster.

"Time to die, Mackenzie. Time to die!"

The bounty hunter went for his guns, both of them. Mac cringed when a shot rang out, but when he opened his eyes, he was startled that the bullets hadn't ripped through him. He hadn't thought Means was that bad a shot, either left- or right-handed.

More shots rang out. The thunder of a galloping horse from behind caused him to look over his shoulder. Desmond Sullivan fired his rifle repeatedly.

Means was distracted by the new attacker, giving Mac time to fumble in his coat pocket and find a cartridge. He stuffed it into an empty cylinder and reached for another when he heard a heavy thud. Desmond's horse ran past him. His eyes following the horse, he saw it pass where the bounty hunter stood, his guns smoking after shooting Desmond from the saddle.

Mac snapped the gun closed.

"He died for you, Mackenzie. Now you'll die!" Quick Willy Means turned his revolvers on his victim. Lead whined past Mac's head. He grunted as a bullet hit him in the side, about where he had been shot before.

Seeing double from the impact, he raised his pistol and fired. One shot. That was all he had. One shot. He fell facedown on the ground, waiting for Means to finish the job he had started. Through the hard ground where his cheek pressed down, he felt vibration. Another horse. He tried to warn Estella away. No words came. All that came for him was darkness.

Chapter 29

Mac was lifted straight up and dropped on a hard surface. He cried out from the shock and pain. His eyes refused to focus for a few seconds, then he saw Hiram Flowers.

"You aren't dead. I wondered . . ." Mac said. His words sounded strange. Flowers poured water over Mac's chapped lips. He swallowed enough to repeat what he'd said. By now he saw beyond Flowers. He lay in the back of a wagon bouncing along. Every bump the wagon hit jolted him and increased his misery.

Moaning, he rolled onto his side and forced himself to sit up. His shirt had been cut away and a fresh bandage circled his waist. It not only covered his fresh bullet wounds but held his bruised ribs in place.

"I fetched Don Jaime and his men," Flowers said. "We ran off the Rurales, then heard more gunfire."

"What about Desmond?" Mac looked around. "He saved my life. He distracted Means long enough for me to reload."

A chill passed through him. Reloaded? He had slipped *one* cartridge into his pistol. One. His life—and Desmond's—had rested on one single shot. Closing his eyes, he called up the image of Ransom and his men, then Quick Willy Means, as if they were players on a stage and he was in the audience. He watched it all as if it had been dipped in molasses.

"Desmond took a bullet in the thigh, but the fall from his horse shook him up even more." Flowers sounded disgusted. "He's in good enough shape to ride, even though *she* protested."

Mac didn't have to ask who Flowers meant. Estella would be nursing her beau every inch of the way.

"We're back in the U.S.?"

"Yup, we are."

"Good," Mac said. He wondered why he had ever considered riding farther into Mexico. He had been greeted with more lead and death than he wanted to consider, even if most of it had followed him. The bounty hunters, Wardell's men, they had trailed him down from New Mexico Territory. Only the Rurales, and maybe Don Pedro inciting the bandidos, had been new dangers. Now all that lay behind him, across the border.

"Are you considering drifting on, Mac? I'm not funning you when I say you've got a permanent job with the Circle Arrow. We can reach Denver, take a train to Kansas City, and then ride on back to Fort Worth."

"Denver," Mac said softly. A thought poked into his head but stayed just beyond the reach of his brain.

"You got any ideas about making sure Desmond gets home?" Flowers asked.

Mac looked hard at the trail boss. This was the first time Flowers had ever admitted he had no answer for a thorny question. Even more surprising, he was asking a chuckwagon cook for advice.

"That's not my problem," Mac said. "Truth is, it shouldn't be yours, either. Desmond's proved himself capable of taking care of any trouble that comes his way. And if what you say's true about Estella, she sees that in him."

"Don Jaime will never let them get hitched."

"They'll light out, and he'll never see his daughter again. You willing to let her go back to the Circle Arrow with Desmond and explain it all to Mercedes Sullivan?"

Flowers groaned.

"I don't have any idea how I'd explain that her son's found a girlfriend and intends to get married. Mercedes is a Methodist, and I reckon Estella is Catholic. How *that'll* play out is anyone's guess." Flowers shook his head. "What are we gonna do, Mac? I can't think of a single thing that makes a lick of sense."

Again a thought rose and—almost—came spilling from Mac's lips. His head hurt so bad it threatened to split open. His bullet wounds and ribs were bound up so tightly they didn't give him much pain. That was something to be thankful for, anyway.

"Where are we?" He turned his head to look through the opening at the front of the wagon. "We're almost back to Fort Sumner!"

"You were out of your mind for a day or two, then settled down for the last few." Flowers peered at him, squinting as if this gave him better insight. "You're looking mighty good, considering what you were like before."

Mac started to respond, then stopped. He grinned broadly.

"I need to talk to Desmond and Estella. And Don Jaime."

"That can be a chore, at least as far as getting Desmond's attention. We're almost back to our herd. When we get there, that'd be the best time before he and Estella hightail it to parts unknown." Flowers cleared his throat. "That's what I expect to happen. Not saying it will, but finding anybody to bet against me isn't possible."

Mac settled back, working over his scheme. The fog had finally cleared and let him see things better now. Try as he might, he couldn't find any drawbacks with the idea. When the wagon rattled to a halt at the Circle Arrow camp, he climbed down and went hunting for Desmond and Estella. Finding them proved easy enough.

Estella had her beau stretched out on a blanket as she held a cool compress on his forehead. His leg was bandaged where the bullet had ripped off a hunk of flesh. Every move the man made showed a touch of pain. Mac didn't doubt Desmond ached all over from falling off his horse, but he also believed much of the apparent pain was feigned to keep Estella fussing over him.

Somehow, Mac couldn't find it in his heart to fault Desmond for doing that. Estella was a lovely woman.

"I wanted to thank you for distracting Means," Mac said. He sank to the ground and sat cross-legged near Desmond. "I was a goner until then."

"You took on a powerful lot." Desmond looked at Estella. "You risked your life to save us. I had to return the favor."

"We're even," Mac said.

This caused Desmond to sit upright. His demeanor changed.

"We're not going to Denver with the herd." He looked at Estella, then back at Mac. "Her pa and my ma don't have any say-so. We love each other."

"Yeah, about that. I've got a proposal that might work out for all of us."

"What is it?" Desmond's suspicious nature showed how much he had learned on the trail drive. Before he would have opposed anything Mac had to say, just on general principles. Now he would listen and if he liked what he heard, agree. That was all any man could do.

Dewey Mackenzie launched into his plan. Desmond remained unconvinced, until Estella warmed to the notion and started talking to him in low, confidential tones. Mac got to his feet and left them discussing what he'd suggested. He had others to corral.

"I don't see what good I'll be," Hiram Flowers said. "That so-and-so isn't gonna listen to anything I have to say. All I want to do is get on the trail to Denver. You coming with us, Mac? I hope so."

Flowers tugged on the reins and brought his horse to a halt. Don Jaime's hacienda loomed in the twilight, spacious and sprawling, more a fortress than a house. The high adobe walls encircled the entire hacienda. Inside were garden views for the rooms facing inward. Whether Don Jaime allowed them inside didn't matter as long as he listened to what Mac had conjured up, more in a fever dream than through rational thought.

"Looks like we've been noticed."

A man carrying a rifle came from the gates protecting the hacienda's interior. The gates stood partly open, letting out a heady aroma of growing plants and flowers. After breathing trail dust, this buoyed Mac and made him even more sure he was on the right track.

"Don Jaime, good evening," he called as the rancher planted himself in their path.

"What do you want?"

"You've paid off the banker? Your ranch is still yours?"

Don Jaime nodded. "Dunphy took the money. Reluctantly. He wanted to sell my land for a big fee."

"To Luther Wardell," Mac said. He saw how the rancher tensed and brought the rifle muzzle around, as if his adversary had appeared in front of him.

"What do you want? You did not work enough for me to pay. You lost a horse. You owe me money, but I will forgive the debt for all you did to protect my daughter."

"Glad the debt's canceled," Flowers said dryly. "I'd hate to tally up all you owe us for protecting you from bandidos, Rurales—and Wardell's killers."

"Mister Flowers here has a proposal for you." Mac walked his horse closer but did not dismount. Don Jaime gave no indication of relaxing.

"I do?" Flowers scowled. "What proposal?"

Mac spoke louder to drown out the trail boss.

"It's a mighty long trail for the Circle Arrow crew to drive the rest of the cattle all the way to Denver."

"It is." Don Jaime lowered his rifle. Mac hoped the man had an inkling of what he was going to be offered.

"You've sold all your cattle. What good is it having a ranch if you don't have any cattle left?"

"It will take two or three years to rebuild."

"There are some heifers and more than a few bulls in the Circle Arrow herd."

"Wait a second, Mac," Flowers said. "You can't offer breeding rights to him. *I* can't without Miz Sullivan's permission."

Mac ignored the trail boss and plowed on.

"You have the land, the Circle Arrow has the cattle."

"Many steers in your herd," Don Jaime said.

"What you need to sell next season while the rest of the herd grows."

"To graze on my land, what will you pay?"

"Nothing," Mac said. "Nothing because there's going to be a merger of your ranch and the Circle Arrow, whether you like it or not."

"A merger? No! I will never permit my daughter to marry him!" Don Jaime jerked the rifle back up.

"You don't have a choice. Estella will sneak away to be with Desmond, no matter what you do. Even if you try to put her in a convent."

"There is one in Mexico City. She—"

"She'll escape. He'll find her. Give in to the inevitable."

"The cattle would be mine? In exchange for the grazing?"

"The money you get is shared. After all, your land will be the western extension of the Circle Arrow back in Fort Worth. Desmond and Estella will be the owners some day—she of your rancho, him of the Circle Arrow—they'll own both."

Don Jaime mumbled. Mac pushed his final argument.

"You want to make it as comfortable as possible for them to stay here, on the old land grant, rather than living over in Texas."

"She would never do that," Don Jaime insisted. "Give up this hacienda for some Texas ranch house."

"I don't know why not," Flowers cut in. "I've never seen a purtier house than the one Miz Sullivan has, a bigger one, or one with more servants."

Mac almost laughed. Mercedes Sullivan did most of the chores herself. The ranch house was nice, but he thought Don Jaime's hacienda might be more lavishly appointed. The trail boss had hit the right chord, though. Don Jaime's complaints melted like ice in the bright New Mexico sun.

"They will marry?" Don Jaime said, glaring. "When?"

"That's up to them," Mac said. "I do know Desmond wants to take Estella back to Texas, at least for a spell, to show off a new bride to his ma."

In a whisper only Mac heard, Flowers said, "I need to get the money from the cattle to her, too. I don't know what the hell I'll tell her about most of the herd being left here to graze for another year."

"Desmond can explain it," Mac told him.

"My daughter, married." Don Jaime shook his head. He didn't have to add, "to a gringo like Desmond Sullivan." He didn't have to. That went unsaid. But he was giving in to Mac's argument, that was obvious.

"The way I see it, the Army will need more beef later in the year. You'll have a herd waiting to be butchered."

"Wardell will sell more to them to undercut my market," Don Jaime protested.

"He can't do that forever," Flowers said. "He has to make a profit somewhere or he'll risk losing his own ranch." He coughed, spat, and said, "You've got the Circle Arrow money behind you now, too. Or Estella does. Estella and Desmond."

"So, where are they? My daughter and her . . . man."

"He's recuperating at our camp, but having a bed would go a ways toward speeding his recovery," Flowers said.

"I will order a room prepared for him. On the far side of the house, away from my daughter's room." Don Jaime went back through the gate and closed it. The sound of the locking bar falling into place echoed through the still night.

Flowers and Mac sat for a moment, then the trail boss said, "I don't know if this is any kind of a deal. Miz Sullivan's not going to take it kindly, losing out on selling so many of the herd."

"She's probably doubling the size of the Circle Arrow. Don Jaime's land grant is huge."

"But there's five hundred miles between the east and west pastures," Flowers said.

"It's going to be up to Desmond to make some decisions. His ma can run the Circle Arrow. Running this spread is going to be hard if Don Jaime won't let loose of the reins. My thought is that he'll come around and let his son-in-law run things while he takes it easy."

"There might be a grandbaby someday to keep him busy."

Mac and Flowers both laughed at that.

They walked their horses away. Mac rubbed his eyes when he saw shadows moving not too far away, as if a man eavesdropped and now ran off. Or it could have been a coyote skulking about.

"I hope Desmond is up to it."

"I think he is," Mac said. "After all he's been through, I *know* he is."

Mac was confident enough in his opinion, but the nearby shadow that had vanished worried him more than a little.

Chapter 30

Luther Wardell paced behind his desk, fists beating at the air. Nothing had worked right. Not a damned thing, and he had planned so carefully. Everyone worked against him in a huge conspiracy, but how did he get even with men like Amos Dunphy? The banker had cooked up some deal with Jaime Abragon to let the man keep his land grant. That had to be the answer. Wardell's men had tried to stop the herd from being sold, and they had failed. Then Ransom had gone to steal the money Don Jaime had received for the herd, and he had failed. Somebody warned the damned Mexican rancher of every move against him. That was the only answer.

Wardell spun and slammed both fists down hard on his desk as his new foreman came into the room, timidly holding his hat and looking like he was going to piss himself at any instant.

"Well? What'd you find out?"

Guy Brooks ran his fingers around the hat brim, then found his voice. Wardell wished Ransom was still here, but the man had been murdered in an ambush by the Circle Arrow cowboys.

"Well, sir, like you said, I followed Don Jaime around town. He didn't do much. He paid off his bill at the general store, then spent a while at the feed store. I couldn't get close enough to hear, but he must be wanting a line of credit to buy feed for—"

"The bank. He went to the bank. What happened there, dammit?"

"Well, now, Mister Wardell, he wasn't in the bank too long, but the banker, Dunphy, came out with him and shook hands. It looked for all the world like they parted on good terms. He must have paid off his loan."

Wardell sank into his chair and put his forehead in his hands, elbows on the desk. How was he cursed with such idiots? Ransom had been trigger happy, but the man had a brain and used it.

"Of course he paid off his loan. He had money from selling his herd."

"About that, Mister Wardell, it happened just like I said. Those Texans hid and shot at us and killed everyone. I was lucky to get away."

"Without a scratch. You shot your way out of an ambush that killed Joe Ransom and a half dozen gunmen and didn't get so much as a scratch." He rocked back in his chair and cursed being saddled with such cowards and incompetents. For two cents he'd put a bullet through Brooks's fat gut and keep shooting him until he spewed forth the truth.

Then he decided that would be a waste of good ammunition.

"I ain't lucky in cards or with the ladies. I musta used up all my luck getting away, Mister Wardell. Really."

"Where'd Abragon go after he left town? Straight back to his ranch house?"

"Straight as an arrow. He went into his compound and locked the gates. I smelled food cooking." Brooks rubbed his bulging gut. "I got powerful hungry 'cause it smelled so good. Them Meskins fix mighty good food. He—"

"You stood outside sniffing at that dog's supper. How lucky I am to have such a devoted employee."

"I am as devoted as they come, sir. Really, I am. But he didn't stay inside. Don Jaime came out wavin' a rifle around when they rode up."

Wardell gritted his teeth. Getting information out of this fool was worse than pulling his own teeth with pliers. He gripped the edge of his desk and forced himself to stay quiet. That lingering silence wormed the facts from Brooks.

"Them Texans. The trail boss and his cook. They rode up, and Don Jaime came out to talk with them. I was close enough to hear them make a deal."

"A deal?" The question burst from Wardell like a bull from the chutes at a rodeo.

"One of the Texas cowboys and Don Jaime's daughter are getting hitched. The herd they didn't sell—"

"That I didn't buy," Wardell said, his belly tightening into a cold knot.

"Yeah, that. They're goin' to leave them to graze on Don Jaime's pasture, then split the money when he sells them."

"He sold every last cow to Don Pedro to save his ranch. I could have bought his land next year because there wouldn't be another herd. But there will be now. The Circle Arrow herd."

"Our cows are prime, Mister Wardell."

"They're not as good as the longhorns. Abragon is going to sell them to the Army over the next year and then still have a big enough herd to drive to market, down in Mexico or up in Denver. He's going to be a rich man because of the damned longhorns."

He closed his eyes. Estella and one of the Texas cowboys. It had to be the red-haired one. Their union was more than of the flesh. Somehow this merged the Circle Arrow and Don Jaime's land grant. After paying so much for those three hundred head he had almost given to the Army, his funds ran low. Dunphy would loan him whatever he wanted, but Abragon held the winning hand with the Texas longhorns pasturing on his vast range.

"Why didn't you shoot the son of a bitch? You were within earshot. A single bullet would have ended this farce." Wardell pushed to his feet and began pacing again.

Killing Abragon accomplished nothing, he realized. The deal between the Texans and Abragon revolved around the marriage of his daughter with the redheaded cowboy. Remove Estella Abragon and her sweetheart and the deal fell apart. Killing Estella Abragon might be all it took for the two sides to break their pact. He hated that idea since she was such a beautiful woman, but sacrifices had to be made if he wanted to keep his ranch and prosper.

If he wanted to expand onto Abragon's land.

"How many men does Abragon have at his hacienda?"

"What? Not so many. He paid them and they all went into town to get drunk."

"Is his daughter at the hacienda?"

"And Desmond Sullivan. That's her boyfriend, sir. Her betrothed, from what the Texans said."

"How many men can you get together?"

"In town? If there's a payoff involved, I can get a couple dozen."

"No, no, not that," Wardell said, his mind racing to other ways of getting what he wanted. "How many of our Big W wranglers can you find right now?"

"Not so many, sir. Three?" Brooks sounded unsure.

He was that kind of foreman, unimaginative . . . and a coward.

"Never mind. Come with me. Make sure your revolver's loaded." Wardell opened his desk drawer and pulled out a holster. He checked the Colt Navy to be sure it carried six rounds in the cylinder, then stood, strapped on the gun belt, and practiced a quick draw. He wasn't anywhere near as fast as Joe Ransom had been, but tonight he wouldn't have to be.

"What're you gonna do, sir?" Brooks shifted nervously from foot to foot.

"We're going back to Abragon's spread and shoot us a couple varmints. Are you up to it?" He squared off and considered throwing down on his new foreman. It would be good practice, shooting worthless—

Brooks spun around suddenly, facing out into the main house.

"What is it?" Wardell came around the desk, pushed Brooks out of the way, and stepped out into the main room. A hiss like a striking rattler escaped his lips, and his hand moved to his six-gun.

"You got us all tangled up in promises nobody wants to keep, Mac." Hiram Flowers slumped as he rode. "I don't know how Mercedes is going to take this."

"Go back to the Circle Arrow with the money from the cattle Wardell bought. Desmond will go, too. Him and Estella. You might be surprised at how she takes the news. Then let things take their course."

"Like spring runoff? Water gushing down a mountain and into a river?"

"New tributaries can be cut if the runoff is strong enough," Mac told the trail boss. "Why don't you go on ahead? I've got a few things to deal with."

"What're those?"

Mac ignored the question. He left Flowers grumbling but not inclined to follow his cook. The trail boss rode on through the darkness, heading for the Circle Arrow herd now slated to be pastured on Don Jaime's spread.

Mac kept his horse's gait at a slow walk to hold down the sound of hooves hitting the dried ground. His head hurt and he worried his vision had doubled from all the falls and wallops he had taken in the past week. Imagining haints in the night wasn't out of the question. A smile curled his lips when he spotted the man on foot, running toward a stand of cottonwoods. His eyes hadn't betrayed him back at Don Jaime's. There had been a man spying on them as they negotiated the merger between the New Mexico and Texas cattle empires.

The only one that mattered to was Luther Wardell. The man riding away at a dead gallop had to report to Wardell. Mac felt as sure of that as he ever had anything in his life. The speed the rider showed leaving in the direction of the Big W ranch told Mac more than he needed to know. This wasn't Wardell himself but one of his errand boys. At the U.S. border where the gunfight had left so many dead, Don Jaime had identified not only Wardell's foreman, Ransom, but also the others as being his henchmen. Wardell sent others to do his dirty work.

Tonight, Mac was going to end the skulking around once and for all.

A half hour later, he dismounted outside Wardell's ranch house and stepped up to the front porch. From inside he heard voices—two. From the snatches of argument he caught, he had trailed Wardell's new foreman from Don Jaime's. He made sure his S&W rode easy, then slowly opened the front door and went inside.

The only sounds in the house came from the direction of the parlor and the office beyond it. He took a deep breath, settled his nerves, and went into the parlor. His spurs jingled and the click of his boot heels echoed in the stillness. Two kerosene lamps in the office provided most of the light, but another small one on a table in the middle of the parlor cast dimmer light. He made certain to keep from being silhouetted by it and turning himself into an easy target.

"What is it?" Luther Wardell came around his desk and pushed his foreman out of the way. He stepped into the parlor. "Who's out there?"

"You sent Ransom to kill me," Mac said.

"How'd you get here?" Wardell jerked around and glared at Brooks. "You let him follow you?"

"He's not much of a trailsman," Mac said. "And you're not

much of a rancher. You spend all your time and money trying to steal Don Jaime's land instead of running your own herd."

Wardell laughed harshly.

"Listen to you. A cook? That's all you are, and you're lecturing me how to run my ranch?"

"A cook," Mac said softly. "That's all I want to be." Louder, he said, "You're going to keep meddling where you're not wanted. I promised Flowers I'd help him look after Desmond."

"The red-haired kid? What's he to you?"

"A duty. A job I never wanted. You might even say he's a curse, but he saved me from Ransom and the bounty hunter that rode with your men."

"Bounty hunter?" Wardell moved farther into the parlor. He pushed back his frock coattails to better get to the gun at his side.

"Quick Willy Means, he called himself." Mac's heart beat faster. Then he settled down. The showdown was going to happen at any instant. He felt it.

"I don't know anybody named that, but you have bounty hunters on your tail? You're running from the law? That means I can claim a reward when I—"

Luther Wardell went for his gun. Mac was faster. And more accurate. The rancher's shot blasted into the floor. The cook's tore through Wardell's chest.

Mac swung around, aiming for Wardell's foreman. Brooks threw his hands up and stepped back. His heel caught on the rug, and he sat down hard. Somehow he kept his hands high above his head. Mac cocked his pistol again and leveled it at the man's face. Sweat poured down Brooks's forehead and his lips quivered in fear.

"Don't come after me," Mac said. "Try and you'll end up like your boss." He lowered the hammer and backed away, then turned. Brooks was too cowed to try shooting him in the back. Mac got out of the house at a fast walk.

He vaulted into the saddle and galloped away. A light came on in the bunkhouse. He wanted to put some distance between him and any pursuit by Wardell's cowboys. Brooks had to tell them something, but his cowardice might keep him from identifying Mac.

He couldn't take that chance. He swerved from the road leading back to where the Circle Arrow crew bedded down. He wouldn't have minded wishing Desmond and Estella well, and not saying good-bye to Hiram Flowers bothered him, too. The trail boss had a passel of problems ahead of him with Mercedes Sullivan, and dealing with Don Jaime had to be a mountain of trouble, if he failed to say the right words.

Flowers had complications enough to deal with. Having his cook chased by Wardell's men or the local law or even the cavalry would just make things worse. And there was no telling how many more bounty hunters Pierre Leclerc had set snapping at Mac's heels.

He rode northward, following the Pole Star until after midnight, then turned so it stayed on his right side. West? If he went far enough, he might end up looking out over the Pacific Ocean. He'd seen the Mississippi River, and it was a huge stretch of water, but he could see across it. An ocean was something else, too vast to understand. That would be a sight.

Or maybe somewhere else would beckon more after a week or two in the saddle. Dewey Mackenzie had plenty of time to figure that out.

And somewhere along the way, he mused, he needed to buy himself a new hat.